The Bottom Line

The Bottom Line

SANDY JAMES

New York Boston

This book is a work of fiction. Names, characters, places, and incidents are the product of the author's imagination or are used fictitiously. Any resemblance to actual events, locales, or persons, living or dead, is coincidental.

Forever Yours
Hachette Book Group
237 Park Avenue
New York, NY 10017
www.hachettebookgroup.com
www.twitter.com/foreverromance

First published as an ebook and as a print on demand edition: May 2014

Forever Yours is an imprint of Grand Central Publishing.
The Forever Yours name and logo are trademarks of Hachette Book Group, Inc.

ISBN: 978-1-4555-7399-8 (ebook edition)
ISBN: 978-1-4555-7522-0 (print on demand edition)

I cannot thank my editor, Latoya Smith, enough for patiently waiting for me to be "ready."

I cannot thank my editor, Latoya Smith, enough for patiently waiting for me to be "ready."

Acknowledgments

I send my thanks out to my agents, Joanna MacKenzie, Danielle Egan-Miller, and Abby Saul, for all they do for me. Love you, ladies.

I'd be lost without my critique partners. Hugs to Cheryl Brooks, Nan Reinhardt, and Leanna Kay for always having my back.

I give my thanks and admiration to Pam Young, Anita Brown, Kathy Atkinson, and Susan Roberts—the inspirations for this story.

And, as always, I have to thank my husband, Jeff, for putting up with me. Love you, honey.

The Bottom Line

Chapter 1

One more change.

After a year of unrelenting upheaval, Mallory Hamilton was ready to get her life back. She only needed one more change.

Giving her short hair another quick tweak, she set the gel aside. Rascal, her tabby cat, jumped up on the vanity counter, where he knew he didn't belong. But Mallory had learned from experience, some silly rules were made to be broken.

She ran her hand down his back as he arched up to get more of her touch. The cat's fur was soft and warm, and she wanted nothing more than to crawl back into bed and let Rascal snuggle against her side like a living heating pad.

"Did you finish your breakfast?" she asked her pet.

Rascal's reply was more purring.

Mallory took one last look in the mirror, smiled, and walked out of the bathroom. Her cat padded beside her, twitching his tail in the air.

The summer had been hot and very dry, matching her mood quite well. Everyone patted her on the shoulder and told her they admired her strength. Truth was she wasn't strong. She was numb. Her life had taken a one-eighty turn so fast, she hadn't had the chance to catch her breath. There simply hadn't been time to cry. Now that the ordeal had ended, she saw no reason to indulge herself in an emotional breakdown. Crying wouldn't change a damned thing.

She'd lost things she couldn't get back, and that was that.

The doorbell rang as she finished buttoning her shirt.

Rascal hopped on the bed, stretching out on the rumpled quilt and kneading his claws against the cloth. Before she headed downstairs, Mallory jerked the shade up so that the sunlight hit his striped brown fur.

"Have a nice nap. I need to talk to the contractor about fixing up this dump."

And her home really *was* a dump.

The doorbell rang again.

"Coming!"

She had to push the front door with her hip to hold it tight while she flipped open the dead bolt. The squeak when she opened the door grated on her nerves. She promised herself she would go to the hardware store and get some oil after the contractor left.

Dressed in a sky-blue polo and jeans, a thirtysomething guy with short dark hair glanced up from the iPad he held in his hand. His sexy smile took her by surprise.

"Are you Mallory?" he asked.

"Yes. I'm Mallory Hamilton. You're Ben? The contractor Robert Ashford sent?"

"Yes, ma'am. He said you wanted some work done on your place." He fished in his shirt pocket and produced a white business card, which he handed to her. "If you show me which projects you'd like done, I can give you an estimate. Then we can talk about a timetable."

She blinked twice when she read the name, but she didn't laugh. She hadn't truly felt like laughing in a very long time.

"Your last name's Carpenter? Seriously? You're a carpenter named Carpenter?"

"I'm a *contractor* named Carpenter." His words were clipped.

She opened the door wider, sorry that she might have offended him. No doubt he'd grown tired of dealing with rude comments about his name. "Please come in. I'll show you around."

His brown eyes wandered the foyer. "DIY?"

"Pardon?"

Ben nodded at the coat closet with no door then at the floor. "Do-it-yourself. The laminate flooring isn't tight enough. I assume the door's in the garage because it was too long to close after you put the floor in."

She nodded. "Along with the trim. The chair rail for the dining room. The sink for the half bath. And—"

He held up a hand. "How about you take me room to room and show me what you'd like done?"

"Gladly."

The downstairs wasn't too bad, except for the great room. The fireplace mantel was only partly stained, and the gas logs had never been installed. That's what the contractor was for.

He followed her up the stairs into the master bedroom. "And in here?"

"Doesn't it speak for itself?"

When he smiled, he had laugh lines that framed his eyes. "It does, but I want to know what *you* think needs to be done."

She pointed at the exposed beam at the apex of the cathedral ceiling. "It's fake, and the corners have split away from the drywall. I like the way it looks in general, so I'd like to see if you can save it."

He nodded and entered more information on his tablet.

"The window needs...*something*. I can hear the wind whistle when storms blow through."

"Any water when it rains?"

"No."

Ben pulled the drape back. "They're newer windows. When did you have them put in?"

"Not sure. Maybe three years ago?"

"They're in good shape, but they weren't caulked properly. Next?"

Mallory led him into the bathroom and froze, utterly mortified. So accustomed to being alone now, she never bothered hiding anything she used on a daily basis. She swept her arm across the counter, scooping up all her stuff and dropping it into the deep vanity drawer.

Without missing a beat, Ben flipped the switch to the exhaust fan, which did nothing in response. "You'll need a new fan. Do you want to keep these light fixtures? They're a bit...dated."

His calm acceptance eased her embarrassment. "They suck."

He chuckled. "Light fixtures are easy to switch out. I'll bet you're tired of six big, naked bulbs staring you in the eye first thing in the morning."

Nothing else naked stared at her, but the lightbulbs still had to go. "Yeah...you're right. I'll need new ones for all three baths."

More taps on his iPad that were probably adding up to a pretty penny.

Didn't matter. She couldn't take her house anymore. Not the way it was.

She needed it to be *her* home now.

The rest of the tour took a good hour. Every disaster she showed him raised her anxiety, especially when his response was to draw his lips into a grim line and nod curtly. Dollar signs flashed in her head. She didn't even want to know what he found in the crawl space or the attic.

They ended up right where they began, and for some reason, the foyer looked worse this time than it had when she'd invited him inside. Her stomach was tied into nervous knots, and she was on the verge of a full-blown panic attack. But she was going to do this.

She *had* to do this.

"So what do you think? Can all this be fixed?" Her voice quivered.

Ben kept working on his tablet.

"I know this house is… old and a big mess, but—"

He finally glanced up. "Relax. There's nothing really *wrong* with the place."

Mallory snorted. "*Everything's* wrong with this place. But it's all I've got and I sure can't afford to move."

In all honesty, she probably could afford to move—she simply didn't want to. The commute was less than ten minutes, and she was close to everything she needed. The library. The pharmacy. Her friends. A SuperTarget.

His gaze wandered the foyer. "The way I see it, this place has a few scars. That's all. Just scars."

"Scars?" She hated that word more than anyone would ever know.

"Yeah. Cosmetic stuff mostly, but the bones are good. Just give it time—give *me* time."

His words pounded through her brain, a steady rhythm that made her insides somersault and her head ache.

A few scars.

Cosmetic stuff mostly.

Give it time.

"What's the bottom line?" she asked, holding a tight lid on her emotions.

"Bottom line is I'll fix things for you, Mrs. Hamilton. I promise."

Those few simple words worked magic by easing her anxiety. Perhaps it was his sincerity. Perhaps it was his smile. Perhaps it was the funny coincidence of his name. "I believe you."

"I need to check some prices, see if I can call in some favors, and get you a price. You realize it's an estimate, right? That when I get to work, I might find more problems hiding underneath the skin?"

She nodded. What was below the surface always caused her the most trouble. With her luck lately, Ben Carpenter would find everything from termite infestation to dry rot.

***

Ben Carpenter's temper rose to a boil the moment he saw Amber sitting on the front porch of his rented town house. Since it was the last week before she started eighth grade, she was supposed to be spending time with her mother. Then she'd come back home Sunday before classes began.

Damn you, Theresa.

His daughter's elbows were propped on her knees, and her chin rested on her hands. She'd gathered her long dark hair into a ponytail, and she wore her usual jeans and T-shirt. A pink backpack lay at her feet.

Throwing the truck into park, he sighed. Not at having his daughter home where she belonged, but because his bitch of an ex-wife had abandoned their kid. Again.

"Hey, ladybug," he said, resisting the urge to gather her into his arms. "Why didn't you call me and tell me you were coming back early?"

Ever since she'd become a teenager, Amber had started keeping her distance. He just hadn't figured out whether it was a teenage thing or if she didn't want to hug her father anymore. She never hugged Theresa, but then again if Theresa were his mother, he'd not only be reluctant to hug her, he'd run away to join the circus.

At least Amber always knew she was safe with her father. He tried to make a stable home, even if they could only afford a rental. She'd decorated her bedroom herself and made it reflect her eclectic personality. Posters of anything from androgynous singers to muscular athletes lined the walls. Since he remembered how important his own privacy had been at that age, he didn't hover.

Amber looked up at him with brown eyes that held enough red to show she'd been crying. "Her phone got turned off 'cause she didn't pay for it." Each word dripped with disdain he was accustomed to hearing whenever Amber spoke of Theresa. "She took mine. Said I was too young to have my own phone."

Of course she took Amber's phone—he paid for it.

"What happened this time?" Ben asked.

"Some of her stupid friends were going to Vegas." She stood and picked up her backpack, slinging the strap over her shoulder. "She didn't say when she was coming back. Just dropped me off, telling me she didn't want to see you. Do you know how many of my friends' texts I've missed?"

He gave her ponytail a playful tug. "Why didn't you let yourself in?"

"I couldn't remember the new code."

"I'm sorry. I wish I hadn't had to change—"

"It's not your fault, Dad. It's hers. She was the one who let herself in and took your checkbook."

Once she followed him into the house, Amber dropped her pack inside the door, flopped on the couch, and grabbed the remote. Then she flipped through channels.

"Well, at least you're home now, ladybug."

What kind of mother does something like this?

"Pizza or Chinese?" he asked, picking up the phone. "If I'd known you were coming back so soon, I could've shopped."

"You never know when I'm coming home."

"Touché."

Amber's gaze shifted from the flat-screen to him. "You know, I hear people say that all the time, but I don't know what it means."

He found a smile. His daughter was, above all other things, the most curious creature on the face of the planet. From the time she could speak, her favorite word was "why," usually followed by a question that revealed an intelligence beyond her years. Most kids outgrew that curiosity. Not Amber. If anything, it grew exponentially with each passing year.

"I think it's a fencing term or something. Flip open the laptop and Google it."

She turned back to whatever show she'd been watching. "I don't want to know that bad. And get Chinese. Sweet-and-sour pork. I had pizza delivered last night when Theresa didn't come home 'til ten."

"Theresa?"

"I stopped calling her Mom."

"Why?"

"'Cause she doesn't act like a mom."

She had him there.

After calling for supper delivery, Ben sat down in his recliner with his iPad and scrolled through the list of things he'd need to do to make Mallory Hamilton's house decent.

Her house reeked of "hubby just moved out." Half the master closet was empty, and she'd barely begun to spread her things into the vacated space. Only one toothbrush in the holder, but there was toothpaste spatter on the backsplash over the second sink. She still had a light line on the third finger of her left hand where her ring had blocked the sun.

What kind of idiot would leave such a nice woman? Pretty, too, although she wore her light brown hair awfully short. At least it suited her round face and drew attention to her best feature—her big, brown doe eyes.

The least Ben could do was fix her home. Her husband—or was it ex-husband?—obviously had no idea how to finish any of the numerous projects he'd begun. Most of what he'd done would have to be started over, but Ben hadn't lied to her when he'd said the house had good bones.

It was a sturdy, roomy home built in the days when houses were supposed to last. No cheap vinyl siding or slab foundation. The crawl space was dry, the floor joists sturdy and well put together. The attic needed more insulation, but it was also clean and dry and the roof had plenty of life left. Once he finished working on repairs, she could stay in that house and make new memories or sell the place for a nice profit. Either option would give her a fresh start, which she surely needed.

Back to that estimate...

After fiddling with the costs, he came to a final figure when the doorbell rang.

Amber popped up and came to stand at his side, holding out her hand and grinning. "Cough it up, Dad."

He pulled out his wallet and handed her some cash. As she went to the door, he frowned at the nearly empty wallet, which matched his nearly empty bank account.

Ever since the economy turned sour, finding jobs hadn't been easy. Ben was grateful to friends and customers who recommended him to potentials, but work was still sketchy at best.

He hadn't told Mallory Hamilton how much he needed this job. If she knew how desperate he was getting she might not hire him.

While Amber took the food to the kitchen island and started setting out containers, he e-mailed his estimate to Mallory, sending it off with a wish and a prayer.

Chapter 2

The first day back is always the worst." Mallory set down her lunch and then dropped into the chair. How in the hell was she going to make it through a full day let alone an entire school year?

After the bell rang, the bustling noise of Stephen Douglas High School's passing period faded to the running steps of a few late students.

Her voice was already hoarse, and her neck and shoulders hurt. The left side of her chest ached, probably because she was using those muscles for the first time in a long time. Once she took her shoes off when she got home, her feet would swell. She needed to retrain her bladder to follow the bell schedule.

And she was almost too tired to move.

Danielle Bradshaw put her lunch bag next to Mallory's then flipped her blonde ponytail over her shoulder. Her blue eyes were filled with anger. "I'd like to know who I pissed off in the guidance office to end up with nothing but freshmen. Seriously, isn't there a law or something?"

"Doesn't the eighth amendment prohibit cruel and unusual punishment?"

"That's exactly what having six classes of freshmen is—cruel and unusual punishment."

Juliana Kelley was the next to come into the small upstairs room where they'd gathered each weekday to eat lunch for the last five years. From the dark circles under her green eyes and the way she kept shaking her head, she was too shell-shocked to speak. But she would. Jules was too much of an extrovert not to.

As usual, Bethany Rogers came in last. She jerked her plastic supermarket bag out of the refrigerator and tossed it on the table before practically falling into her seat. "I made it through three whole periods before I had to send someone to the office."

"A new record," Danielle said, raising her Diet Coke in a mock toast. "What happened?"

"David Mason told me to go fuck myself when I told him to put his phone away and quit texting."

Juliana breathed a disgusted huff and shook her head again.

"He's a senior, right?" Danielle asked.

"Yep. Another overprivileged, the-world-belongs-to me senior," Beth replied.

"Maybe I'm not so bad with freshmen after all." Danielle sipped her drink.

Mallory let her gaze settle on her friends—the Ladies Who Lunch, as they'd dubbed themselves the first year they'd all been assigned the same lunch period. For five years, they'd made sure the principal always scheduled them together, calling in favors when they had to so they could have this time. They shared their meals while they shared their lives—both in and out of school. These women were her life support, especially Juliana.

Tears stung her eyes. "I never had the chance to thank all of you." She hated to cry in front of anyone.

"No thanks necessary. You'd do the same for us." Juliana patted Mallory's hand. At least she wasn't scowling now.

"You *have* done the same for us," Danielle added. "When I had my appendix out, I didn't have to cook for two weeks because of all of you."

"'That's what friends are for,'" Bethany chimed in, her big, brown eyes sparkling as she sang the words from the old song. The woman could be cheerful in the face of a global apocalypse.

Giving help was easy. Accepting it was the real trick.

"I may not have to say it, but I want to say it." Mallory sighed, sniffing hard to hold back the emotions she'd learned to keep tightly caged. "You got me through the worst. When Jay left—"

"We know." Juliana gave her a lopsided smile, her green eyes full of empathy that said *I know* rather than *We know.*

She was the only other one in the group who was divorced. She'd married in college, realized after several discouraging years she'd made a huge mistake, and had been solo ever since. Jules loved dating and hated commitments.

When Jay left, she'd told Mallory she was happy that she was getting her life back. Since Mallory tended to agree with that sentiment, she'd understood. The only difference was that Juliana's ex-husband was also a teacher at Douglas High, and she had to see him any time she went near the gymnasium, which she made sure wasn't often. At least Mallory never had to see Jay Hamilton. And her life was better for that blessing.

Perhaps she and Jules saw eye to eye because they were close in age—Mallory was thirty-three to Juliana's thirty-four. Danielle and Bethany were both twenty-nine and still single.

Mallory pulled out her yogurt, salad, and banana, then turned the bag upside down to let the plastic spoon and fork slide out.

She'd started eating healthier, seizing control of the one thing in her life that truly needed repair. She'd gotten too thin—at least that was what most people said when they saw her after the months away for summer vacation.

Danielle drowned her salad in ranch dressing and stabbed a hunk of lettuce with her fork. Instead of eating it, she pointed the fork to emphasize her words, making drops of the dressing drip on her salad. "I have a minimum of thirty kids in every class. How is that fair to them or to me?"

"We all have thirty-plus kids per class," Mallory replied. "Funding was cut. Again."

"Screw the legislature." Bethany scooped some hummus on a cracker and shoved it in her mouth. Her hair was short, although not as short as Mallory's. It also was a mass of curls that most people envied but Beth hated.

"I refuse to spend this whole lunch hour bitching about the unfairness in education." Juliana had evidently overcome her shell-shock. She leveled a smile at Mallory that screamed she was up to something. Again. "We're still having a mixer at my church every Saturday and—"

Mallory waved her off. "No way, Jules. I'm not dating."

"Why on earth not?"

"Are you serious?"

"Mal…it's time to put all this behind you."

"I *have*. I just don't think a date is what I need right now. I've got a house to fix, students to teach, and peace and quiet to enjoy."

"Look, it's just a mixer," Jules coaxed. "You haven't been out in ages. Not since—"

"I had two dates this month. Remember?"

"You had two *disasters*. Just come with me. Please?"

While she'd rather have a root canal, Mallory finally gave her friend a curt nod. It was probably time to come out of her cave once and for all.

She needed to learn to live again.

"What about the house?" Danielle asked. "Did you talk to Robert?"

One of the industrial tech teachers, Robert Ashford, built custom homes as a second job. Whenever a teacher needed work done, anything from painting to adding a room, Robert would handle it or recommend good and trustworthy people to hire. Mallory had reached out to him, and he'd sent Ben Carpenter, the carpenter.

"Yeah. I had a contractor look at it yesterday. He e-mailed me an estimate last night, but I'm utterly terrified to look at it."

"I'm sure Jay will pay for part of it," Bethany said.

Sometimes her optimism bordered on naïveté. If Bethany actually believed Mallory's ex would give her a single dollar, she'd crossed the border.

"Are you kidding?" Mallory screeched.

"No... I mean... don't you get alimony or something?"

"There's no alimony in Illinois," Jules replied.

"He gave me the house—"

"And the mortgage," Danielle chimed in.

Mallory had to smile at that. "The house was all I wanted, and it's got tons of equity. I don't want another penny from him anyway." She'd promised herself not to dwell on her skunk of an ex, so she segued to a new topic. "I'll work up some guts and check that estimate when I get home. Maybe I can find enough money to get my house finished."

* * *

The estimate hadn't caused a coronary. Yes, it was high, but it was also pleasantly lower than she'd anticipated. She stared at the business card, dredging up the courage to call the number and commit. With a sigh, she dialed.

"Ben Carpenter."

"Mr. Carpenter? It's Mallory Hamilton."

"Hi, Mrs. Hamilton. Glad to hear from you. I assume you received the estimate."

Although it was the second time he'd called her that, she didn't correct him. After all, a simple name shouldn't make her heart hurt. Even the kids at school still called her Mrs. Hamilton. Perhaps she would eventually go back to being Mallory Oldham... but not yet. "Call me Mallory. Please."

"Fine. Mallory. So what do you think?"

"I think my house is a flippin' mess."

He chuckled. "A flippin' mess, yes. But a *fixable* flippin' mess."

Just what she wanted to hear. "How soon can you start?"

"I've got a couple of other projects right now..."

Damn. "I was hoping you could get started right away. I'm sick of this place looking like... like... this."

Silence reigned for a few long moments. "If you don't mind me being there in the evenings for the first two weeks, I guess I could start work tomorrow. In a couple of weeks, I can give you more time during the day."

She felt like an ogre. What she was asking was akin to someone wanting her to teach night school after teaching all day. The guy probably had a family he cared about. A wife. A kid or two.

She wouldn't abuse what she'd judged as his good nature. "I shouldn't have asked. That was very selfish of me."

"No, it's okay. I can handle it."

"Won't that make an awfully long day for you?"

"Actually, yes. But I could *really* use the extra money."

The way he stressed the "really" made her overactive imagination run amuck. She speculated about his need for money, blaming anything from gambling to drug addiction. As if a guy that handsome and healthy could be using drugs.

But she was going to be giving him access to her home. Shouldn't she know more about him?

No. Mallory trusted Robert to send her a good contractor, not a psychopath.

"What time tomorrow?" she asked.

"What time do you eat supper? I don't want to interrupt your routine."

"Trust me, you won't be interrupting anything. After school, I'm grading papers, numbing my brain with reality TV, or snoring, and you won't disturb any of those activities."

"Sounds...invigorating. Then maybe I could get there around five or five thirty?"

"Sounds fine, Mr. Carpenter."

"If I'm going to call you Mallory, the least you can do is return the favor."

"You want me to call you Mallory?" At least her rather offbeat sense of humor was coming back. Maybe one day she'd be the old Mallory again. Maybe one day she could put everything behind her and move on.

Maybe one day she'd be whole again.

"I'd rather you call me Ben. I'd hate to be known as Mallory Jr."

She loved his feisty retort. "Fine. Ben."

"See you tomorrow, Mallory."

"See you tomorrow, Ben."

No sooner had she ended the call when her cell vibrated again. Juliana's picture stared back from the phone.

"Hey, Jules. What's up?"

"The mixer. This Saturday. You and me, babe."

Mallory groaned. "I'd hoped you'd forgotten about that."

"Stop being a stick-in-the-mud. I don't want you to find a happily ever after. I don't even want you to find a happy-for-tonight. I just want you to get your ass out of the house."

"Fine. Fine. I'll try. But I'm not promising to stay long. And I'm not setting up any dates with any guys."

"We'll see about that."

"Jules..."

Mallory could almost see Jules holding up a hand in surrender. "Okay. You win. How about we go out for a bite Saturday evening and then go together?"

A snort slipped out. "Like I don't know what you're up to. If let you drive, then I'll be at your mercy on when I can leave."

"Saw right through my scheme, did ya?"

"How about we meet at the restaurant instead?"

"A solid plan. Oh, hey... wear the new makeup. It's supersexy."

Mallory had gone for a makeover at an expensive boutique. She didn't bother wearing the good stuff for school, not caring if her complexion was wan or her eyelashes were short and sparse. What did her students care? She ran her fingers through her short, gelled hair, thinking for the first time in a long time about how much fun it might be to put on the Ritz and dance the night away.

Maybe Juliana was right: she should get back into the swing of things.

"And dress nice—something like you'd wear to parent-teacher conferences."

"Damn. You mean I can't wear my French maid outfit with the fishnet thigh-highs and black f-me stilettos?"

"*Ooh la la*. I say go for it. Might get you a few phone numbers."

Mallory snorted again. "Not if I don't stuff my bra." None of her clothes fit right anymore, and if she lost any more weight, she'd have to either take all her waistbands in or go shopping. She hated shopping. That part of her femininity had never kicked in.

"You look fine, Mal."

"I look bald and skinny, Jules."

"Then go ahead and stuff your bra."

She shook her head, even if Juliana couldn't see her. "Not quite there yet."

Chapter 3

Mallory had just put the last of the dishes in the dishwasher when the doorbell rang. Ben Carpenter was here for his first day of trying to save her house.

She opened the door and managed a smile despite her exhaustion. "Hi, Ben."

"Hey." He stepped inside, setting a gray toolbox just inside the open foyer closet. "Did you have a good day at school?"

The question seemed so ordinary for him. Jay had seldom asked about her day. Then again, he'd never seemed very interested in her job. Hearing about the inner workings of a high school was probably boring as hell to most people.

There she went again, making excuses for her ex-husband's perpetual cold shoulder. Would she ever be able to break the habit? Would she ever learn to expect more from a man than taking her and her feelings for granted?

"My day was fine. Thanks for asking. Have you decided where you're gonna start on this disaster?"

"I'm not starting tonight." The grin he gave her was impish, so in contrast to the hard, masculine lines of his face.

Ben wasn't classic "handsome." No patrician nose. No prominent jaw. No fierce brows. But his brown eyes sparkled with life, and she loved the shadow of tawny stubble on his chin and cheeks. He was lean, but his arms were muscular enough to keep her attention. His backside was sublime in those weathered jeans.

Since he didn't react to her obvious gawking, he probably knew he was appealing to women and was accustomed to their stares. Besides, she was perfectly safe looking. She wasn't on the market despite Juliana's interference. Her dating life had died last winter, and she was content to let it rest in peace. She'd even be glad to erect a tombstone in its honor.

No man would want to haul around the baggage that now accompanied Mallory Hamilton, nor would she ever ask one to. Besides, she was fine alone. Just fine.

"What do you mean you're not starting now? I thought you said you'd start the renovations tonight," she said.

"I did." A crooked smile crossed his lips. The guy clearly loved to tease.

"Now you're just confusing me."

"Didn't mean to. I'm here to start, but you have something to do first."

Mallory chuckled. "I can pretty much guarantee you that anything I do you'll have to redo."

"Not this task. You'll be great doing this."

It had been so long since she'd played flirty little word games with a man. Ben's bantering was so natural, she couldn't help but smile. "Then what task do I have to do?"

"Every woman's favorite, the one that gives them the most pleasure." He winked at her.

Heat spread over her face, and she opened and closed her mouth, unsure of whether she should say anything.

He laughed at her embarrassment. "Shopping, Mallory. You need to go shopping with me."

"Very funny, Ben."

"I thought so." He opened the door and gave her a half bow. "After you."

***

It wasn't until they walked into Home Depot that Ben realized what he'd been doing with Mallory.

For God's sake, he'd flirted with her.

He wanted to blame her. After all, she'd somehow broken through the shell of ice he'd wrapped around himself where women were concerned. He'd teased Mallory as though they were on a first date.

The blush had burned bright on her cheeks when he'd joked with her, and it was a good sign that he hadn't offended. He reminded himself he was her employee, not her date.

So why was it so easy to see himself in that role?

When she reached for a cart, Ben shook his head. They'd need a four-wheeler and at least three trips to his truck for all the stuff he'd be buying to start on her house. He hated shopping with a passion, even at a hardware store. By taking her to pick out what she wanted—the colors, the fixtures—he could get almost everything done in one fell swoop and only have to pop back a few times for stuff he hadn't anticipated.

The first four-wheeler he grabbed had three wheels working and one that didn't even touch the floor. He pulled another out of the queue and pushed it up the first aisle as Mallory walked at his side.

"Do you have a list?" she asked.

"In my head."

"Then we're in trouble. Whenever I go shopping with a list in my head, I forget what I need and come home with a bunch of stuff I hadn't planned on buying."

He enjoyed how at ease she was with him. "Doesn't matter. I'll just bill you for all of it, needed or unneeded." He stopped at the laminate selections. "Do you like the color you've got in the foyer now?"

"Not really."

"Then why did you choose what's there?"

"Jay picked—why does it matter? It's partly done. Can't you just use the boxes that are left and save a little money? I mean... sure, I like other colors better, but..."

"Box, not boxes. There's only one, boss." After a quick visual scan, Ben frowned. "They don't stock that color anymore." She needed to hear the whole truth. "The flooring you've got down now isn't installed correctly, so I'll have to pull it up. I might be able to save some boards, but not likely. Whoever hammered them in didn't use a tapping block, so the tongues and grooves are ruined."

She heaved a weary sigh. "Why doesn't that surprise me?"

Clearly there was a story there. Although he was dying of curiosity to know if he'd assumed correctly—that she was recently divorced—he refused to ask, not wanting to press her. "Look, there isn't even a full box left of the old stuff, and it's crap anyway. You need something that will last, especially in a high-traffic place like a foyer."

"I sure wouldn't call my foyer 'high-traffic.' The only people who come in through the front door are you and Girl Scouts selling cookies. After tonight, I figured you'd be coming in through the garage like my friends do."

He liked the sound of that—the notion that while he worked for her they would be friends. After he checked the stacks of laminate, he found the right brand: great quality and decent price. "Why don't you look these over and pick a color you like?"

"Oh, I know what I'd like. But you need to tell me what's in play."

"Start here." He touched the first of the laminate samples that he felt comfortable using. "Stop here." He tapped one further down the display.

Mallory perused each of the samples, running her fingers over the surfaces before coming back to the same walnut hue.

Ben wouldn't rush her. This project was rapidly taking on an importance to him. Mallory had been through a rough patch. He suspected she'd recently been through heartbreak and was trying to rebuild her life. If he could help her do that by working on her place, he'd be satisfied. Just as he wanted his town house to be "home" for Amber, he wanted to turn Mallory's house into her "home" down to the last nail.

Her hand rested on a dark sample, the one he would've picked were it his house. "I saw this on a renovation show on HGTV. I really liked it. What do you think, though?"

While he loved the color of the stain, he wanted her to choose for herself. "Doesn't matter what I think, boss."

"I'm not your boss. Not really."

"Seemed easier than calling you 'client.'" Funny, but he didn't like thinking of her as either a client or his boss.

"How about Mallory?"

"Fine... but it still doesn't matter what I think."

She shifted her gaze from the laminate to him. "You're the one who has to work with it."

"You're the one who has to *live* with it."

A smile bowed her lips. "Fine. I want the walnut."

"Walnut it is."

When she reached for a box, he moved to stop her. Too late. She lifted one end, promptly dropped it, and then hissed out a breath.

The urge to scold her tickled his tongue, but he refrained. The boxes were heavier than they looked, and she'd misjudged what she could lift. "Let me do that. That's what you're paying me for."

She nodded, her lips a grim line as she dropped her left shoulder and held her left arm close to her middle.

"Are you okay?"

"I'm... fine."

"Did you strain something in your shoulder?"

Her reply was a brisk shake of her head.

"We can do this later..."

"No." She took a deep breath. "No, I want you to have what you need to start working. I'm—I'm fine."

The word "liar" almost slipped out. Instead, he frowned and loaded boxes of walnut-colored laminate onto the cart. If she wanted to pretend she hadn't strained something, fine with him.

"Where now?" she asked. Her hand had fallen away from her left side, which he hoped meant she felt better.

"Time to pick out some light fixtures."

"Oh goodie," Mallory drawled.

"Hardware stores not your thing?"

"Not even close. Neither is shopping. Although... it will be fun to pick out things I like."

"Yes, ma'am. That house will be exactly what you want it to be. But I thought all women loved to shop." Then again, Ben tended to judge most women based on his ex-wife. That was clearly a dumb thing to do with his new boss.

One of these days he'd have to drop the walls around him and try to let someone new in. Maybe he'd be lucky enough to meet a woman with a good sense of humor and a sweet nature.

Like Mallory Hamilton.

"You really hate to shop?" he asked to distract himself from his wayward thoughts.

"Yep. But I'll let you in on a little secret." She crooked her finger until he drew closer. "Teachers melt at an office-supply store." Her voice was a mischievous whisper, and her face glowed when she smiled.

"I'll have to remember that."

* * *

"You've only got the one car?" Ben asked.

Mallory nodded, although the question seemed a bit odd. None of the projects she'd hired him to do were in her two-car garage.

The place was next to empty since the day Jay decided he wanted a divorce. He'd packed up his clothes and his tools and just…left. While a little warning might have been nice, she'd come to believe the direct cut had been for the best, especially considering everything else she'd been dealing with. Let the new girlfriend deal with him and hope to hell she never needed him to man up when the going got tough. Being a mature adult wasn't Jay's forte.

She approached the divorce the way she did most things. Head-on. No weeping. No gnashing her teeth. No self-pity. He wanted out of the marriage? *Good-bye and good riddance.* She wouldn't waste any more tears on Jay Hamilton.

"Do you mind if I set up in the unused side?" Ben asked. "It's a pain in the a—um...butt to have to load and unload some of my stuff. I'm going to use quite a few things for a while."

"You won't need them for your other jobs?"

He shook his head but didn't expand with a true reply.

She'd heard once that women talked more often than men, that females used three times as many words. Ben certainly didn't waste any. He'd talked to her at the hardware store, but then he'd grown eerily quiet. Sure, he asked questions about the items he wanted her to pick out, but nothing more. No more teasing or chitchat. The ride home had been filled with nothing but the twang of country music on the truck's radio, another overemotional song about love gone wrong. He'd all but disappeared as he unloaded the things he'd need to bring the "money pit" back into its heyday.

"Fine, then," she replied. "Just set up wherever is best for you. Where are you going to start?"

"I thought about that a lot. If you don't have a preference—"

"I don't," she insisted. The whole place needed work. What did it matter what got fixed first?

"Then the foyer."

She waited for him to explain why he'd chosen that.

He didn't.

"Why not one of the bathrooms?"

"The floor in the foyer's dangerous. The bathrooms are just ugly."

"Dangerous?"

"The laminate boards weren't joined together tightly, and the whole floor floats. It slides. Didn't you notice?"

"Yeah. I guess I just got used to it."

"When you put it in you forgot to add a foam underlay. I'll have to pull the whole thing up and start from scratch."

As if she'd ever let Ben think she would be that irresponsible. "I didn't put it in. Jay did."

"Jay?"

"Never mind."

Since Ben didn't tend to elaborate, neither would she. The whole sordid nightmare still humiliated her every single time she thought about it, so she tried to keep it where it belonged, in the past.

"I'll be able to get this pulled up and prepped tonight. I'll install the new flooring tomorrow. Sorry, but this won't be the first time you're inconvenienced, not by a long shot."

"Meaning?"

"I'll have to turn off electricity, water, stuff like that while I fix different things."

She'd survived much, much worse than a little inconvenience. "I only want to be able to walk on one level from the stairs to the kitchen instead of traversing all those wooden speed bumps."

"Your ex is the one who made such a mess of the DIY?"

"Yeah." *He made a mess of a lot of things…*

"I'll get rid of the speed bumps. Promise." Ben's chuckle was warm and genuine. Mallory tried not to notice.

Her whole body flushed hot, but she couldn't tell if it was from yet another hormone flux or Ben Carpenter. One of her medicines made her suffer from hot flashes, night sweats, and mood swings. While she could easily blame turning crazy on Jay leaving, she hadn't even started those pills when he moved out.

With a curt nod, Ben headed out the front door.

At least when this guy walked out, he'd come back.

Chapter 4

Mallory couldn't stop frowning, hardly believing she'd actually shown up at Bayside Church's Saturday singles mixer. She wasn't looking for a companion right now. Maybe someday.

The things I do for friends...

On the other hand, she wasn't sure how long she could wait for male companionship, which explained why she'd allowed Juliana to cajole her so easily. Being around Ben in the evenings seemed to have reawakened her hibernating libido. Sex hadn't crossed her mind for a long time. Even before Jay left a year ago. Now it was all she could think about.

But she wasn't looking to find someone tonight. It was too soon. Far too soon. Besides, the prospects of great single guys in Cloverleaf, Illinois, were few and far between.

Except for Ben Carpenter...

"I'm staying an hour, Jules." She held up her index finger. "*One* hour. Then I'm heading home."

Her words did nothing to diminish Juliana's smile. "We'll see."

As usual, Juliana would get her way. "At least there's a bar."

"Damn right, or I wouldn't be here." She waved to some guys

who stood clustered around the large-screen TV, mostly ignoring it—probably because it wasn't showing any sports. "You need to start living again, Mallory."

"I'm living just fine."

An inelegant snort popped out of Juliana. "You're sleepwalking through life. You go to school, you go home, you sleep, then you do it all again the next day."

"I didn't go to school today."

"Stop being a smart-ass, although it's nice to see you're getting back to yourself." She tossed Mallory a wink. "The divorce has been final for months and you're getting healthier and stronger. What does it hurt to meet a couple of new guys? Dance. Flirt. Remember that you're a beautiful woman and—"

"Beautiful? With hair shorter than most of the men here and…and no—"

"Don't even say it, Mal. You're going to fix that, remember?"

With a sigh, she nodded. Flirting wasn't on her agenda, but she'd talk to a few guys even though the last thing in the world she wanted was to open up to a new man. Not yet. Not while she wasn't whole.

"Let's get a drink and mingle." Juliana grabbed Mallory's hand and dragged her to the bar.

"Let's get several drinks."

They stood close to the dance floor and nursed their white wines while Mallory watched a small group of men who were drinking beer from long-neck bottles and laughing every now and then. The whole scene reminded her of the awkward dances she'd been to during middle school. Girls to one side; guys to the other. Both groups trying to work up enough courage to ask someone to dance.

One of the men gave her and Juliana a half wave, and Mallory smiled in return. Robert Ashford was here, so at least there would be one more familiar and friendly face. He tapped the shoulder of the guy next to him whose broad back was to the women and gestured his brown bottle Mallory's direction. Then the man turned to look at them.

Ben Carpenter. Her *carpenter.*

"Wow." Juliana nudged Mallory's arm. "That one's a looker. Tall drink of water, too. Think I might ask him to dance."

"You can't." Was that a note of jealousy in her own voice?

"Why not?"

"He's the guy working on my house. Ben Carpenter."

"You have a carpenter named Carpenter? That's priceless." Juliana stared at him for a few long moments. "You get to see him every day?" She let out a low whistle. "Maybe I need to find some projects for him to do at my house."

"He's got a full-time job and works on my house evenings. He doesn't have enough time to do anything for you."

"Careful, Mal... You're sounding possessive, which makes me very, very happy. This one might have a chance. You already know him, and it's obvious you're interested."

Mallory shook her head.

"Why don't you give this guy a shot? The way he's grinning at you, I'd say he's interested, too." She nudged Mallory with her shoulder. "Go on. Go ask him to dance."

"I'm still having my wine."

When Mallory took a sip, Juliana tilted her glass up so she'd have to finish it before snatching the glass from her hand. "You're done now."

Her throat burned from drinking the wine so quickly. "I can't ask him to dance."

"Sure you can."

"I can't! I'm not—he wouldn't want me. At least not yet."

"Don't make me smack you for saying something that stupid." Juliana shoved her with her shoulder, a little rougher than the last time. "Go. Oh…wait. Looks like you won't have to."

"What are you—" Mallory's eyes flew wide. "Lord Almighty, he's coming over here." She swallowed hard before the reality of the situation hit her, calming her anxiety. "He's coming over here for you, Jules. You look spectacular tonight, by the way."

"Don't I always?" She winked. "But I'll bet you another drink he's gonna ask you to dance, not me. He hasn't taken his eyes off you."

As if anyone would even consider her when Juliana was right under his nose. "You're on."

Ben stopped in front of them and smiled that lopsided smile that made Mallory's stomach somersault. He was staring right at her. "Who's on, and what are you on for?"

"Mallory just bet me—"

She stopped Juliana from being her wicked self and blurting out what they'd bet upon by kicking her gently. The woman didn't have any kind of filter between her brain and her mouth.

"Hi, Ben. How are you?"

"I'm great, Mallory." His gaze shifted to Juliana. "Hi, I'm—"

"Ben Carpenter. Mallory already told me all about you." Jules held up the two wineglasses. "I'd shake your hand, but…"

"Double-fisted drinker, eh?" His chuckle was warm, but his eyes returned to Mallory.

"Not at these prices," Juliana replied.

"You look nice in pink," he said to Mallory.

Her whole body flushed hot in response to his intense stare. He was clearly choosing skinny, little her over Juliana.

A first.

Although Juliana was her dearest friend, whenever Mallory was with her, she felt rather invisible even before all the changes. Perhaps it was the long red hair. Natural red, too. Not a brassy bottle red. Her eyes were a sparkling green. Her Irish heritage shone through in her curvy shape. The only thing missing was the accent, and Jules could even affect one of those when she put her mind to it. Heaven knew she'd trotted it out to use on guys she met in bars just for kicks and giggles.

Still, despite all of Juliana's beauty and charm, Ben wasn't staring at her.

His hands were halfway in his back pockets, and he rocked on his feet as though nervous. She'd never seen this side of him before. "I don't suppose you'd want to...I don't know... dance?"

"You're asking *me*?" Juliana laughed and held up the wineglasses. "Thanks, but my hands are full."

"I wasn't...Oh." A nervous laugh made Mallory smile at his unease. "You knew I meant Mallory." He turned those brown eyes on full power, melting something inside her. "D'ya wanna dance?"

The question came out so quickly, it sounded like one long word.

She took mercy on him and indulged herself in her only chance to ever be in his strong arms. "Sure. I-I'd like that."

* * *

Ben let out a long, relieved breath. He hadn't been that nervous since asking a girl whose name he now couldn't even remember to the junior prom.

He stretched out his hand. "Then come on. Dance with me."

After a moment of hesitation that made his heart skip a beat, Mallory put her hand in his.

The dance floor wasn't crowded, but there were enough other couples so he didn't have to feel as though all eyes were on them.

Robert was leaning against the wall, grinning like a damned fool. He'd already teased Ben ad nauseam about how Mallory would fall in love with him while he fixed up her house. The joshing was probably Ben's fault. He'd made what he'd hoped were subtle inquiries into how long ago Mallory had been divorced and whether there was a chance of Mr. Hamilton ever returning to the picture. Robert told him her husband had walked out without a word of warning almost a year ago.

Dumb bastard.

The song changed right as Ben was about to show her that he really couldn't dance well. Only country line dancing made him comfortable, usually because he was among a bunch of other drunk, wannabe cowboys and cowgirls who missed steps as often as he did. Thankfully, the DJ put on a slow song, the type that made holding her close acceptable. Since she seemed reticent, he guided her arms around his neck and set his hands on her waist.

She's thin. No doubt the stress from the divorce, and it wasn't as though he didn't like what he saw. But he wanted to help her stay healthy. He'd already formed a game plan to fatten her up a smidge, aiming to do something he'd never done for another woman.

He'd cook for her.

After Theresa left, money had been tight, so he'd stretched dollars by learning to cook. Amber had joined in, learning along with him. She was good. He was great. He could make one of his specialties for Mallory.

Since when had he needed to think of lame excuses to get a woman interested in him?

Most women liked the way he looked. His ego loved how their gazes lingered and how often they approached him instead of forcing him to make the first move. He wasn't a tomcat, but since his divorce, he'd taken a few of the more interesting ladies up on their offers of intimacy. They were one-night stands—always at their places—that meant nothing to him except a satisfying physical release. He'd left instead of spending the night. While he made sure they enjoyed themselves, he'd never once considered starting another relationship.

His first marriage had been hell, and Amber needed stability. He wasn't about to start parading women in and out of his daughter's life. The few liaisons he'd had were private, and he hadn't truly thought of seeking out a new mate. Marriage was for other guys.

Then Mallory Hamilton had called to ask his help. A week of getting to know her while he fixed her foyer floor and put a new toilet and vanity in her downstairs half bath, and he'd found himself besotted.

As they swayed with the music, Ben couldn't seem to get her to loosen up. Holding her was akin to dancing with an ironing board. He let his hands drift up to rub small circles on her back, and she slowly eased her rigid posture. By the time a second song began, she was relaxing.

"This is my favorite song," he whispered in her ear so she'd keep dancing. Then he dared to press his lips to her earlobe.

When she shivered and nodded, he smiled, grateful she couldn't see his grin. She might mistake it for smug instead of for what it was—relieved. Her divorce was still fresh. She'd need time and patience to learn to trust another guy. Although he wasn't at all sure Mallory would be anything more than a passing fancy, at least her surrender meant he'd have a chance to find out if she could be something more.

Ben loved her scent. Light. Utterly feminine. He tightened his embrace, wanting to press her against him so he could savor the feel of her in his arms.

"I—I didn't think you'd ask me to dance." Her voice was hushed.

"Why?"

"Because of Juliana. She's so much more…"

"You mean the redhead?"

"Yeah."

"She's so much more what?"

"Pretty."

Giving her a squeeze, he rubbed his chin on the top of her head. She was a little bit of a thing. Couldn't be more than a couple inches over five feet. Delicate. Feminine. "Are you fishing for a compliment?"

She bumped his chin when she tilted her head back to glare at him. "No! I wasn't…I mean…"

Ben flashed her a grin. "I was teasing. But you're prettier. Besides…I know you. I don't know anything about her."

"It's a mixer. You're not supposed to know anyone here."

"I don't like mixing much."

"Then why did you come?" She'd stopped dancing, so he did the same. Her eyes kept searching his, making him wish he knew what she was looking for so he could try to be that man.

"I came because Robert told me you'd be here."

"How did he know?"

The conspiracy wasn't supposed to be a secret, so he spilled. "Because your friend called and told him."

Mallory leveled a frown at Juliana. "Figures."

With a finger under her chin, Ben coaxed her to look at back at him. "What's it matter? I'd been trying to work up the courage to ask you out anyway. I just figured I'd wait 'til I wasn't working for you anymore."

"Really?"

He held tight to his frustration and nodded.

Was she pleased that he'd gone out of his way to spend time with her? Not that he didn't see her every weekday evening. But this was...different. They weren't trying to talk around the buzz of his saw or the pounding of his hammer.

"The song's about over. Want to go get a drink and sit and talk?"

Her hesitation hurt his ego, as did her taking a step back.

"C'mon, Mallory. What do you have to lose? Get to know me, and if I'm not a nice guy, I'll go back to being just your contractor. Deal?" Ben held out his hand.

Her eyes found his. There was a sadness there that tore at his heart before a slow smile curved her lips. Then she gave him a nod and put her hand in his. "Deal."

Chapter 5

A vibrant Ben wasn't at all what Mallory had expected.

Since she'd been the one to chitchat with him as he worked she'd believed he was a quiet, restrained guy. She hadn't formed too many conclusions on what he was like on a more personal level because he hadn't opened up. Now, as they talked, she tried to learn all she could about Ben Carpenter.

While he drank another beer and she sipped a fresh white wine, they bantered much like she'd enjoyed the first day they'd met. Things between them were easy and fun, something she hadn't enjoyed with a man since…well, ever.

She'd always kept her guard up around guys, suspicious of their true motivation when they showed an interest in her. Sure, that smacked of a self-esteem problem, but she blamed a chubby childhood for that flaw. Perhaps she could someday think of herself without picturing the girl her aunts often claimed had too pretty a face to hide under all her baby fat.

On the other hand, the trials life threw her way had toughened her, made her look at herself with a new set of eyes—eyes that appreciated her finer qualities. She had a good heart. She was faithful to those she loved. And she had a passion for life. There was substance to her that many shallow women lacked. Perhaps her new inner strength was what attracted a guy like Ben Carpenter.

Mallory relaxed, enjoying the conversation until he abruptly turned the mood serious. "When was your divorce final?"

Her temper spiked at the notion someone was talking behind her back. "Who said I was divorced?"

He shrugged.

"How do you know I'm divorced? Robert told you, didn't he?"

"Actually, I figured it out on my own first. He just confirmed it."

"How could you figure it out?"

Ben's smile helped her anger ease. "Well... first clue—the DIY projects at your house. Women don't do those too often. From what I've seen, when they do start them, they also finish them."

"That wouldn't be enough to tell you I'm divorced."

"Clue two, the tan line on your ring finger."

Mallory whipped her hand up and looked at it, really looked. The white line left behind after she'd removed her wedding ring was now as bright as a flashlight shone in her eyes.

Her prickliness evaporated. She'd been so private about all the changes in her life, and the notion that she was nothing but fodder for gossip had fired her blood. She didn't want sympathy or pity from anyone, especially Ben.

"Clue three... you mentioned a guy named Jay who's conveniently not around."

I'm a fool. "Oh..."

"For how long?"

"Six months."

"So I'm your first date?"

"This isn't a date, Ben. It's a chat with my contractor."

"Why'd he leave?"

Lord, the man asked the most brazen questions. "How do you know *I* didn't leave *him*?"

"Because you're not the type of woman who'd walk out on a marriage."

They'd known each other for so short a time, how could he possibly have formed any conclusions about her?

At least this conclusion is good.

"Fine," Mallory said with a curt nod. "He walked out and I'm really glad he did. You know those vows you take? The ones that are supposed to be for a lifetime? Well, Jay thought that he was in for nothing but richer and health, and instead he got poorer and—" She shrugged.

Ben quirked an eyebrow.

She waved his unasked question away. "Let it go."

"For now."

While she wanted to say "forever," she followed her own advice. "So let's turn the inquisition around and focus on you."

"Fine. What do you want to know?"

"What happened to *your* marriage? All I know is you're divorced and that you've got custody of your daughter." She'd learned that much from the times they'd talked while she'd helped him out. Her favorite thing so far had been to stand on the new laminate flooring so it wouldn't move whenever he had to tap in a stubborn board. He'd teased her that she didn't weigh enough to keep it in place. She'd countered by picking up her cat, smiling at him, and saying Rascal was enough added weight.

"I'm divorced because Theresa's a selfish woman who doesn't even care about her own daughter."

"Amber, right?"

"Yeah. Amber. She just turned thirteen."

"Fun age."

"Not from what I've seen."

"I was kidding. I wouldn't teach middle school for a million dollars a year."

Ben's mouth thinned to a line. "Are all girls that age so...so emotional?"

Mallory let a laugh spill out. "Mister, you ain't seen nothin' yet."

He rolled his eyes. "Super. Just what I wanted to hear."

"Give it four or so years. She should become human again—right before you send her off to college."

"Parents?"

He'd switched gears so fast he'd lost her. "Pardon?"

"Your parents. Where do they live?"

The sadness was still there. Probably always would be. As was the fear. "Mom died a few years back."

"I'm sorry."

"Yeah, well...so was I."

"She must've been young."

"Fifty-five. Breast cancer doesn't care about a woman's age." She gave her head a shake to erase the memory. "Dad sold the house and moved to a retirement community in Florida. He loves it down there. Says he can reach just about anywhere he wants to go with his golf cart." Since she wasn't up to twenty questions about her life, she fired one at him instead. "Where do your parents live?"

"Chicago. They've been in the same house for the whole forty years they've been married. Raised two boys and more dogs and cats than I can remember."

"That's wonderful." *Like a marriage should be.*

The conversation strayed into idle musings until another slow song popped up. Most of the other people at the mixer headed toward the bar with the exception of four couples who'd obviously discovered they felt an attraction. They stayed to dance, and she envied them. The newness. The excitement. The fun of discovering each little new thing about a person.

Then she realized that was exactly what she was doing with Ben.

How had she let him in so easily? The walls around her heart she'd built after Jay left—the walls that made her strong enough to face everything on her own—had budged. They weren't down, but there were already cracks and breaks she wasn't sure she could plug.

Ben stood, holding out his hand. "Let's dance, boss."

"I told you, I'm not your boss."

"All right, then...*Mallory*." His warm baritone washed over her like the brightest of sunbeams. "Dance with me, pretty lady."

Her eyes found Juliana. She was deep in conversation with a bald guy who had the best biceps Mallory had ever seen.

You go, Jules.

Mallory took his hand. "Fine. One more song. Then I need to go."

Ben checked his watch. "So early?"

"I'm really tired. Okay?"

"Whatever the lady wants."

This time, she went easily into his arms. Why fight the attraction? Nothing was going to come of it, so she might as well borrow as many tender moments as she could before Ben disappeared from her life. There were weeks of work left on her home, which meant she could get to know him better without having to date him. It also meant that if they didn't click, she'd be stuck seeing him every day for quite a while.

Was she making a big mistake?

She didn't think so once he wrapped his arms around her. His warmth was as wonderful as a fluffy blanket straight from the dryer. His shirt was soft against her cheek when she found the courage to lay it against his chest. When his chin dropped to rest on her head, she sighed in contentment.

"See," he said, the word rumbling in his chest. "This isn't so scary, is it?"

"No," she replied. "It's not."

The song ended, and while she simply wanted to stay in his embrace, the time for fantasizing had ended. This wasn't a grand ball, and she sure wasn't Cinderella.

* * *

When Mallory stepped out of his arms, she might as well have moved a mile back. The distance was chilling, as was the way she suddenly masked the emotions she was feeling.

Ben had felt a connection. Their conversation had been easy, and the way their offbeat senses of humor complemented each other made him believe they might be good together.

Then she'd stepped back and raised that firewall of hers so quickly he couldn't even fight it.

"I need to go." She tried to walk toward her friend.

His hand snaked around her upper arm. "Wait. What's wrong?"

Her responding yawn was as phony as the ones Amber gave him when she wanted to skip school and faked exhaustion. "I told you, I'm tired. Need to catch up on my sleep on the weekends."

He glanced over to Juliana and saw she was engrossed with a man. "If you came with your friend, you're out of luck. She's gonna be busy for a while. Maybe I could drive you home? You won't even have to give me directions."

She didn't rise to his teasing this time, which made him even more convinced he'd done something wrong. The problem was he didn't have a clue what it was.

"No, thanks. I drove myself."

"Then let me walk you to your car."

"You don't have to do that. This is a mixer, remember?" She shooed him away with the back of her hand. "Go mix."

"I've mixed with the only woman I care to mix with."

At least Mallory smiled. "That sounded kinda dirty."

A small crack in the wall. He'd try his best to crawl through. "Only *kinda* dirty? I'll have to try harder next time."

Reaching for her hand, he hoped she'd let him lead her to the dark parking lot—the perfect place for a test kiss.

He'd always believed in finding out if there was any chemistry before taking the next step with a woman. This time, he'd reversed the order, getting to know Mallory before checking to see if they were compatible physically. Since they'd clicked, Ben was dying of curiosity to see if that connection extended to the physical.

"C'mon, Mallory. Let me walk you to your car. It's dark out there. I need to know you're safe."

"Fine." Her gaze found her friend. "Juliana's obviously not ready to go."

"Obviously," he drawled.

"You don't have to bother, you know."

"No bother." He swept his hand toward the door. "Lead the way."

Her SUV was about as far away from his truck as she could've parked.

Mallory stood at the driver's door and gave him a hesitant smile. "I should go."

"I had fun, Mallory."

"Me, too."

Her face lifted when she smiled at him. The moonlight bathed her skin, making her glow. The crickets' song broke the silence that had descended upon them.

The perfect scene for a first kiss.

Leaning in, Ben gave her time to pull away if she didn't welcome his attention. Her eyes widened then her lids lowered to half-mast. He was smiling when his mouth found hers.

The softness of her lips against his was painfully sweet. Moving slowly, he put his hands to her waist and pulled her closer, close enough her body pressed against his.

She tasted sweet, like wine, and he wanted more. Tickling the seam of her lips, he took quick advantage when she opened to his tongue.

Chemistry.

He'd wanted to know if they had any. The first brush of her tongue across his told him everything he needed to know.

They had enough chemistry to blow up a laboratory.

Mallory rose on tiptoes, so he held her closer, wrapping his arms around her, and finally lifting until her feet dangled. He wanted to devour her, to drink in all her sweetness. Her response was heated, frantic. She looped her arms around his neck and laced her fingers through his hair, tugging as though she couldn't get enough of him.

They were playing with fire, one that could quickly flare out of control if he didn't call a stop to it. But…*damn.* He loved kissing her.

He turned, leaning his back against her Escape while he ravaged her mouth. She shifted, rubbing against his erection. He groaned, hugging her tighter. Everything inside him screamed to take her home, to beg her to let him make love to her.

Ben finally found the strength to drag his mouth away, and he let Mallory slide down his body. She stopped when her small feet were on top of his. She weighed next to nothing.

He had to smile at her bemused expression. The woman looked thoroughly kissed.

He had to stop this now or he wasn't sure he'd be able to regain any control.

"I—I should go," Mallory whispered.

"Yeah." If he tried to say anything more, he'd probably sound like a blabbering fool.

"See you Monday?"

Ben nodded while she chirped off her alarm. He opened her door and waited until she slid behind the wheel.

"Okay, then. Bye."

He couldn't help himself and leaned back in to brush one more kiss over her lips. Then he closed her door.

As she drove away, he noticed the magnetic pink ribbon—the one for breast cancer awareness he'd seen on lots of other cars. After hearing about her mother, he understood its significance.

He went to his truck, ready to leave. There was no sense in going back inside since the woman he wanted to spend time with was on her way home.

At least Monday was only two days away…

Chapter 6

Mallory opened her thermal lunch sack and pulled out her salad and packet of dressing.

Juliana eyed the items and then glanced down at her rather smushed peanut butter sandwich. "Wanna switch?"

"Nope. You know how much I love my Caesar salads." Setting her fork and napkin on the table, she reached in for the most important part of her lunch. "Ah…caffeine. How I need you."

The Diet Cherry Coke didn't reply to her compliment.

"I thought you were giving that stuff up," Bethany said as she plopped down in an empty chair. "Weren't you supposed to be eating healthier?"

"I'm having a salad," Mallory replied. "That's healthy enough. Don't you dare ask me to give up the only thing that keeps me moving during the day." She popped the tab and then took a long swig. The refreshing cherry-cola taste filled her mouth.

Juliana gave her a mock toast with her Diet Coke. "Me, too."

"Me, three." Danielle shut the door to the private lunchroom and pulled out the last chair at the round table. "Two cups of coffee at breakfast, and I'm barely functioning." She fished a Diet

Coke out of her bag. "Without this, I'd fall asleep at my desk by the end of the next period."

The women ate in companionable silence, but Juliana would turn inquisitor once she was able to talk. For several minutes of reprieve, Jules was occupied with chewing through a peanut butter sandwich that appeared to be pretty heavy on the peanut butter. But her eyes were full of questions, and Mallory ate her salad, waiting for queries about Ben.

Danielle beat Juliana to the punch. "So… Mallory. Heard you hooked up with a cute guy at the mixer this weekend."

"I didn't *hook up* with anyone." Scooping another forkful of lettuce into her mouth, Mallory glared at Jules.

"Don't look at me—I didn't tell her," Juliana insisted after swallowing the last of her sandwich.

"Heard it from Robert," Danielle explained. "Said the guy was a friend of his who went there looking for you."

"For the love of… I didn't hook up with Ben!"

"Ben?" Bethany tilted her head. "You mean your carpenter?"

"My contractor."

"You hooked up with him?" Beth wolf-whistled. "When you let loose, you really let loose."

"She didn't hook up with him," Juliana said.

"There! I told you so," Mallory said with a nod. "Thanks, Jules."

"No hookup 'cause he scared her away."

"Juliana!" Mallory had thought about calling her to tell her about the kiss she'd shared with Ben. They'd exchanged some texts because she'd been worried about Mallory's abrupt departure, but Mallory hadn't been ready to talk about everything that happened after the mixer.

"He didn't scare me away," she insisted. "I was just feeling a little… tired."

"You ran away like a frightened rabbit because he pushed too hard," Juliana retorted. She studied Mallory for a moment. "What did he do to you?"

"Nothing. I mean...not really." Mallory knew that answer would not suffice, so she caved. "We kissed."

"He kissed you?" Juliana's surprised tone grew loud. "Way to go, Mal!"

A sly smile spread over Danielle's face. "You liked him kissing you."

"I suppose I did."

"Good for you," Bethany said. "Maybe you've finally turned a corner."

With a shake of her head, Mallory said, "You're all making too much out of it."

Juliana snorted. "Then why are you blushing?"

"Is he a good kisser?" Danielle leaned in. "Details. We need details, woman."

"Details?" Mallory feigned confusion.

"Come off it," Danielle said, popping open her fruit cup. "You know the routine. What's the number?"

While she'd always enjoyed listening to her friends talk about their latest dates—especially enjoying their rate-his-kiss-on-a-one-to-ten-scale ritual—Mallory hesitated. The kiss had been more than a simple kiss. In those few moments in Ben's arms, while her senses were filled with him, something inside her had come back to life...something that she feared was dead and gone when Jay left.

Ben had made her want him. He'd made her heart pound, her head spin, and her body flood with heat. Once she'd gotten home, she'd savored the excitement he'd inspired and settled down to reread her favorite romance novel. Her sex drive had been abruptly reawakened. She wanted to drown in those wonderful feelings she'd feared had disappeared forever.

"Earth to Mal," Juliana said.

"Sorry. Lost in thought."

"That good, huh?" She winked at Mallory. "A ten?"

A twenty. "A solid nine."

Juliana snorted again. "So did he call?"

"Why would he?" Mallory asked. "I'll see him when I get home tonight."

"You were necking with the guy in the parking lot of—"

Mallory cut Juliana off. "I wasn't necking with him. We kissed. That's all."

"A solid nine," Danielle repeated with a chuckle.

Bethany pitched in her two cents. "I think Jules is right—he should have called."

They were right. He should have called. After a kiss like that…

Now she was being stupid. Just because he'd made her toes curl didn't mean she'd had the same effect on him.

***

Mallory set her grocery bags down on the table. "Ben? You're here?"

She hadn't expected him so early. When she'd come home from work to see his truck in the driveway, her heart skipped a beat. Since he had the code to her new garage door opener, he could always get inside. But he'd never arrived ahead of her before.

"Ben?"

He didn't answer, so she called again. A little louder. "Ben? I saw your truck."

This time a muffled reply came from upstairs.

Hurrying up the stairs, she almost collided with the ladder that rested below the open attic entrance. "You're early today."

"Finished my day job," he shouted. Squeaking rafters accompanied his voice.

"What'cha doing up there?"

His face appeared, grinning down at her. "Wiring for the ceiling fan in the master."

"What time did you get here?"

"About an hour ago. Wrapped up everything at the Peters place. I'm yours full-time for the rest of this week."

Ben disappeared. There were several shuffling noises then his work boots came through the square opening.

Mallory held the ladder, worried he'd fall.

Once his body was out of the attic, he slid the panel back into place and climbed the rest of the way down. "Should be able to have that fan done tonight."

"Thanks." She put her groceries away, ready to kick off her shoes and relax. "I'll leave you alone."

He folded up the ladder as she went back downstairs, casting a couple of worried glances over her shoulder.

Two weeks had gone by since the church mixer. Since then, things between her and Ben had gone right back to client and contractor. He hadn't mentioned the passionate interlude in the parking lot, so she refused to bring it up. She'd gotten carried away in the heat of the moment and let her feelings get tangled up with a guy who obviously wasn't all that interested in her.

She shoved the containers of yogurt into the fridge and turned around to find Ben right behind her. "Um…hi."

He was still grinning. "Hi."

Heat rose on her cheeks at his intense stare. "Um…I need to—"

Ben cut her off with a quick, no-nonsense kiss. "Look, Mallory…I'm sorry."

"Sorry? For what?" Although she tried to make her tone nonchalant, it was breathless enough to reveal how rattled the kiss left her.

"We should have talked. You know…after."

"After what?"

She'd never seen someone who could arch one eyebrow so effectively.

"Okay…you got me." A smile tickled her lips. "There's nothing to apologize for. We kissed. No big whoop."

"Oh, it *was* a big whoop. That's the problem. I shouldn't have kissed you."

Stepping around him, Mallory pulled cans of peaches and pears out of another plastic sack. His words felt like a slap to her pride. "Let it go."

He was behind her, hands on her shoulders. "I don't want to let it go."

She tried to shrug him away.

He wouldn't budge.

"Look, Ben…it was just a kiss. That's all. Just a—"

When he spun her to face him, she let out a surprised gasp that he captured with his lips.

This one lasted a little longer, but Mallory pulled back first. Staring up into his dark eyes, she tried to figure out what was flying through his thoughts.

"Can we talk now?" he asked as his hands framed her face.

"About?"

Ben chuckled. "About why I can't stop kissing you." He stroked her cheeks with his thumbs.

"I—I guess."

Taking her hand in his, he led her to the sofa, tossing aside the throw pillows. "Sit."

Mallory obeyed, edging a little farther down when Ben plopped down beside her.

"We're going to have to stop tiptoeing around each other," he said.

"I didn't realize we were."

He scoffed. "How about we set down one important rule from the start?"

"Start of what?" Not that she was playing coy. She truly had no idea what was happening between them.

Was this a beginning? A relationship? A partnership?

Or was she overthinking everything?

It had been too long since she'd had to gauge what a guy was thinking. If her friends were correct in their assessment of men in general, all Ben could be thinking about was sex. She could never be naked in front of a new man. That was entirely out of the question.

No man would want her now anyway…

"This…this…" He heaved a sigh. "Touché."

"What was that rule you mentioned?" Not that she needed to know.

Ben Carpenter was her contractor—the guy fixing her house. He'd never want to be something…more. Nor did she need something more.

"One of the things that drove me crazy with my ex was her lying," he said. "If we're gonna…do this, I think we should promise to always tell the truth. Deal?"

"Do this? What is this?"

He rested his hand on her knee. "Honesty, remember? I think we should promise to always be honest. Agreed?"

Mallory thought about it, realized he was right, and gave Ben a curt nod. "Agreed."

"I love kissing you."

"I love kissing you, too."

"I'd like us to get to know each other better."

While part of her wanted to squeal with delight, the other, saner part of her cautioned that Ben wouldn't want her if he knew everything there was to know about Mallory Hamilton. Not that she wasn't a good person. There was simply too much baggage. "I see you every weekday."

"No," he retorted. "You see me work every weekday."

"So?"

With a frustrated sigh, he ran his hand over his face. "I want to take you on a date. Okay?"

She shrugged even as her heart jumped to a faster cadence. After Jay left, she'd been thrown into a hurricane of change. In all the time, she hadn't felt a single attraction to another man. While some of that might have been the chemical changes in her body, it could also be explained by her losing faith and trust in the male gender.

"You like me." He punctuated the statement with a firm nod.

"I suppose..."

"I like you."

"Then why haven't you said anything for two weeks?" she asked. "You've been here all that time since the dance and haven't said a word."

"Same reason you didn't. I was rattled by the kiss. I just didn't know what to say."

"And now?"

"Now, I finally worked up some guts," he replied. "I want to see how we get along on a date. Just one date, Mallory. Okay? What've you got to lose?"

To know Ben was attracted to her, perhaps with the same intensity she was attracted to him, touched something inside her. "A date. Wow. Um..."

He squeezed her knee. "Seriously. What do you have to lose?"

"A great contractor."

"Ah...now I get it. You don't want to get personal with me 'cause you're afraid I'll quit working on your house."

She nodded, although he was barely scratching the surface. Getting to know him better frightened her in almost too many ways to acknowledge.

"How about I make you a promise," he suggested. "Go on a date with me. One real date. If we click like we did at the mixer, super."

"And if we don't?"

"Then we just go back to being client and contractor." Ben held up his hand as if to shake hers. "Deal?"

Since the arrangement he suggested meant she had nothing to lose, she shook his hand. "Deal."

When she tried to pull her hand back, he refused to release her. Instead he pulled her closer.

The kiss started out gentle. Easy. Nice. But when a growl rose from his chest and his tongue invaded her mouth, Mallory surrendered.

She loved his taste, and her body caught fire—a surprise because she'd all but chalked up her reaction to their parking lot kiss as an anomaly born of Ben being the first man she'd kissed since her divorce.

Oh, how wrong she'd been.

As his mouth lingered on hers, his tongue stroking and probing, his words floated in her head.

I was rattled by the kiss.

At that moment, Mallory was a hell of a lot more than rattled. She was in lust so deep, she had to force herself not to crawl on his lap and lace her fingers through his hair.

Dredging up every ounce of her control, she eased back. At least she was spared embarrassment since Ben was breathing every bit as choppy as she was. They stared at each other for several moments before they both grinned.

Without a word, he stood up and walked to where he'd left the folded ladder. As he carried it out of the house, he whistled a tune.

It took her a moment to realize it was "Light My Fire."

She was smiling as she put the rest of the groceries away.

Chapter 7

Open house.

The longest day of the year.

Mallory shoved her keys in the ignition, ready to be home and thanking God her house was only a few minutes' drive. She'd go ahead and kick her shoes off if she wasn't afraid her feet would swell up on the trip. If she couldn't get her shoes back on, she'd have to walk through the sawdust in the garage, probably jamming splinters in the soles of her feet.

Ben had begun working on the dining room, adding wainscoting and crown molding. He'd set up some terrifying circular saw that looked right out of a horror movie, and the sound it made as he cut the fresh wood reminded her of a dentist's drill on steroids.

The place was starting to shape up nicely. Her only worry was that once the work was finished, Ben Carpenter might walk right out of her life. Luckily there was still plenty to do.

The garage door was up when she got home, but Ben wasn't in the garage. His truck was parked a couple of houses away, so she hauled her exhausted body out of the car and walked through the door into the laundry room. "Ben?"

"In the kitchen!"

The smell hit her the moment she opened the door—the mouthwatering aroma of simmering tomatoes and pungent spices. "Is that—"

"Chili," Ben replied. "A little on the spicy side. I hope you don't mind."

"You...cooked?"

"I'm a chili snob. It has to be spicy or I won't even bother. Something I learned when I lived in Texas. I made corn bread, too. Helps tame the heat." He opened the oven, peeking at the pan on the middle shelf.

Mallory was too stupefied to move. "You...*cooked*?"

"I cooked." Moving around the kitchen as though he spent plenty of time there doing something other than home improvement, Ben stirred the pot of chili, stopping to give it a quick taste.

Jay's idea of making supper was to grab something from a drive-thru. Even the other men she'd dated before her marriage had avoided a kitchen until it was time to eat.

He picked up a big bowl of salad and carried it to the kitchen table, the one he'd obviously taken the time to clear of all the unread magazines and the mail she'd let pile up for far too long. Two places had been neatly set with silverware, glasses, and napkins.

"I—I don't understand."

"You said you had open house and were gonna be late. I figured..." Ben shrugged and turned back to the stove.

"You thought I'd be hungry."

"Yeah. Chili's easy and quick." He grinned over his shoulder. "Next time I'll make you a rack of lamb. That's my specialty."

Is he for real?

Finally finding the will to move, she toed her shoes off and dropped her purse next to Rascal's bed. Then it dawned on her that her cat hadn't greeted her. "Where's Rascal?"

"He headed upstairs when I started cooking. I don't think he liked me messing around your kitchen."

"Probably because you didn't feed him." She should call him down, but she wanted to keep enjoying the sight that had greeted her.

Funny, but her feet didn't hurt anymore, and she wasn't nearly as tired.

"Want a beer?" he asked, wrapping his fingers around the refrigerator door handle.

There wasn't any beer inside. Then again, there hadn't been any items to make chili, either. "Did you shop?"

He chuckled as he grabbed two brown bottles. "Yeah, Mother Hubbard."

"Mother Hub—Oh...But my cupboard wasn't all that bare. I just shopped."

"Salad stuff and yogurt ain't gonna cut it, Mal. You need protein to put some meat on those bones."

Instead of taking offense, she smiled. "I'm trying to eat healthier."

"Healthier doesn't mean rabbit food." He popped open the beers, set them on the table, and then took another taste of the chili. "Perfect, at least as perfect as it can be without aging overnight. Ready to chow down?"

"Absolutely." Mallory picked up the bowls he'd left by the stove. "Want me to serve?"

Ben took them from her hands. "Nope. Go sit down. You're exhausted. I'll get everything together."

"But—"

"Sit down. Let me finish getting dinner ready."

"I can help," she insisted. "I can—"

"Sit!" He softened the rebuke with a grin. "Let me take care of you."

Although it felt odd, she sat in the chair he pulled out for her and waited for him to do all the things she should've been doing. The only others who had gone to so much trouble for her were the Ladies Who Lunch. To have a man cook a meal felt…odd. "So is this that date you asked for?"

Scooping chili into the bowls, he chuckled. "Hardly."

That had been her only explanation: he'd changed his mind about them going out on a real date and was substituting a quick bowl of chili. "Then why?"

"Because I knew you'd be exhausted and figured you needed to come home to something more than yogurt and salad." After he set the bowls on the place mats, he grabbed a bag of shredded cheddar cheese and a tub of sour cream. "Wasn't sure how you took your chili…"

"Wow. This is all so…wonderful."

The timer started its annoying beep.

"Let me get the corn bread, and we can eat."

***

Mallory washed while Ben dried. Since it was his fault they had to hand wash, he didn't complain. A new dishwasher had been added to his list of renovations, but he was moving room by room. The kitchen was after the dining room.

That list had started so simple, and he'd been correct in his first appraisal. The place had great bones. Everything else, however, was shit. Thanks to his frugal nature, he'd been able to do far more than he'd anticipated. Didn't hurt that Mallory had seen the slow but steady changes and scraped together more money for the renovation budget.

She had great taste and knew exactly what she wanted done. A refreshing change from the ladies who couldn't make up their minds on paint colors or what type of countertop to pick. Mallory never hesitated to tell him what she wanted, and she also took into account his suggestions. She was the perfect person to work for.

"Thanks, again," she said as she handed him a glass. "I'd be glad to finish the dishes so you can get home to your daughter."

"Nah. I always finish any job I start."

Ben had never enjoyed this kind of domesticity with Theresa. Not that he wanted to compare Mallory to his ex. Hell, they weren't in the same league.

He'd seen the dark circles under her eyes when she'd come home for a short time after school. She'd put away some groceries, mostly yogurt cups and lettuce. He'd almost suggested she catch a nap, but she'd said something about having to go back to school for an open house, probably the same type he'd attended for Amber over the years.

It had never dawned on him how exhausting it was to be a teacher. Whenever she was home, she was grading papers. The woman seemed to have no clue how to relax. No wonder she always looked so tired.

After she'd headed back to work, he discovered she'd left one grocery sack on the kitchen table. A frozen dinner, one of those diet things that probably had nothing but an ounce of meat and a few wilted vegetables. No way he'd let Mallory eat that after working her ass off all day.

Ben pitched it in the freezer and made a list. After he'd mounted the last of the crown molding and put up his tools, he'd booked to the grocery. Chili was quick and easy, and according to Amber, it was one of his best dishes. He'd barely finished the meal when Mallory had returned.

Her wide eyes and openmouthed gape had been worth every minute of his effort.

They'd enjoyed easy conversation as they ate, discussing the plans for the master bath and how much equity the house was getting now that it was slowly coming together. Nothing of great importance had been done, yet her home was infinitely more comfortable. And natural. Just like when they'd danced.

Ben dried the last of the silverware while Mallory cleaned up the sink. When he laid the damp dishtowel on the counter, she grabbed it and headed to the laundry room. He followed as though she were some irresistible force. The woman had him firmly under her spell, and he didn't care if she knew it.

After she tossed the towel in the washer, she turned and almost plowed right into him.

He cradled her head in his hands, stroking her temples with his thumbs as he smiled down at her. "Did you enjoy your supper?"

"Yes. Thank you." She nibbled on her bottom lip. "Are you sure this wasn't the date?"

Instead of answering, he drew her closer. Then he settled his lips against hers. A quick kiss. Nothing more. Even if he wanted to ravage that sweet mouth, she was tired. Besides, he had no business starting something neither of them was ready to finish.

When he pulled back, her chocolate eyes stared up at him, filled with curiosity.

"What, Mal? What do you want?"

"I want to know why."

"Why what?"

"Why you went to all this trouble."

That statement answered every question he'd ever have about her ex. "Because you needed someone to take care of you tonight."

Her eyes still searched his, and he wished he knew exactly what she was looking for. Since she'd obviously been married to an inconsiderate jerk, she might not realize that some guys took care of the women they loved. If he asked her what she wanted from him, she was likely to raise that firewall that had just begun to drop. So instead of guessing, he kissed her again. Another short kiss, but sweet nonetheless.

When he pulled back, her eyes were closed and her lips curled in a smile.

"I should go," he said, unable to mask the sensual huskiness of his voice. The kisses hadn't left him unaffected, either. "It's getting late."

"Your daughter will be worried."

"Nah. I called her hours ago. She was munching on leftover Chinese and finishing a paper for her English class."

"You can stay. If—if you want. We could…I don't know… watch some TV."

What he wanted to do was sweep her into his arms and carry her up the stairs. Then he'd make love to her until she fell into a blissful slumber.

He really needed to grasp a little self-control. She'd just freed herself from a marriage that was clearly one-sided. The best he could hope to be was a rebound guy.

Ah, but he had other plans in mind. Sure, the timing might suck. Didn't mean they were doomed from the start.

That thought brought a smile to his face. "I should go." *For now.*

Mallory gave him a quick nod. Damn if she didn't look dejected, and damn if that didn't make his smile broaden.

"How about Saturday?" Ben asked.

"What?"

"Saturday. We could go to the mixer at Robert's church again."

"You want to go on a date to a singles mixer?"

"Sure. We can dance. I love dancing with you."

"But don't people go there to meet new people?" At least she smirked so he didn't have to address her rhetorical question.

"This town doesn't have a lot of good places to go on a first date," he insisted.

"What about a movie?"

"Two hours of sitting together and not talking?" He shook his head.

"Miniature golf? Or does the prospect of me beating you frighten you?"

He enjoyed her sense of humor. "Puhleeze… You'd get mad when I beat you."

When she laid her hand against his chest, he sucked in air like a teenager with his first girlfriend. Her smile meant she'd heard. "Well, then I guess a dance it is."

Chapter 8

After seeing how crowded the mixer was, Mallory wished Ben had chosen something more intimate.

"There are a lot of new people." She was glad to see Juliana, although she was well occupied with a tall blond who appeared to have spent a little too much time in a tanning bed.

Didn't he know those things caused skin cancer?

From the speed her hands were moving as she spoke, Jules was relating one of her many adventures, probably a humorous tale about the pitfalls of traveling overseas with students. Why the woman let herself get roped into chaperoning the school's biennial trip to France, Mallory would never understand.

She'd always wanted to see Paris, had even added it to her bucket list. As soon as the renovations were done and paid for, she'd start saving for that goal. But she sure as hell wasn't going with students tagging along. She wasn't even sure she'd share the trip with Juliana, Bethany, or Danielle. This was something she wanted to do for herself. If she was extra frugal, she might even be able to squeeze in a few days in London on the same trip.

Her gaze wandered the large room. Of all the new people, the majority—a good two-thirds—were women. She had to swallow her apprehension when all of them seemed to stare at Ben. Not that she could blame them. Dressed in a baby-blue polo and Levi's that fit him perfectly, he certainly stood out from the other guys. Many of them were older forty-to-fiftysomethings, balder, wider in girth, and casting an air of desperation. The blond talking to Jules was an exception, as was Robert. At least there were two friendly faces in the crowd she could ask for a ride home if Ben decided to search for greener pastures.

"More women than men tonight." Mallory tried to keep her tone from revealing her attack of nerves. She ran her fingers through her short hair.

"Yep. But you're my date," Ben replied, giving her other hand a squeeze. "You dance with me. Only me." A few seconds passed by before he added, "Right?"

She squeezed back, touched that he seemed as insecure as she felt and secretly enjoying the possessive tone of his voice. "I don't want to dance with anyone else, Ben. Only you."

Robert raised his beer bottle in a silent toast when his gaze fell on them.

"Not even Robert?" Ben teased.

"Not even Robert."

Mallory couldn't stop the heat rising on her cheeks as Robert leveled an intent gaze at them. She'd always kept her private life out of school. With the exception of the Ladies, she wasn't even sure most of the faculty knew about the divorce or—

"It's a slow song, Mal. Wanna dance first? Then we can grab some drinks and talk to Robert and your friend. Julie, was it?"

"Juliana. Or Jules."

Ben held out a hand. "So can we dance?"

"Sure." She let him lead her onto the empty dance floor,

looking around to see if anyone was gawking at them. With no one else out there, she felt as obvious as if a spotlight shone on them.

Ben tugged her into his arms. While she loved being so close to his strong body and arousing scent, she couldn't force herself to relax. Every eye had to be turned their way. She hated to be everyone's focus, at least anywhere but her classroom.

Leaning down, he whispered in her ear. "What's wrong?"

"Why would you think something's wrong?"

He snorted. "You're as rigid as a two-by-four."

"Nothing's wrong. Really."

"Ah, ah, ah." His warm breath caressed her skin. "We have a rule about that. Remember?"

She released a sigh, wondering how often her promise to always be honest with Ben would bite her in the ass. "Fine. I don't like being the center of attention."

"Is that what you think you are right now, the center of attention?"

"I don't think I am. I *know* I am. Every woman here has already zeroed in on you and is probably plotting how to get you away from me." She raised her chin so she could see his face. "By the way, you look great tonight."

A smile reached his dark eyes. "I'm supposed to tell *you* that. Which, by the way, you do."

With a shrug, Mallory dropped her chin. Jay had given her compliments all the time. Words didn't mean much when there weren't feelings backing them up.

Ben raised it with his finger. Then he touched his lips to hers. "I came with you, Mal. I'm leaving with you." He gave the air a quick sniff. "Love the perfume. What is it?"

She found a genuine smile. "Twirl."

With no warning, he let go of her and did a quick spin. "Ta-da!"

How long had it been since she'd laughed?

She gave him a playful slap on the chest, resisting the urge to run her fingertips over the firm muscles she found there. "No, silly. The name of the perfume is Twirl."

Chuckling, he pulled her close again, and she surrendered to the love song by laying her cheek against his shoulder. How easy it was to pretend that he belonged to her, that the safety she found in his embrace was something more than a fleeting comfort.

But he didn't belong to her. She wasn't ready for a real relationship. Not until she was whole again.

Ah...but for tonight, he was hers.

The song ended, but Ben made Mallory stay with him on the dance floor when another slow tempo song filled the air.

A brazen bottle blonde tapped her on the shoulder. "How about I cut in?"

Trusting that he didn't want to be disturbed any more than she did, Mallory shook her head. "I don't think so," she replied, loving Ben's responding grin.

"But—but this is a mixer," the woman insisted. "You're s'posed to be meeting new people. Two dances with one girl isn't fair. Probably against the rules."

"Yeah, well..."

Ben flashed her a crooked smile. "Sorry. I guess the lady and I don't play by the rules." Then he did a few turns, moving them farther away from the intruder.

The possessive gesture made Mallory deliriously happy.

A chuckle made his chest rumble, a sound she heard clearly because he pressed her head back down on his chest. "Rather pushy, wasn't she?"

"A little." *A lot.*

Content, she hardly noticed when the next song began.

"Wanna grab a drink?" he asked. "Disco isn't my thing."

What she wanted was for the DJ to stop playing songs that were recorded before she was even born. "Mine, either."

He wrapped his hand around hers and led her toward the bar.

Juliana cut them off before they got there. "You two having a nice time?"

"Yeah," Mallory replied. She rubbed her cheek against Ben's upper arm, loving how tall he was and how warm she felt just being close to him.

The smile on Jules's face was the faux one she plastered on when dealing with clueless parents. "Gonna make this a weekly habit? I'm sure the new ladies would love that."

"Why not?" Ben smirked. "Seems like you're here every Saturday."

The sparks flew between them, but not the same type that Mallory shared with him. This tension was pure hostility, and she didn't have a clue as to what caused it. They seemed fine at the last mixer.

"Too cheap to spring for dinner and a movie?" Jules asked. Since sarcasm was a lifestyle for her, that reaction wasn't surprising.

Ben's was. "You've got me all figured out."

Horrified that her best friend and her date were getting off on the wrong foot and having no idea what caused the antagonism, Mallory scrambled for the right thing to say. "Ben likes dancing. Not too many places to do that in Cloverleaf. So…here we are."

"You're a dancer, Ben?" Jules asked.

"Not particularly. Just wanted a place where Mallory and I could come to listen to some good music, have a drink, and dance a little."

Mallory leaned in to whisper to Juliana. "What's wrong with you?"

Jules shrugged.

"Stop being an asshat. Okay?"

With her lips pulled to a solemn line, Jules nodded.

What was she trying to accomplish? Judging from Ben's stiff frown, all she was doing was pissing him off. Perhaps one day Juliana would learn exactly how abrasive she could be.

Mallory needed a minute alone with Juliana to figure out what was going on in her friend's head. "How about a glass of wine, Ben?"

"Preference for red or white?" he asked.

"White. Please."

Jules finished her drink and handed the glass to the blond, who was still hovering at her side. "Do me a favor, Patrick? Refill?"

His whole face lit up like a child on Christmas morning. "Sure thing, honey." He trotted after Ben.

Mallory barely waited until he was out of earshot. "What's with you? For pity's sake...you wanted me to go out with him."

"I *did*. Now I'm not so sure."

"Why not?"

She took a long time before answering. "I just wanted you to get back into the swing of things. I didn't think you'd like the guy. You're not ready for that."

"What are you talking about?"

"Who do you think you're talking to?" Jules asked. "I know you better than anyone, and I saw the way you were dancing with him."

"So what?"

Jules heaved a sigh. "You were supposed to date him a couple of times, have a nice time, and then cut him loose. That's all. Not... not... *this.*"

"This *what*?"

"This relationship. You're already in too deep. I don't want you to get hurt again, Mal."

Her temper rising to a slow boil, Mallory knit her brows. "You're assuming an awful lot after watching a couple of dances."

"I told you, I know you. I know exactly how you think. I'd bet my bottom dollar you didn't tell him everything. Right?"

"It's our first date!" Mallory insisted. "Besides, he knows about Jay." As though that would satisfy Juliana...

Thankfully, Ben and Patrick came back with glasses of wine and bottles—Patrick's beer and Ben's water.

Juliana threw her a this-is-far-from-over look that made Mallory glad the next day was Sunday. She'd have a day's reprieve from any more interrogation or insinuation.

Ben handed Mallory her drink and then gave Juliana a wan smile. "Look... I'm not sure why you were giving me a hard time, but... I'm sorry I rose to the bait. I was out of line."

Jules huffed and took her drink from Patrick, who kept nervously shifting his weight between his feet.

"I know you're Mal's friend," Ben continued, "but I just don't know why you're being so... so..."

"Hostile?" Jules shook her head. "I didn't mean to be so rude. Just looking out for Mallory."

"Then we have something in common," Ben added. "Because I'm looking out for her, too."

"Here's to friends, old and new." Mallory raised her glass, clinked it against Ben's water bottle and then held it out for Jules, hoping she'd catch the hint.

After a couple of tense seconds, Jules clinked her glass against Mallory's. "To friends." She arched an eyebrow at Ben.

He touched the lip of his bottle to her glass. Then he looked over his shoulder to see Patrick walking away, shaking his head. "Didn't mean to scare off your date."

With a dismissive wave, Juliana said, "Just met him. Guess he decided I'm not his type. How about we get some pretzels and sit down for a nice long chat?"

***

Mallory folded her hands in her lap after Ben threw the truck into park.

Thankfully, he and Juliana had worked past their earlier dislike. While she had no doubt Juliana was simply trying to protect her, Mallory didn't need that kind of protection. Sure, she might have been fragile when her world went in the crapper, but she'd pulled herself up, dusted herself off, and got on with surviving. Jules had helped her all along the way, but the time had come for Mallory to truly live again.

At least by the time they decided to call it a night, Ben and Juliana found some common ground—they both spoke fluent sarcasm. Mallory even had a fleeting thought they were better suited to each other than she was to Ben. Not that she would ever give him up.

He killed the engine and then smiled at her. "Want me to come in?"

She gave her head a quick shake. "Not tonight. I'm really tired."

"Me, too. Just enjoyed myself so much, I didn't want to call it a night. Not yet."

"You enjoyed yourself?"

"Yeah. A bunch. You're a great dancer."

"Oh, please." Although she rolled her eyes, she smiled. "I'm amazed I didn't break any of your toes."

"As little as you are? No way. Probably wouldn't even leave a bruise." He had slowly turned toward her as they talked. Now he eased closer.

Funny, but she was doing the same. With a sigh, she admitted to herself she wanted him to kiss her.

Bullshit. You want him to carry you inside and screw your brains out!

A giggle bubbled out.

Ben smiled in response. "Sure you don't want me to come in?"

Hell, yes. "Not tonight." She nibbled on her bottom lip as she squirmed.

The heat inside her grew with each move he took in her direction. Unfortunately, she was already stifling yawns left and right. If he came in and tried to keep up conversation, he'd probably think she found him boring. And Ben Carpenter was anything but boring.

He slid the rest of the way, cupping her cheeks and lifting her head. "I had a nice time."

"So did I."

"Then you'll go on another date with me? I'll even pony up the dough for a movie. Popcorn, too, if you play your cards right." Giving her no chance to reply, he brushed his lips over hers.

When he pulled back, Mallory let a frustrated growl rise from her throat.

Ben grinned and kissed her again. A little deeper. A little longer.

She was tired of waiting. Her tongue pushed between his lips, stroking his as she looped her arms around his neck. He held her by the waist, pulling her close enough she might as well have been sitting in his lap.

The kiss was thorough. Sweet. Hypnotizing. His taste was becoming familiar, something she craved as much as chocolate. She let his tongue chase hers back into her mouth, then she grasped it between her teeth and gently tugged.

Ben lifted her, bringing her up and over until she straddled his hips, never breaking the kiss.

Mallory tunneled her fingers through his hair, letting whatever was causing her libido to run rampant take control. Tearing her lips away from his, she kissed his cheek, working her way over to his ear. She traced the ridges with her tongue, then took his lobe between her teeth.

His hands settled on her hips, pressing her down. His rigid cock was easy to feel, and the contact made shivers race the length of her spine.

She licked his neck, wondering if he'd get upset if she nibbled on his skin enough to give him a small hickey.

Suddenly his right hand settled on her left breast.

"Stop!"

Chapter 9

The moment Ben placed his palm on Mallory's breast, she reacted as though she'd been hit by lightning.

She shoved herself back with both hands on his chest, scrambling off his lap. Sitting there, her eyes were full of fury he didn't comprehend as she panted for breath.

"I—I don't understand."

Sure, she was a little flat-chested. He'd felt the padding in her bra and immediately dismissed it.

So what?

Boobs weren't a big turn-on for him anyway. He'd never fixated on body parts, usually admiring the whole package from hair to eyes to a really sexy smile. Why did all women with small breasts feel so inadequate?

"I—I have to go." Her words were clipped and filled with more emotion than simple anger.

"Mallory… stop. Please. I'm sorry." Why he was apologizing, he had no idea. But it seemed to be the right thing to do.

She grabbed her purse from where it rested on the floor of the truck. "I have to go."

He wasn't ready to let her out of the truck, so he didn't click the lock open in case she started trying to go. "I don't understand what happened. I mean... that was so... nice. Why'd you push me away?"

"I have to go." She jerked on the door handle, her eyes growing wide when she found it locked. "Please let me go." Her voice quivered as though she'd burst into tears if he didn't obey.

Ben frowned, but he responded to the fear in her voice by opening the locks. "Whatever I did, I'm sorry."

Her eyes, full of unshed tears, found his.

"Mallory... don't go. Talk to me."

With a shake of her head, she scrambled out and then slammed the door. She hurried to the garage door, punched in the code, and waited while it rose. Before it was all the way up, she ducked underneath and made her way into the house.

Although his first instinct was to follow and demand she explain her odd reaction, he simply sighed. Watching her go, he was both confused and frustrated. She'd felt the same fire. He was sure of it.

So why did she run away?

Since she hadn't shut the garage door, Ben stared at the back of her car. His thoughts whirled with questions. Was she afraid to get close to another man because of her divorce? Was she angry at him or at herself since the kiss had come close to getting out of hand? Did he piss her off by trying to touch her breast?

She'd been turned on, too. No way he could've been that off in reading her response. He might not have a wealth of experience with women, but Mallory had been an active participant—a *very* active participant. He hadn't imagined her tongue in his mouth and his ear.

Afraid she'd forget to put the door back down, he got out of his truck. Marching to the garage, he ran his hand over his face, fighting an inner battle over whether to close the door or march inside and demand to know what made her run.

Think, Ben. Think.

The gentleman in him won the fight, and he punched in the five-digit code.

After watching the door descend, he clenched his right hand into a fist, trying to calm his rising anger. He hadn't done anything wrong. They were both adults. She'd responded to his kiss with a passion that seemed to match his own.

This doesn't make any sense.

The truth hit him the instant he unclenched his fist, trying to remember the shape of her breast against his palm.

Padding. His hand had found padding, not the natural texture or softness of a woman's breast. Nor had she reacted the way other women had. There was no recognition of his touch. No murmur. No reaction. Except anger.

Ben was sure he felt padding.

No, not just padding.

A fake breast.

"Oh my God."

He remembered her saying that her husband had experienced nothing but "poorer and sicker" in their marriage. And in his mind's eye, Ben clearly saw that pink ribbon magnet on the back of her SUV.

That ribbon wasn't just for her mother.

It was for her.

An angry roar built in his chest, but he smothered it, unsure of where he should direct that rage.

Mallory?

For what? For having the temerity to win his affection after his repeated promises of keeping women at arm's length? Or for so easily stealing his caring only to have the audacity to threaten to take it away just as quickly by having cancer?

No, his anger was directed inward. He was stupid on so many levels he let out a scoffing laugh.

You fucking idiot.

He'd let her in. Without an ounce of self-protection, he'd let her crawl right inside his mind. If that wasn't stupid, he didn't know what was. After all his promises, all the oaths he'd made to himself about keeping his life and Amber's uncomplicated, he'd dived right back into the deep end.

Ben hopped back in his truck, sitting behind the wheel for a good, long while, mentally kicking himself in the ass. Repeatedly.

He was blind, too. Stupid and blind to ignore all the clues Mallory had dropped along the way.

He'd dismissed her thinness as an emotional response to the divorce. Some people, especially women, were comfort eaters, but there were also those who wouldn't eat at all when stressed out.

Sure her hair was short, but not short enough to scream *chemotherapy.*

Yet his own stupidity became obvious whenever he thought back to her reaction when he first entered her bathroom to give her the estimate on fixing her home. The stuff he saw had made a deep blush rise on her cheeks, and she'd rapidly scooped it all into a drawer. He struggled to remember as many items as he could.

Prescription bottles. Tubes of antibiotic ointment and scar-lessening cream. And a falsie, a fake breast, probably the same one his fingertips had brushed when he'd tried to deepen their intimacy. He'd been ignorant enough to believe she just wanted to look like she had bigger boobs.

After smacking his forehead against the steering wheel a couple of times, Ben turned the key and brought the engine to life. He broke every speed limit getting back to the church. He was tired of feeling stupid, and Mallory's friend would surely have the answers he so desperately needed.

He marched inside and quickly spotted her leaning against the wall, chatting with Robert.

Did he know too?

Was Ben the only one in the dark about Mallory's breast cancer?

The redhead—what was her name?—caught him stomping across the floor, head down, like a bull that had seen a red cape. Her eyes widened, and her mouth fixed into a harsh frown.

She spoke before he could think of how to ask the questions pounding through his brain. "I thought you two headed home." Leaning to the side, she looked past him. "Where's Mallory? Did she go to the restroom or something?"

"She's at home."

"Home?"

"Yeah, home."

She stared at him for a few long moments then her eyebrows gathered in irritation. "What in the hell did you do to her?"

The accusation stung, probably because he felt guilty, as though he'd crossed some invisible line or invaded Mallory's privacy. "I…um…We…" He was more flustered than he'd ever been where a woman was concerned. Which meant—

Mallory was already important to him. Much more important than he'd realized. "She has cancer, doesn't she?" It hurt to say the words aloud. "Breast cancer. Right?"

"I can't talk to you about Mallory's personal life."

"Yes, you can. I have a right to know if she has cancer."

"A right?" She scoffed at him. A fiery temper accompanied the red hair. "What *right* do you have? You're renovating her house. You barely even know her. Why would her health matter to you anyway? Why would *she* even matter?"

"She matters. Okay?" He raked his trembling fingers through his hair. "Look...I just need to know for sure. I know what I... felt when I—" A frustrated shout was gathering in his throat. He wanted to hit something. Hard.

"When you what?" Green eyes searched his face. "You felt her up!"

"It wasn't like that," Ben insisted. "I like her, Julie."

"It's Juliana or Jules. Not Julie. And I don't give a shit if you declare your undying love. I still can't tell you. If you want to know, ask Mallory. Or, better yet, just drop it."

"Why do you hate me?" he asked. "Hell, you don't even know me."

She held her tongue.

"Seriously...what have I ever done to you?"

"This isn't about you," she insisted. "It's about Mallory. She's not ready for you."

"What are you talking about?"

"You don't know Mallory." Julie glared at the men. "Not like I do. She copes by locking everything up inside in a deep, private place."

"That's ridiculous," Ben said with a shake of his head.

"You don't know much about women, do you?" Jules worried her bottom lip. "She's been hurt enough. Okay?"

"You think I don't know that?" He set his hands on his hips. "I'm at her house almost every day, fixing the messes her bastard ex made."

"I'm not talking about her house."

"Neither am I." He waited, hoping he was getting through to her. Then his patience reached its limit. "You're really the type of woman who's going to make me beg?"

"Had," Robert blurted out.

"What?" Ben shifted his gaze to his friend.

"Had. She *had* cancer."

Juliana punched Robert's upper arm. "Traitor."

"Why? Because I told him something he'd already figured out?" Robert inclined his head toward Ben. "The poor guy obviously likes her. He deserves to know the truth."

Had cancer. The words were the closest thing to good news Ben had heard in a long time. "She's cured? Did surgery cure her? Did she have chemotherapy? Radiation? How does she know the cancer's gone?"

"I don't know all the particulars," Robert replied. "Jules? What's the latest?"

She folded her arms under her breasts and dug in her heels. "What if she did?"

This conversation was making Ben crazy. "If she did what? Still have cancer?"

"Yeah. Would you like her if she still had cancer?"

The insult cut deep. "What kind of guy do you think I am?"

"I have no idea. That's why I'm trying to figure you out. You could be a serial killer for all I know."

"He's not a serial killer," Robert insisted. "He's a good guy. That's why I sent him to help Mallory in the first place."

"Fine," Juliana conceded. "He's a good guy. But would he want her if she still had cancer?"

"Of course I'd want her!" Ben lowered his volume when people began to stare. "I'm not that kind of guy, Juliana. My ex-wife's a basket case, and I didn't leave her. *She* divorced *me*."

Her eyes finally softened. “Tell me what happened with Mal.”

Robert shook his head. “I’m bowing out now. You two don’t need me eavesdropping on something this personal.” His eyes shifted to a gaggle of women across the hall. “Besides, I see a rather attractive blonde in need of my handsome company.” He strode away, still shaking his head.

“What happened?” Juliana asked again. “When you felt her up, I mean.”

“I didn’t—” But that was exactly what he’d done, so he owned up to it. “She pushed herself away and got out of the truck. So left me so fast, I’m amazed she didn’t leave skid marks.”

“You frightened her.”

“She didn’t act afraid. She acted pissed.”

Dropping her arms and relaxing her at-attention stance, Juliana leaned back against the wall. “Pissed is frightened for Mallory.”

“Why would she be scared of me?”

“Because she knew you’d figured out she had cancer. She’s been very private about it. Even when her hair fell out from the chemotherapy, she wore wigs that looked like her old hair. When she abandoned the wigs, she just said she decided to cut it really short so she didn’t have to mess with it anymore. I’ll bet only a handful of the staff at school knows everything she’s been through. She needed it that way.” She shrugged. “They might even attribute the physical changes to her sudden divorce.” Then she closed her mouth so quickly, her teeth clacked together.

“Mal told me she was divorced. You’re not revealing some deep dark secret. Actually, I’d already figured it out.”

“Did she tell you her skunk bastard ex left her three days after her diagnosis?”

The news took a few moments to sink into his brain. “He left her because she had cancer?" That guy deserved the beating of his life, and Ben would be happy to deliver each and every blow.

What kind of cold-hearted bastard did that to his wife?

When Theresa was at her worst, which could be pretty damned bad, he'd never once considered breaking the vows he'd taken. He protected Amber at all costs, but he didn't abandon Theresa. She'd walked out. Several times, actually. The difference was the last one stuck.

His heart went out to Mallory even more. Then and there, he took a new vow—to make her house the most beautiful one in Cloverleaf, no matter the cost.

Juliana nodded. "The Ladies Who Lunch helped her through her surgery and chemo."

At this rate, he'd never stop feeling ignorant. "The what?"

"We have a group of friends who've eaten lunch together every day for years. Named ourselves after a song from the show *Company*. We all saw it once in Chicago and laughed about that song being so much like our crazy little group."

Ben nodded toward the bar. "Let me buy you a drink, and we can talk."

She hesitated when he took a step that direction. "I really shouldn't...Mallory wouldn't like—"

"Look, I like Mallory. I want to make this better, and I hope she still wants to get to know me as much as I'd like to know her. But I can't do that without your help." When she still hesitated, he closed his eyes and heaved a sigh, trying hard not to let his shoulders droop in defeat. Then he opened his eyes. "Please?"

With a curt nod, she led the way.

* * *

"What was I thinking?" Mallory asked Rascal when he jumped up on the bed and pawed at her hand until she petted him. "I'm not ready for this."

She hadn't gone on that date for any reason other than to get Jules off her back about reentering the world. Well, maybe a couple more reasons, one of which was to prove to herself that she could still interact with people.

For the last year, she'd been something of a hermit. Not that it was all her fault. A person sure as hell didn't feel like socializing when she was in the midst of recovering from a mastectomy and suffering the side effects of chemotherapy.

Everything had happened so fast, she wasn't sure she'd truly accepted all the ramifications. The loss of her breast. The early menopause brought on by the meds. The fear of what the future might or might not bring.

She hadn't cried much, although she'd worked her way through the five stages of loss her oncologist had warned her about.

Denial only lasted a day. Confronted with all the evidence, staying in denial for too awfully long would have been absurd, especially when the doctor was urging her to act quickly.

Anger got her through the surgery. It was so much easier to face the pain and the loss by being pissed off. Being a teacher made her empathize with people and treat them well. Not after her surgery. She'd bitched at the nurses, thrown sarcastic comments at her surgeon, and greeted her visitors, her friends, with smart-ass quips or sullen silence.

Bargaining was supposed to be the third stage. Just like denial, it had been fleeting. Mallory had only asked for a favor from God once. Now that she thought about it, she felt ashamed for that request being born of vanity. The day she started chemotherapy, she'd prayed that she'd beat the odds and keep her hair. Long and sleek, the color of sable, that hair had always been the thing that made her pretty.

Exactly one week after her first dose of the toxic yet life-saving drugs, chunks of her hair had come off right in her hands as she'd shampooed. That brought bargaining to a swift conclusion.

Depression was next. Her time in that awful stage had been short but intense—a crying jag the three days after Jay had her served with divorce papers. Jules had ended that nonsense by taking her out on a clothes-and-makeup shopping spree that ended at a bar with a never-ending supply of raspberry margaritas. With Jules's help, Mallory had drowned her depression. Her other friends took a similar tack when she finally bit the bullet and shaved the tufts of hair not affected by chemotherapy. The hair grew back, as everyone promised, but it was a different shade of brown and tended to curl.

Acceptance. She'd reached that the day she'd made herself take off her shirt and stare at her new body in the mirror. Since her breasts had always been on the small side, the changes weren't all that jarring, not nearly as awful as she'd expected. Her insurance was going to pay for reconstructive surgery.

And that, as she always said, had been that... until last night when Ben Carpenter had tried to touch the fake breast that she'd used to fill out the empty A-cup on the left side of her bra.

She'd overreacted. Juliana was sure to scold her when they had lunch on Monday. It was a bit amazing her phone hadn't been ringing all night with texts or calls from her. At least Mallory would have a reprieve Sunday, unless Jules started firing curious text messages her way.

Then again, Juliana had been worried about Mallory falling for Ben too quickly. So like her to flip-flop on her opinion. Jules always chalked it up to being a Gemini and having two sides to her personality.

Had Ben gone home when Mallory ran away?

For all she knew, he might still be sitting outside her house.

A quick peek out the window disproved that hypothesis.

What did he think of her now? Would he send an e-mail that said he couldn't finish the work he'd started on her house? They didn't have a written contract or anything…

This was all her fault for letting emotions get the better of her. With a bit of luck, he might simply think she'd been freaked out over him trying to get that intimate after nothing more than a few weeks of deciding to get to know each other better. She was pretty sure a guy touching a woman's boob wasn't a big thing to most people. From the way Juliana, Danielle, and Bethany talked about dating, there were a lot of men out there who thought sex was a natural conclusion of a first date. Not that the Ladies Who Lunch agreed. Mallory's friends had discriminating taste in guys, which meant they didn't date all that often.

After the date she'd had tonight, she doubted she'd ever have another with Ben Carpenter.

She snorted before stroking her hand down Rascal's back again. His rumbling purr always made her smile, even through the worst of the worst. How many times had she been too weak to do anything except sit on the cold tile of the bathroom floor and wait for another wave of dry heaves to make her lean over the toilet and pray she'd survive chemotherapy? Every single time, her cat had been there, rubbing against her, warming her feet, letting her know someone still loved her.

Even if her husband didn't.

Fuck you, Jay Hamilton. You and the horse you rode in on.

Mallory leaned down and rubbed her nose against Rascal's,

one of the affectionate cat's favorite things. His purr grew louder, forcing a smile on her lips.

That smile faded when she thought about Ben again.

She had entertained fantasies about him, erotic fantasies. All she thought she would ever be to him was a skinny lady who needed help fixing up her mess of a house.

But he'd come looking for her at the mixer and cooked her that wonderful supper the night of open house. Then he'd asked for a bona fide, old-fashioned date.

That gave her warm fuzzies all over until she remembered her overreaction to his touch.

If she hadn't freaked out, he probably wouldn't have thought anything beyond assuming she padded her bra. Instead, she'd shoved him away as though he'd burned her. No doubt he'd driven away, heading right back to the hall to play Twenty Questions with Jules or Robert.

Would they tell him the truth?

Maybe. Maybe not.

What did it matter anyway? The best Ben could ever be to Mallory was a rebound guy. Jules had told her the first man a woman connected with after her divorce could only be a stepping-stone to other relationships. A rebound guy wasn't ever supposed to be permanent. So even if she and Ben clicked in a way Mallory knew was unique and more than a little special, nothing could come of it.

Leaning over, she flipped off the lamp and lay there in the dark, watching the new ceiling fan slowly spin. She'd known the exact model she wanted the moment she saw it at the store. The blades were a beautiful shade of chestnut that complemented her furniture. As soon as Ben had put it in, she'd quickly discovered the soft humming noise helped lull her to sleep.

Now she always thought about him right before she drifted off.

Rascal moved closer, spun in a complete circle, and then settled up against her side.

Mallory closed her eyes, wishing she could wind back the clock to before she'd skittered away like a frightened bird darting at the first noise. If Ben had been destined to be her rebound guy, she would have at least enjoyed the time they could have spent together.

And from the way the sparks flew when they kissed, he'd probably have been a hell of a lover.

Now she'd never know.

It was better that way.

Chapter 10

Sipping coffee on the porch, Mallory looked out on her backyard.

This was the first year she hadn't planted a garden since she and Jay moved in eight years ago. She'd been thrilled to have a yard after years of being in cramped apartments. When she was still living with her parents, she and her mother would plant seeds that gave the family fresh food in the summer. As the tomato plants exploded with fresh tomatoes, they'd make salsa and Italian sauces to use all winter long. One of the many joys of growing up in rural Illinois.

The large square of dirt had gone untended for the better part of the year. Now it was a mixture of weeds that surely included some poison ivy. She'd have to clean the mess out soon, which meant she'd catch a nasty case of poison ivy rash and end up on prednisone and anti-itch cream. But next year, she could plant her tomatoes, zucchini, and eggplants again. Some okra and kohlrabi, too.

And flowers. She hadn't planted her spring flowers, either. Purple had always been her favorite color, especially the rich purple of well-tended petunias, which could keep producing flowers lasting into the fall. There was a flower bed on each side of the big porch, and there were ceramic pots of many different sizes at spots throughout the front landscaping. Flowers planted there usually bloomed the whole summer to give her home a splash of color.

Instead of gardening, spring had been full of doctors and hospitals and pain. Flowers had barely crossed her mind unless someone brought a bouquet when they visited. While she'd appreciated their thoughtfulness, watching the beautiful flowers wilt and die made her sad, the opposite reaction of what the giver intended.

Perhaps this year she should plant pink petunias. Somehow that seemed more fitting—her way of supporting the pink ribbon movement. Her friends all wore pins showing their support of her, but Mallory had never worn one. She'd wanted to play things low-key. Her only pink ribbon was a rather innocuous magnet.

Thankfully, the worst of the symptoms had hit during summer, so her students hadn't been forced to watch her decline right before their eyes like all those bouquets. Once school started, people surely whispered, but she looked more and more like the old Mallory, so the speculation soon fizzled out.

No. She wasn't going to plant pink petunias next summer.

Maybe one day, far in the future when she no longer felt embarrassed talking about her disease, she'd find herself participating in breast cancer awareness walks and wearing pink ribbons. She'd acknowledged her illness with the magnetic ribbon on the back of her car. Since she'd placed it there after her mother died, no one would think it marked her own struggle.

Snapping up, she almost splashed herself with coffee as a thought startled her.

The ribbon! Ben had to have seen the ribbon!

That didn't mean anything, though. No, he couldn't have connected her running away with a silly car magnet. He knew about her mother's death, and most men weren't observant enough to connect that many dots.

The doorbell made her startle again, partly because she wasn't used to the new tune it played and partly because she wasn't expecting Sunday-morning company. She set her cup on the table as Rascal jumped off the other chair and followed her to the front door.

Pulling aside the curtain, she froze. Ben stood on her porch, holding a bouquet of multicolored flowers and looking as sheepish as a boy of sixteen on his first date. His gaze found hers, and a lopsided smile formed on his lips.

Her heart leapt to a faster cadence, something that also happened whenever he came to work each evening. Since he'd seen her through the skinny side window, there was no way she could pretend she wasn't home. Whether she wanted to have an awkward conversation or not, it was going to happen. Now.

Mallory opened the door and waited for him to say something.

His gaze dropped to her cat. Rascal had gone right to him and started rubbing against his leg. Ben picked Rascal up and set him back inside. Then he walked into the house, making her back up a few steps. He seemed to swallow up all the space.

"I came to apologize." He thrust the bouquet at her.

She took it, giving the single rose in the arrangement a quick sniff. "These are beautiful, but you don't have anything to apologize for."

"I scared you away."

Unable to bear his close scrutiny any longer, she headed down the beautiful walnut floor of her foyer into her mess of a kitchen.

She grabbed a white vase from a cabinet, filled it with water, and arranged the flowers.

He stood on the other side of the island, bracing his hands against the old-fashioned butcher-block countertop that would get switched out sometime soon. "Can we talk about stuff?"

Mallory shrugged, carried the vase over to the kitchen table, and found a place to set it down among all the books, mail, and newspapers. Since he hadn't worked on the kitchen yet, she'd let it go back to a disaster after he'd cooked for her.

As he completed each room, she treated it as though she were spring cleaning and made that room like new again, probably as a way to *feel* new again. This was her fresh start. Jay was gone. The cancer was gone.

Good riddance to both.

The only change she dreaded was when he finally got around to the kitchen because she'd have to deal with all the stuff she'd accumulated over the years. There were still a few things in boxes because they'd been wedding gifts too weird to use.

Garage sale time.

When she turned around, she bumped right into him.

He settled his hands on her shoulders. "I really want to talk about…everything."

Working up her courage, she lifted her chin to stare into his eyes, fearing she'd see what she feared most—pity. Pity meant he knew. Pity also meant he didn't understand.

But it wasn't there. His brown eyes definitely weren't full of pity…and yet she couldn't place the exact emotion she found. She dropped her chin to her chest.

Ben lifted it back up with his knuckle. "I didn't know about the cancer, which makes me as dumb as a box of rocks."

"So Juliana told you."

"No."

"Robert, then."

"Not really."

"Then how did you—"

"I figured it out while I stood on your driveway, wondering why you ran away and wanting to know what I'd done wrong." His smile melted something deep inside her.

She shook her head, grateful his hand fell away from her chin to settle back on her shoulder. "You didn't do anything wrong," she insisted.

"I did. I didn't pay enough attention. When I touched…I mean when I tried to touch…I should have known." He caressed her upper arms.

Desire raced through her, settling between her thighs. She didn't know what to think of that reaction, since it conflicted so much with her postsurgery body.

After the mastectomy, she'd taken meds that wiped out her own natural estrogen production. Her sex drive had dropped to zero. Zip. Nada. Not as though she had much of a chance to test it out, but the urge was gone, and she'd feared it might have disappeared forever. Her beloved Rabbit vibrator, the one Bethany gave her years ago as a gag gift, had gone into hibernation along with her libido. The fact that she'd kept and used it spoke volumes of the lack of sex in her marriage.

Funny, she'd never given that problem much thought. Was it because she hadn't wanted Jay more often? Or was it because he'd been a rather selfish lover?

Probably both.

But Ben had reawakened her sex drive. With a vengeance. At that moment, it took all of Mallory's self-control to keep from sweeping the mess of newspapers and bills to the floor, grabbing him by his shirt, and forcing his back against the table. Then she'd straddle his hips and let nature take its course.

A nervous giggle slipped out as that visual tumbled around her brain.

Ben frowned. "What's so funny?"

She shook her head, biting her lip so she wouldn't laugh again.

His features hardened. "You're laughing at me?"

That quickly sobered her. "No. No, Ben. Not at all."

Thankfully, Ben let his shoulders relax and his eyes regained their normal warmth. "At least you're smiling now. I'm really sorry, Mal."

"I told you…you didn't do anything wrong."

"Then how about we start over?"

"What?"

"How about we start over?" He took a step back and held out his hand. "Hi, I'm Ben Carpenter. I'm a friend of Robert's, and he thought we might want to go out on a date."

"Don't you mean *another* date?"

"All right. Another date. You know…that thing couples go on to see if they might have some stuff in common?"

Everything inside her finally relaxed. Ben might not have come right out and declared it didn't matter if she had one breast, nor did he say that her cancer wasn't going to scare him away. But the fact he was still standing in her kitchen, asking her to go out again, was every bit as good as if the words had spilled out of his mouth.

"I'd like that," she replied.

He brushed a quick kiss over her lips.

She wanted more but kept quiet because she wasn't sure what he would think if she let him know exactly how much she wanted another of those deep, wet kisses.

Let the second-guessing begin.

That was the hardest part of getting to know a new man: constantly worrying about what he thought and analyzing everything he said and did.

Did Ben want her to be brazen? Did he want her to play coy? Did he want the virgin or the whore?

Why were men so damn complicated?

Mallory glanced down at her T-shirt and yoga pants. "Since I'm not really dressed for it now, when did you want to go on this date?" She smiled. "Can't be on a weeknight. I have this guy who comes to work on my house those evenings. Wouldn't trust him all alone with my stuff."

"Oh, I don't know. Heard he's pretty dependable."

"Yeah, but..." She let her gaze wander the pathetically dated and disheveled kitchen. "With all these high-end fixtures, he could assume I have money stashed away somewhere."

"Or he might not be interested in your money at all. He could call pretending to be sick one of those evenings...especially if he has something better to do."

"Then I'd just have to dock his pay."

"Since it's Sunday, how about tonight?"

Was he still teasing or serious? "Tonight?"

"Sure. Some great new movies are out this week, and we won't have to fight the Saturday crowd."

"Or we could go out for a nice supper and come back here and watch one of my movies. When I was sick—"

Oh, shit. Would Ben begin to pity her if she talked about her cancer?

They were trying to establish a relationship. At least that's what Mallory thought they were doing. She didn't want his sympathy to play a part in whether he learned to care for her or not.

And screw a duck if she didn't suddenly realize she already cared for him.

How had *that* happened so fast?

"Mal? What were you gonna say? When you were sick… what?"

His concerned tone brought her back to the conversation. "When I was sick, my friends gave me a pile of DVDs to keep me from being too bored while I recovered from the mastectomy."

There. She'd said it. Now she needed to wait for his reaction.

It wasn't long in coming. "When I fell off a roof and broke my leg, I was grounded to my recliner. Got so bored I thought I'd lose my mind." Neither his tone nor his words contained a note of sympathy.

She couldn't stop herself. She threw her arms around his neck and kissed him. Soundly.

***

Ben groaned, his breath knocked out of him when Mallory jumped him. Before he could react, her mouth was on his.

As though he'd let such a wonderful opportunity pass him by. He returned her ferocious kiss, rubbing his tongue over hers when she thrust it into his mouth.

God, he loved how she didn't hold back. With the exception of her hasty exit the night before, Mallory was unabashedly passionate, never waiting for him to be the first to deepen a kiss.

He gave as good as he got, drinking in her taste and her wonderful scent as the kiss went on and on. The touch of lips. The caress of tongues. The exchange of breaths.

Easing her back, Ben trapped her against the island. As he continued to ravage her mouth, he glided his hands down her arms and her sides to settle on her waist. Unable to stop himself, he held her tight while he ground his pelvis against her.

His cock was so hard it ached. Were Mallory Hamilton any other woman, he'd be carrying her upstairs. He harbored no doubts she'd allow it. From her uninhibited response, the way she undulated her hips to rub against his erection, she'd not only allow him to make love to her. She'd eagerly participate.

Until he got anywhere near her chest.

As much as he wanted her, he had to slow down. Not only did she need to know that he liked her, the whole package of Mallory, he also needed to take it at a more relaxed pace. The woman needed time, and he'd be sure she got it. He had no intention of being her rebound guy. When he made love to her it would be because she wanted him every bit as much as he wanted her.

There was a lot to consider, but while she was kissing him, his logic disappeared.

Easing back, Ben breathed hard and fast. "God, Mal…you're the best kisser I've ever known."

Her lips were swollen and red when her fingers flew to touch them. "R-really?"

First hurdle: helping her find her self-worth after her divorce. Her ex had to have been the biggest asshat in history. "Absolutely."

Second hurdle: convincing her she was still desirable, even after what cancer had done to her body. "You have no idea how hard I'm fighting myself not to take you upstairs and make love to you."

"I-I'm not…ready," she whispered in a voice choked with emotion.

"I know." Ben smiled and then tapped her nose with his fingertip. "Besides, it's too soon." Then he stepped back.

Her eyes were wide as saucers. "Too soon?"

"Yeah. Too soon. You know it, too."

"I—I suppose."

He took her hand. "I don't want a quick fuck. You don't, either."

The way she winced when he'd said "fuck" told him to be more careful with his choice of vocabulary. Maybe schoolteachers never liked to hear curse words, even from adults. Since he wasn't a guy to swear often, except in his thoughts, where he cursed like a seasoned sailor, that would be an easy change. At least he didn't have to face a third hurdle.

"No, I don't," she said. "But I figured we might want to go ahead and…do it. That way I'd know if you were…I don't know…disappointed?"

And now he had a third hurdle: to figure out how her mind worked, because her last statement made absolutely no sense. "Why would I be disappointed if we f—Um, if we made love?"

"Because of my surgery."

"Oh…" Trying to think of the right thing to say to allay her fears, he tossed around responses. Then he realized he wasn't sure what tack to take.

Did he pretend she wasn't missing a breast? That seemed absurd.

Did he tell her he didn't care? That wasn't the truth.

He did care, but not because he thought she was somehow less than a woman. His concern revolved around whether he could contain any reaction he had when or if he saw her scar.

"Look, Mal…I want to talk about this, about everything. If we're going to try to be a couple—"

"That's what you want?"

"Well…*yeah*. Isn't that what you want?" He'd lost all control of the conversation and had absolutely no clue what she was thinking. That third hurdle was going to be the highest and most challenging.

She shrugged. "Jules says the first relationship after a divorce can only be a rebound."

Jules again. Of course she'd claim he'd be nothing but a rebound guy. The woman annoyed him as much as jock itch. "What's that supposed to mean?"

Mallory pulled a chair away from the table and sat.

Ben followed suit. He shoved the small pile of magazines aside and took her hand. "Tell me what you meant."

"All you can be is a rebound guy. If I fall for you, you'll eventually dump me."

"She said that?" Juliana needed to have her head examined. That or she was severely misguided about men and relationships.

Mallory nodded.

"Okay...look. Here's what I think," he said. "You and I have something kinda special going on here. Agreed?"

"Agreed."

"Then how about we don't worry about what everyone else says or thinks and just figure it out as we go...by ourselves. Deal?"

A slow smile settled on her face, finally reaching her eyes. "Deal."

Ben stood, bent down to give Mallory a quick kiss, and then cupped her chin. "So if we're still on for supper, how about I pick you up around six?"

"That would be wonderful."

Chapter 11

Ben sat across the table from Mallory, wishing she'd talk about something other than the unusually dry weather or her students.

The date had started off well, just as well as their last one. She'd opened the front door before he even rang the bell. The choice to go through the front instead of the garage had been deliberate—a way to separate "Work Ben" from "Date Ben." Since she'd been waiting, it was clear Mallory understood that they needed some sort of division between their professional and personal relationships.

And that was exactly what he hoped they were starting. A relationship. A real relationship where both partners were committed to making their pairing work rather than having one partner—him in the case of his marriage to Theresa—pulling all the weight.

Mallory had agreed on his choice of heading to Santiago's to eat. Everyone from Cloverleaf loved the place, especially their all-you-can-eat pasta special. Other than Santiago's, the only restaurants in the small city were chains that seemed generic and boring.

Now that they sat across from the table for two, nothing but a flickering candle in a jar between them, the silence was uncomfortable.

"You know, I suppose now's the time to tell you one of my odd traits, my worst odd trait actually," Ben said, sitting back in his chair.

"Oh? And why exactly do you think we should start this date with you telling me something bad about yourself?"

With a quick shake of his head, he replied, "Didn't say it was bad. Just said it was the worst of my odd traits."

Her smile was so warm and genuine, he couldn't help but smile in return. "Okay…then what is your worst odd trait, Ben Carpenter?"

"When I see an elephant, I have to say something about it."

"Elephant?" Her gaze darted around, settling on the artwork hanging on the walls, moving from painting to painting.

"It's not up there, Mal."

She quirked a brow.

"It's sitting here between us."

"Ah…the one in the middle of the table, right?"

He nodded.

"You want to talk about my cancer."

The sadness in her voice made Ben regret bringing it up. His blunt nature had offended more than a few people over the years, but he'd never been a guy who dealt well with ambiguity. His marriage had been nothing but a roller-coaster ride, and he was sick of that kind of volatility. Knowing where he stood was more important to him now, so important he would ask the difficult questions and say exactly what needed to be said.

This wasn't just about him. Or Mallory. Amber had a part to play in this little drama. His life wasn't truly his own anymore.

To let a new lady in could mean casting Amber back into a storm. Mallory was the first woman he'd even considered allowing to interact with his daughter. So many things about her, from her sweet personality to her kindness to her beautiful face, were impossible to ignore.

That thought spoke volumes about his growing attraction to Mallory, which also led him right back to the damned elephant. If she wasn't well, if she wasn't in remission, there was no way he'd let his daughter become attached to her. Amber had lost so much already.

Ben's stomach knotted at the thought of Mallory being in danger. Living with that kind of fear was simply unacceptable. Yet he had to acknowledge that the fucking cancer might be hanging over her head for years to come, and that made it dangle over his head as well.

Seeing the haunted distance in her eyes made him regret acknowledging the obvious for once. "I'm sorry. I was too blunt. Told you it was my worst odd trait."

"No." Her gaze came back to lock with his. "I understand."

"I'm not sure you do."

"Of course I do. You're worried you'll fall for me then I'll up and die on you."

Her words were like a punch to the gut. "And I thought *I* was blunt."

She shrugged. "Cancer makes a person learn to deal with stuff instead of avoid it. I got over the denial stage pretty fast."

He gave her a curt nod but kept the rest of his concerns, especially about Amber, to himself. He'd jumped all the way to step fifty when their relationship was only on step three or four. No sense getting all worked up over something that might never happen.

* * *

Mallory took a deep breath and decided Ben should know everything. Part of her wanted to start off on the right foot by letting him into her crazy world, but another part of her wished she didn't have the wealth of knowledge about such a terrible illness.

From the moment the Breast Center at St. Ignatius Hospital had called to say she needed to come back in for another mammogram, her life had become almost unrecognizable. Instead of grading papers and meeting parents, she'd been reading literature about cancer, chemotherapy, and radiation while making choices that could mean the difference between life and death. Instead of enjoying a few weeks of sun and relaxation, she'd been cleaning clumps of her hair out of the shower and vomiting often enough her throat had been raw. Instead of planning for her future, she'd been contemplating her own death. All at age thirty-three.

She sure didn't feel thirty-three anymore, but at least she had a good prognosis, so death wasn't perched on her doorstep, waiting like a vulture for her to give up. Being with Ben gave her yet another reason to look to the future.

Before she dove headfirst into the water, she decided to check the depth of it first.

"What do you know about breast cancer?" Mallory asked.

Ben shrugged. "Next to nothing."

"Well, get ready for a quick education. What did Juliana tell you?"

"I told you. Nothing really."

"But you knew anyway?"

He nodded as he fiddled with his empty wineglass. "Felt like an idiot when I finally put it all together."

"No, don't feel that way. I tried hard to hide it. Some of the people at school don't even know. I tend to be a...private kind of person. Come to think of it, I doubt too many even know I'm divorced, since I kept my married name."

"Interesting choice." He had the most incredible dimple in his left cheek. "Why not go back to your maiden name?"

Mallory shrugged. "Figured switching from Mrs. Hamilton might raise a few eyebrows, so I subtly started correcting the Mrs. to Ms. instead. Didn't have to change things at school like schedules and my door plaque. It was just...easier."

"When were you diagnosed?"

"You really do cut right to the heart of things, don't you?"

It was Ben's turn to shrug. "I told you I've got some odd traits."

"I had the mammogram last May. They called me two days later and asked me to come back for another. I just figured they'd screwed up the pictures since the machine was so tight on my boob, I'd squirmed a lot." With a wry smile, she added, "Those things squeeze your boob tight enough you wonder if it will ever fill back out again. If guys had to do that to their...um... their..."

"Their balls?"

"Yeah. Those. Well, if they did, they'd come up with some better way to check for tumors."

Ben moved the candle to the side of the table when the waiter brought over a large bowl of salad. The guy shredded some parmesan cheese over the top, then Ben dished out some of the salad with the big tongs and handed her the plate.

"Wow. You're handy with those. I usually drop lettuce everywhere," Mallory said, accepting his offering.

He served a generous portion for himself and set the plate in front of him. "I'm getting kind of handy around a kitchen."

"From what I've seen, you're kinda handy everywhere in a house."

"I meant that I can cook."

"I knew that. You cook better than I ever could." Afraid her teasing was coming across as dumb, she shoved some salad in her mouth, grateful her taste buds had finally come back to life. The salad was good, as were the buttery breadsticks, and the tastes were so pleasing, she feared she'd end up filling up on them before the fettuccine Alfredo even arrived.

"My dressing's better," Ben said as he set down his fork.

"You didn't like this one? I did. Very Italian."

"It's okay for bottled. I make mine from scratch. It's all in the choice of olive oil and how finely you chop up the garlic."

A man who made his own salad dressing? Surely she hadn't heard him right. "What else do you make yourself?"

"Salsa. Always better with fresh tomatoes. I also make my own ground beef. The stuff in the stores is too likely to have E. coli." His dark eyes found hers. "You're ignoring the elephant again."

With a sigh, Mallory nodded. "They biopsied the lump the day of the second mammogram. I'd just walked in the door coming home from the Breast Center when the phone rang. I was back at the hospital an hour later. I was still loopy on pain meds when the doctor told me it was definitely cancer. Juliana was there with me, and she had to explain everything when the drugs finally wore off."

"Where was your husband?"

She shrugged, not wanting to talk about the other elephant yet.

"How old are you, Mallory?"

"You really aren't afraid to ask questions, are you?" Trying to lighten the somber mood that always accompanied a discussion of her disease, she grinned. "How old do I look?"

Was he growling? Good Lord, that's all she needed: a guy with a bad temper and no sense of humor. "Do we really have to talk about this?" she asked.

The waiter interrupted, bringing them their entrees and grating more cheese on her fettuccine and Ben's spaghetti Bolognese. She'd had no idea what "Bolognese" was when he'd ordered it, but from the looks of the food, it was a lot like regular meat sauce.

"Is there anything else I can get for you?" the waiter asked Ben.

"Mal?" Ben asked. "Need anything?"

"No, thanks." She twirled her fork around, gathering the fettuccine into a small ball. "This looks wonderful. Nothing like fresh pasta. The box stuff always comes out kinda clumpy when I make it."

"You need to add some olive oil to the water and wait to drop the pasta in until the water is already boiling. I always make my own pasta instead of using the crap they put in boxes."

"You really *do* know how to cook! Most guys can only do one dish. Figured chili was yours."

"You doubted me?"

She put her fork down against the side of her plate. "Look, Ben…I'm not sure exactly *what* I believe about you."

"What's that supposed to mean?"

"We've known each other a couple of months, but we don't really *know* each other."

"That's why we're on another date. To talk. To see if we click. After those kisses—"

So that was the catalyst, the kisses they'd shared. The ones she'd let get entirely out of hand.

Why were all men so preoccupied with sex?

Her heart sank at the thought that he'd only asked her out to get in her in bed. "I'm not having sex with you." The words came out much louder than she'd intended, and a few heads turned their way. "Sorry. I just...If the only reason you asked me out again is because of kissing—"

"Hotter-than-hell kissing," Ben corrected. "But that's not why we're here. You'd recognize that if you'd drop your firewalls long enough to—"

"Firewalls? What firewalls?"

He leaned back in his chair and simply stared at her for a moment. "You've been through hell this year, haven't you? Maybe I'm expecting too much too soon."

That made absolutely no sense to Mallory. "What exactly *were* you expecting, Ben?"

"A chance."

"A chance to do what?"

"Make you love me."

Chapter 12

I beg your pardon?" Mallory's voice was a harsh whisper.

Ben watched the color drain from her face. His fault for being so direct, but he was what he was. After all of Theresa's stupid manipulative games, he'd approached this new relationship with honesty and openness that some women might not appreciate. He just hoped Mallory wasn't one of those women.

"Look, Mal…I meant what I said. I want to make you love me."

"Are—are you saying you…love me?"

He hoped his laugh didn't come across as condescending. "No. Not yet."

Her eyes were alight with curiosity. "Then why?"

"Why what? Why would I say something so direct?"

She nodded.

"Because of the kisses."

"We're back to that?" she said in a hurt tone. "I'm not sleeping with you just because…well, because…"

"Because of the kisses?"

"Yeah. I'm not like that."

When he grinned at the indignation in her tone, her eyes became nothing but angry slits.

He held up a hand. "Please don't get mad. I wasn't smiling because I disagreed with you. I know you're not like that. Ever think that's one of the reasons I went to the mixer to find you and why I took you on a date? I wanted to be with you someplace where I wasn't your contractor."

"I have no idea what you think, Ben. I'm starting to realize I don't know anything about you at all."

"Ah, but you do," he countered. "We've spent enough time together for you to know a lot about me."

After a glance down at her plate of fettuccine, she smiled. "Fine. You tell me what you think I already know about you, and I'll eat this while it's still hot. Now that I can taste stuff again, I'm not letting something this delicious go uneaten."

"You couldn't taste?"

"Nope. Side effect of chemotherapy. Short-term, thankfully. I missed chocolate more than my hair."

He chuckled, glad to see she was willing to give him a chance and open up a little. "I've got a better idea. How about we just go ahead and ignore the elephant long enough to eat? Then we can get dessert to go and head back to your place. We can have a glass of wine, some of Santiago's legendary tiramisu, and sit down for a long chat."

* * *

"Red or white?" Mallory asked, looking over her selection of wine.

It was limited at best. Bethany was the oenophile, and she always griped about Mallory buying wines simply because they were on sale. Wine just wasn't her "thing." The few wines she enjoyed were horribly sweet. Drinking some of the stuff Beth had made her taste seemed no better than sipping vinegar.

There were four bottles in Mallory's refrigerator: two red, two white. Bethany had explained that not all wines should be refrigerated, but Mallory hadn't paid too much attention. It was easier just to put them all in. Besides, now that she lived alone, the fridge was nothing but a big, empty cavern.

Why did wines all have different names? She didn't want to mispronounce them and appear ignorant.

"Just red or white? Nothing more specific?" He set the box with their desserts on the table, kicked his shoes off, and made himself at home in the mess of her house. He dodged the piles he'd left when he'd wrapped things up on Friday, making his way through her kitchen.

"Yeah…um…I think." She shrugged. "I'm not much of a wine person."

"Let me guess…you like alcohol that doesn't taste like alcohol. Piña coladas. Raspberry margaritas. Wine coolers."

She nodded and smiled.

Right behind her now, he played with her hair, running his fingers through her curls. "Want me to pick one?"

What she wanted was for him to kiss her again. When her sex drive came back, it returned with the intensity of a hurricane. His simple touch made her body temperature shoot up and her pulse beat faster. "Sure." The word came out a choked squeak.

Ben leaned closer, looking over her shoulder as his fingers stroked the nape of her neck. "Grab that moscato. Not that I'd normally team it with tiramisu, but if the lady wants sweet, she'll get sweet."

Plucking the bottle from the refrigerator door, she stepped

away from him to put the wine on the island. She fished a corkscrew from the drawer. Rascal rubbed against her legs, probably thinking she was going to feed him. "You already ate, kitty cat," she scolded.

Rascal must have known a rejection when he heard one because he headed down the hall with his nose in the air, tail twitching behind him.

Ben held out his hand. "Let me open it."

Handing him the tool, she murmured, "Thanks."

"You're welcome."

So they were back to saying nothing of importance and exchanging pleasantries.

Two steps forward, one step back.

Dinner had been a roller-coaster ride, alternating between raw emotions and pleasant chitchat. She wasn't sure which she enjoyed more because she was happy just to be in the amusement park of life again.

The last few years she and Jay were married, even before the cancer, they'd fallen into a relationship that was comfortable. But not in a good way. They'd been moving through life as though sleepwalking, never feeling any excitement or anger or passion. Just... *boring.* And distant.

Then her life was thrown into the deep end, and the man who should have been her lifeline, the one thing who could have helped her through the ordeal, left. She'd wanted to fight, to scream, to thrash things out, anything to try to save the marriage. Until he'd said the one thing she'd had no response for except to stare at him in mute resignation.

It's too real, Mallory. It's just too fucking real.

Damn right it was real!

So much for "in sickness and in health." He'd announced his

intention to leave on a Thursday and had a mover in their house the following Saturday. She'd stood vigilant over what they could and couldn't take, but Jay was nowhere to be found. Pretty typical of him to make an enormous mess and then leave others to clean it up.

She'd only seen him twice since the divorce, and after he moved out of Cloverleaf, she'd breathed a relieved sigh. She no longer had to worry about bumping into him at the grocery or the bank, especially when her head had been bald and her body ravaged by surgery and chemotherapy.

She hadn't had time to mourn the death of the marriage, and even if she had, she wouldn't have wasted tears on Jay Hamilton's sorry ass. Time, distance, and cancer had given Mallory perspective, and her conclusion was that the marriage had died years before her diagnosis. Neither of them had been willing to admit it, but the fact remained: they'd drifted too far apart to be able to find each other again.

The pop of the cork brought a smile, reminding her that one chapter of her life had closed, but another could very well be opening. She grabbed two mismatched wineglasses from the cabinet and set them in front of Ben.

He poured a generous amount in each glass, picked up one to hand to her, and then took the other. "Let's go sit on the couch. Okay?"

"Sure. It's probably the only furniture without tarps on it."

Ben winced. "Yeah…sorry about that."

"I wasn't scolding. I'll be glad when you're done with the fireplace. Then I can start a fire with a flick of a switch."

"Told ya so. Gas logs are great."

Mallory sat down with her bent knee on the cushion so she could face him.

He mimicked her action, giving her his full attention as he sipped his wine. "A little sweet, but good."

She took a taste and was glad to find he was right. "Do you want me to get a couple of forks so we can eat the tiramisu?"

"Not yet."

Another sip kept her from letting any stupid words slip out of her mouth. The intimacy of the scene, the way the tension between them sizzled, had erotic images popping through her brain. Heated kisses. Intimate embraces. Hushed words of desire. Skin on skin.

"Can we talk about the elephant again now?" he asked.

The inevitable question. She shrugged. "I suppose... If you want to know about the cancer—"

"I do, but that's another elephant for another time."

"Then what—"

"Us. I want to talk about *us*."

"Oh..." She sipped more wine, loving the warm trail it blazed down her throat and working up her courage. She wanted to ask him the litany of questions that had crowded her thoughts since he'd declared he was determined to make her love him.

Could he have meant it?

Jay had been quick to declare his love, but it turned out to be fleeting and shallow. Could she trust her own judgment now?

Her gut told her yes. Ben was nothing like Jay, from talents to temperament. Age and cancer had given her wisdom and insight. Ben wouldn't behave like her ex. She was sure of it.

"I meant every word."

"Are you a mind reader?"

"Nah. I only answered the question I'd be thinking in your shoes."

"You just surprised me." More than surprised. Near to stupefied.

"Yeah, well..." He shrugged. "Surprised myself a little, too."

"Why?"

He set his glass on one of the few bare areas of the coffee table. Then he reached for hers and set it down as well. "I told myself I'd never get into something heavy again, not while my daughter would be impacted by it."

"Then why now? Why me?"

"Because the thought of treating you like any of the other women I've dated just seems wrong."

She glanced away. "You feel sorry for me because of the cancer."

Ben nudged her to face him and then shook his head. "Because you're not like the others. Never once did I consider a future with a new woman—as much for my daughter as for myself. Amber didn't deserve to live with that kind of upheaval again."

"Your ex was that bad?"

"Oh yeah. But with you...it seemed obscene not to reach for something more permanent. You're not the kind of woman a guy dates and then moves on, and you wouldn't ruin my daughter's life. You'd enhance it."

"What makes you think that?"

"Fishing for a compliment?"

Her eyes widened. "No...I—I—"

"I was teasing, Mal." His fingers wrapped around hers. "You're a good person. You understand kids, too. How could someone so sweet not enhance Amber's life? Look, I really did mean what I said—I want us to try the relationship thing."

Mallory searched her mind, trying to push aside the terror at opening up emotionally again. Physically would be no problem. The stroke of his thumb against her palm was driving her to distraction. But just because she wanted to sleep with Ben didn't mean she was ready to do anything more than date.

She just didn't know. "This could complicate things, Ben."

He threw her a lopsided smile that set off his dimple. "'Complicated' usually means something fun's about to happen."

"Or something sad..."

"I try to be an optimist."

Optimism had driven her since her diagnosis. "I do, too, although cancer tends to bring out a person's pessimistic side."

"I can only imagine."

"Juliana kept telling me everything would be okay, and I always figured positive thinking helped me fight harder." His fingers dropped to her knee, stroking small circles. His touch worked as well as the wine to help her relax. "I'm cancer-free now."

"Yeah?"

She nodded. "I'm not going to let my whole life be about a disease. I won't be a victim. I'm still me, not just some patient."

"A survivor."

"Yeah, a survivor."

"Have you dated much?" he asked.

"Since I found out about the cancer? Or since the divorce?"

"Either..."

Honesty. The right way to start a relationship, and damn if he hadn't made her believe that was what they were doing. "I went on two dates. Neither of them worked on any level."

"Not your type?"

"Not even close. My heart wasn't in it. Both guys brought me home right after dinner, and I was beyond grateful."

"Are you ready now? To date, I mean."

The very question she'd been asking. "You know...I think I am."

"With me?" His voice cracked.

"With you."

***

Mallory's smile hit Ben like an electric shock. It had been a long time since he'd felt the kind of attraction now holding him hostage. Even when he'd met Theresa, their connection hadn't made heat rush through him, creating a primitive desire to touch, to claim, to mark her like an animal wanting to let others know she was his mate.

Had he contracted some weird virus?

Sure, he worried about Amber. Yet, the more time he spent with Mallory, the more he was certain she'd be as good for his daughter as she was for him.

All Amber had known was a woman who changed her mind as often as her clothes—a mother who put her own selfish desires before anyone else. While he'd loved Theresa, he probably wouldn't have married her if she hadn't gotten pregnant with Amber. His daughter was the best thing he'd ever done in his life, so there were no regrets.

The woman sitting next to him, opening up, sure wasn't the Mallory he'd known so far. What he wanted now was to unearth all there was to discover and to see if he was right in judging her as unique.

Hearing her two simple words declaring she felt the same was—

Come off it, Ben! She never said she was panting after you the way you're panting after her.

Just because he was in the throes a thirty-five-year-old's version of a heavy crush didn't mean she was.

He shifted, trying to get into a more comfortable position. His erection wasn't making it easy.

"I hate this couch, too. Really uncomfortable." Mallory's

brown eyes sparkled with humor as they dropped to the front of his pants.

He snatched a throw pillow and put it over his lap. "Um… sorry."

She stared at the pillow. "Why would you be sorry about that?"

How was he supposed to answer her? Having a boner hadn't been this embarrassing since junior high, when his teachers seemed to have radar for knowing the most humiliating time to call him to the board to work a math problem.

"I-I'm afraid you'll think I just want to have sex."

Leaning closer, she grabbed the pillow and tossed it like a Frisbee. "We already established that this wasn't about sex."

Thank God he'd gone to a lot of effort to tell her he wanted a relationship and that she'd believed him. Otherwise he'd have a terrible time trying to convince her of his sincerity while sitting there with a hard-on and gaping at her with hunger in his eyes.

But wasn't that same hunger in her eyes?

On her knees now, she put her hands on his face and drew him forward. Her mouth inches from his, she smiled. "We never established that sex wasn't included in the package."

Her lips were so incredibly soft and warm when they pressed against his. Unsure of whether he should turn loose the passion he was barely restraining, he let her take the reins. All he had to do was follow her lead.

She pulled back, her gaze searching his.

If only he knew what questions were flying through her mind…

"They *were* special, weren't they?" Mallory asked in a breathless whisper.

His brain had turned to oatmeal the moment she touched him. "What was special?"

"The kisses."

The incredible kisses that haunted his thoughts and dreams. "Yeah, Mal. They were special."

She was smiling when she kissed him again.

Ben was past teasing. He picked her up by the waist and helped her straddle his thighs, never breaking the kiss. When he had her settled, he splayed one hand between her shoulder blades while the other cupped the back of her neck. With a tickle of her tongue, he opened his lips to her.

She tasted every bit as sweet as she had before. Even sweeter now. Her tongue was wild, gliding across his, tracing his teeth. Just when he feared she was pulling back, her teeth nipped at his bottom lip. He opened wider, and her tongue plunged inside again.

Mallory Hamilton was an enigma. She'd always seemed so quiet, so reserved. Prim and proper.

Not now.

She'd turned aggressor, and Ben loved every moment of it. Her hands were everywhere. His biceps. His neck. His cheeks. She tangled her fingers through his hair and tugged gently, the sting adding to his pleasure. Spreading her legs a little wider, she pressed her core against his erection, drawing a ragged groan from deep in his throat.

If he didn't slow things down, he'd be carrying her straight to her bedroom. While he wanted that more than anything, he feared she'd stop trusting in his feelings and return to believing this pairing was nothing more than sex.

That…and this had to be her first sexual experience after her surgery. It might take her a while to warm up to him and realize that he honestly didn't care whether she'd lost her breast or not. He needed to convince her he wasn't that shallow.

Yet his good intentions kept getting waylaid by Mallory.

She tore her mouth away, swirling her tongue around his ear and then licking her way down his neck. Kissing and nibbling down that sensitive flesh, she worked her way to his chest, her fingers fumbling with the buttons of his shirt.

With supreme effort and taut self-control, he grabbed her wrists. "Wait."

They both gasped for breath, staring at each other while Ben tried to calm his body.

Mallory looked into his eyes, and the passion he saw reflected there almost made him change his mind. It suddenly seemed like an excellent idea to kiss her again.

So he did.

Her aggressive nature took hold, and she deepened the kiss. Wiggling her wrists free, she started on his shirt again.

"Wait." He wrenched his mouth away. "We can't do this. Not yet."

"Why not?"

When she leaned in for another kiss, he turned his head. Her lips brushed his cheek. "I promised you. Remember?"

"But *I* didn't promise *you*."

"You don't mean that. We can't... not yet."

"Why?"

His brain scrambled for something tangible. "I—I didn't bring any condoms."

Her whole body stilled. "You really meant it, didn't you? This isn't about sex."

"You doubted me?" Ben practically screeched. What kind of game was she playing?

She shrugged. "Yes... and no. I guess I can really trust you now."

"This was a test?"

She shook her head adamantly. "No. Not at all. It was my hormones reasserting themselves. But…it did show me something."

Holding back his anger, he asked, "What exactly did it show you?"

"That Ben Carpenter is a man of his word."

Chapter 13

She felt like shit.

Mallory hadn't realized how bad she looked until three pairs of concerned eyes fixed on her the moment she sat down for lunch. So much for keeping things to herself…Her fault for not realizing the women she saw almost every day knew her far too well to let her keep anything from them.

"What's wrong?" Juliana asked.

Lying to them was nothing but wasted breath, so she decided to let them in on her decision. "The surgeon put a stretcher in after school on Friday. Blew it up a little more this morning. Hurts like hell."

"Surgeon?" Jules knit her brows. "Stretcher? What are you talking about?"

"Yeah…um…I've been meaning to tell you all something." Mallory took a breath, bracing herself for their reactions. "I decided to go ahead with the breast reconstruction."

"I thought you wanted to wait awhile," Juliana insisted. "You said you weren't ready to put yourself through another surgery."

"Yeah, well." She shrugged before flinching at the pain it caused.

As usual, Jules assumed she understood everything perfectly. "You're doing it for *him*. That's why you didn't talk to us about it first. Shit, Mal…you've only been going out with the guy a couple of months."

"I can't believe you didn't say a word." Danielle's hurt tone felt like a slap.

What was she supposed to say? These women had helped her through the worst experiences of her life. Why was she keeping the best experience, her growing attachment to Ben, such a big secret?

"I'm not doing it for him," Mallory insisted. The throbbing in her chest was incessant, and she seriously considered taking some of the Vicodin the doctor had given her for the pain. She'd decided to try to muddle through without it, especially while she was at school.

"What's a stretcher?" Danielle asked, fishing her lunch out and setting the items on the table.

"A balloon thingy," Mallory replied. "It's under the skin. Gets blown up to stretch my skin enough for the implant to fit."

Cradling her left arm close to her, she popped the top on her Diet Coke with her right. Maybe the caffeine would help. A quick check of the clock said it was too soon for more ibuprofen. The Vicodin was sounding better and better. The only thing preventing her from hunting the bottle down that moment was that the painkiller made her too sleepy to do her job. She would also hate the irony of telling kids to stay off drugs while taking her own.

"I know you better than anyone, Mal," Jules said. "You don't have a vain bone in your body. You wouldn't put yourself through that kind of pain just to get your boob back. You're doing it for him."

"Cut her some slack, Jules," Bethany said. "She's in a new relationship."

"So?"

"So... would you want to sleep with a guy if you were afraid he'd be turned off by you having one boob?"

"That's not why I'm having the surgery. Besides, I haven't slept with him." *Not yet.*

Danielle's eyes widened. "You mean he hasn't seen your scar? I assumed..."

"I haven't slept with him."

Not that she hadn't wanted to. Sweet Lord, they were like a couple of teenagers whenever they found privacy, which wasn't often enough. He worked so much, and he was such a good father, one who believed in spending time with his daughter. Mallory couldn't fault him for that. She'd known far too many students who barely saw their parents, and they always suffered for that neglect. His time with Amber took time away from her, and she was juggling an odd sense of jealousy at their relationship, especially when she and Amber were still trying to get to know each other.

"But you want to. That's why you're doing this." Jules took a big bite of her celery stalk and glared at Mallory.

The way Juliana was acting was precisely why Mallory hadn't called her to discuss the procedure. She'd shared all the rest of the ups and downs of her two-month relationship with the Ladies, but with each new tale, Jules's annoyance rose another notch. She'd been Mallory's best friend since the moment they first met, and she had to feel as if Mallory was putting Ben before her.

That wasn't true—at least not entirely true. Starting a new relationship was difficult at best. Sure, Ben was an easy guy to like. He was polite and sweet and so very patient with her. But the fears she harbored because of Jay's abandonment were always there, right below the surface.

Jay had disappeared because of a diagnosis. What would Ben do when he saw what remained of the left side of her chest?

"I'm doing this for me," Mallory maintained. "I'm tired of my clothes not fitting right. I'm tired of worrying whether my falsie is gonna slip out. I'm tired of looking in the mirror and seeing that…that…scar. I want my body back."

At least Juliana had the sense to appear somewhat contrite as she munched on her celery. She wasn't the kind of person who liked having her bad behavior pointed out. Any type of criticism always elicited a pout before she realized her error.

"We need to decide who's driving next weekend for the Miracle Mile trip," Danielle said. "God, I've looked forward to that. Just two days of shopping and eating out."

"Shit. I'm sorry. I—I forgot."

"Forgot?" Danielle cocked her head. "We do this every fall break. I didn't think we'd need to remind you."

"I know we always go. I should've remembered," Mallory replied. "Look, I can't go. I let it slip my mind. I'll be in Chicago…with Ben."

"Ben?" Bethany shifted her gaze to Jules as though she was the one who should be asking. "Why are you going to Chicago with Ben on our Miracle Mile weekend?"

"I got tickets for us to take Amber to a gymnastics exhibition. First time I get to spend some time with her."

Bethany cocked her head. "I thought you'd met her."

"I did. But it was just a McDonald's supper after one of her gymnastics lessons."

"You're really not going with us?" Danielle's tone was more hurt than angry, which only made Mallory feel worse.

"I'm sorry. We'll do it next year. Okay?"

"Just like our trip to Brown County," Jules said with a huff. "What were you doing with Ben *that* weekend?"

"I said I was sorry." Mallory was in too much pain to eat anything else. That and her rising anger made her stomach churn.

"You've been sorry a lot lately." Juliana drilled holes through Mallory with her sharp eyes.

"You don't want to change your life for him." Bethany popped her soda open, though her gaze never left Mallory's.

"What are you talking about? How am I changing my life?"

"I've seen it happen before," Beth replied. "You're spending all the time with him that you used to with us. You're making you boyfriend more important than anything else, including your best friends."

"It's a new relationship, Beth. It takes time to get to know each other."

"It shouldn't take *all* your time," Danielle said. "It should be something that feels natural, something that enhances your life. Definitely not something you have to do every single minute of every single day."

"Definitely not something to have major surgery over," Juliana added.

As if Mallory's nerves weren't already shot to hell worrying about whether Amber would accept her…They'd have to spend a lot of time together on the trip—a two-hour drive to Chicago and another long ride back. Mallory couldn't help but worry that she'd say or do the wrong thing and make Amber dislike her.

Then what would Ben do? Leave her to please his daughter?

That thought was unbearable.

Her feelings were already so tangled up in Ben Carpenter, she wasn't sure how devastated she'd be if he left. She couldn't even think about it without getting nauseated.

And now the people she depended on, her *friends*, were picking a fight. A missed trip to spend money they really didn't have on clothes, shoes, and purses they didn't need?

Why couldn't they understand how much time went into developing a new relationship?

On the other hand, all three of them were making good points, and she'd be a hypocrite if she didn't accept criticism any better than Juliana. Mallory had given Ben more time than she had the friends who'd helped her through everything life had thrown her way. After everything they'd done for her, they deserved better.

Mallory heaved a sigh. "I'm sorry. You're right. I didn't mean to make you think I was choosing Ben over you guys."

"It's okay," Bethany said.

"No," Jules insisted. "It's not."

"She said she was sorry." Danielle, as usual, was trying to keep the peace. "Now tell us about the surgery."

Thankful for the diversion, Mallory did what she should have done in the first place—she confided in her friends. "I'm going to have it over Christmas break. Gives me plenty of time get the skin stretched enough and to recover without missing school."

"What can we do to help?" Bethany asked. Her kindness was as exceptional as her continued optimism.

"I'll let you know," Mallory replied. "Right now, I just need some painkillers and a long nap. This stretcher hurts like fire."

Beth's eyes were full of concern. "How often do you have to have it inflated? I'd hate to think of you feeling like this all the way to Christmas."

"It's supposed to ease when the skin expands. At least I hope so." While her instinct was to rub it to make the throbbing stop,

Mallory had immediately learned that wasn't helpful. Not in the least. What she needed was Vicodin and ice packs, both of which she could have as soon as the school day ended. "I have to have it inflated a few more times at least until the skin's stretched enough for the implant."

"You're not having silicone, right?" At least Juliana could do something besides get mad at her.

Mallory shook her head. "Saline. I don't think anyone does silicone now. Too many problems."

"Are you sure you want this? That you're not doing it for him?"

"He has a name, Jules. He's my boyfriend now. Can't you accept him?"

She rolled her green eyes. "Fine. *Ben.* Are you sure you're not doing this for Ben?"

"I'm doing it for a lot of reasons, including Ben. Okay?"

With a curt nod, Juliana closed up her container of vegetables and reached for her Snickers bar.

Mallory considered asking for a bite. Maybe chocolate would help the pain.

"Tell us about the thing you're going to," Bethany said. "Something about gymnastics?"

"Amber takes gymnastic classes," Mallory replied. "She loves the sport. When Ben told me he was thinking about taking her to Chicago for some big exhibition, I asked if I could get the tickets."

"You're trying to bribe the kid." Jules had never shied from telling everyone exactly what was on her mind.

"I hadn't thought about it that way. Yeah, I want her to like me. But a bribe?"

Mallory hated to admit it, but perhaps it *was* a bribe. What was she supposed to say? That she craved being with Ben? That he was dark chocolate to her, an addiction so overpowering she couldn't fight it? That keeping him meant winning over his daughter?

At least they'd have a long day to spend together. He'd taken another contracting job, one Robert helped him find that seemed to require overtime every day. The work on her house had ground to a screeching halt, but she never complained. The place wasn't going anywhere, and she knew he'd get to it as soon as he could.

Ben had never come out and said it, but he didn't have a lot of money. He was raising Amber with no help from his ex-wife. She'd seen an eye-popping bill for Amber's braces sitting on the truck bench. Did he even have insurance? Medical or dental?

The trip to Chicago might be too much of a luxury for him to manage, so Mallory bought the tickets and insisted they take her SUV instead of his truck. That way she could pay for the gas, too. Ben got to take his daughter to something she really wanted to see, and Mallory got to be his knight in shining armor.

But a bribe?

Juliana was drumming her fingers on the table, her sign that she was waiting for Mallory's concession of the obvious.

"Fine! It's a bribe. Okay?"

Jules only nodded as a smile tugged at the corners of her mouth.

* * *

Ben reached across to put his hand on Mallory's thigh, hoping to ease whatever fears were tumbling through her mind. "It'll be fine."

She gave him a brisk nod, but her hands still trembled as she drove.

Why had she worked herself into such a bundle of nerves? She'd already met Amber. They'd had one supper together, although that had been fast food and a rather quick episode. Despite his daughter's misgivings at his dating, especially exclusively, Amber had been cordial.

Perhaps that was the problem—Mallory wasn't used to kids being merely *cordial.*

A couple of times when they went out, she'd bumped into students, current and former. They'd fawned over her, telling her how much they loved her class or missed seeing her. Amber had been polite but quiet.

"Amber's looking forward to the trip." *There.* That reassurance would help Mallory get past her anxiety.

She didn't make a peep.

"It was great of you to get tickets. I wish you'd let me pay you back."

"No, Ben. I wanted to do this. For Amber."

"Think you can bribe her into being your new best friend?"

"You think I got the tickets to bribe her into liking me?"

His sense of humor needed an adjustment. "I was just teasing. Trying to get you to loosen up a little. What's got you so worried?"

"I'm not."

"Mal…" He hated to remind her of their "rule," fearing sounding like a scolding parent.

"I'm not worried. Honest. I'm just…in pain." After pulling up next to his house, she jammed the car into park.

"Pain?" He gave her a quick head-to-toe appraisal. Nothing seemed out of place. "Headache?"

From the way she hesitated, it was easy to see she was trying to decide whether to tell the truth. He had no idea what that meant.

"Are you sick to your stomach?" he asked.

She shook her head.

"Why won't you tell me?"

After a long sigh, she finally gave in. "My chest hurts."

"You're having chest pains?"

"No. Not like that. Can we drop this?"

"When you're in pain?" He gave his head a shake. "Honesty, Mal."

"I'm having my breast reconstructed." Her voice was hushed.

While she'd told him about her cancer and her chemo, she'd never once told him she was considering having more surgery. Then again, once she'd shared the story of her diagnosis, mastectomy, and recovery, he'd assumed the topic had been laid to rest.

Ben was at a loss. Not only didn't he understand why her making plans to have her breast reconstructed would be causing her pain *now*, he wasn't sure why she even thought she needed to have the procedure.

For all the weeks they'd been together, he'd never made a move to touch her chest. Their passion hadn't dimmed. Far from it. Whenever they kissed, sparks flew. He hadn't pushed her for more, not because he didn't desire her. She'd wound him up so tight, there were a few times he'd returned from a date to take matters into his own hands so he didn't implode. Or explode.

Soon. At least that's what he'd hoped.

Now he was afraid he'd pushed too hard. Why else would she be thinking about having surgery to repair her breast? She had to assume she needed to be "fixed" before they made love.

"Are you doing this for me?" Ben needed to know she wasn't going to put herself through surgery to please him.

"No."

"Seriously, Mallory. I don't want you doing this for me."

Her brown eyes grew stormy. "Why would you think I'd do it for you?"

There were plenty of reasons, none of which he wanted to voice. What if her feelings didn't run as deep as his? No way he'd bare his mind to her. It was far too soon. Hell, he wasn't even sure exactly *what* he felt for her.

He shrugged.

"You sound like my friends," Mallory grumbled, popping open her seat belt. She was out of the SUV before he could figure out what she meant.

She waited on the stoop, although only the storm door was closed.

Amber stood just inside, shoving her arms into her jacket.

Ben reached around Mallory to pull the door open. "Go on in."

She stepped inside. "Hi, Amber."

Jerking up her zipper, Amber replied, "Hi." She didn't smile until Ben was inside. "Can we stop and get a drink for the road?"

"Um... Mal's not feeling so hot, Amber."

His daughter's brown eyes fixed on Mallory. "You mean we're not going?"

"She's—"

"Fine," Mallory insisted. "She's fine and ready to go. I've been waiting to watch these girls since the Olympics."

"I thought you said you were hurting." Ben didn't want to disappoint his daughter, but he wasn't going to let Mallory go on this trip and exhaust herself, especially when the pain was so clearly written on her face.

Although he'd never told his daughter that Mallory was a cancer survivor, Amber must have seen the same thing he did. "It-it's okay." Concern laced her tone. "I mean... if you feel rotten... Chicago's a long trip."

"I'm okay, Amber," Mallory said. "I had a migraine, but I'm better." Her steady gaze dared him to contradict her.

Since he really didn't want to disappoint Amber and because Mallory was insisting, he gave in. "Let's roll."

After he locked up, he came up behind Mallory before she crawled into the driver's seat. He wasn't sure what was happening that made her hurt, but it had to involve her left side being made ready for surgery. He wanted to make things easier for her. "Would you like me to drive?"

She glanced over her shoulder, nibbled on her lip for a moment, then nodded. She handed over the keys and walked to the other side of the car.

Ben adjusted the mirrors, loving being behind the wheel of her Escape. He fired up the engine, smiled at Mallory and then Amber. "Chicago, here we come."

Chapter 14

Gymnastics had been her favorite sport growing up, so at least Mallory found common ground with Amber. That alone made the trip worth the time, the cost—even the pain.

They talked quite a bit on the ride to Chicago about the changes in the sport since Mallory had taken lessons back in elementary school. Their conversation had been easy and pleasant. But once they arrived at the arena, she couldn't enjoy the exhibition because her chest hurt so damned bad.

Ben kept a close eye on her, making her struggle to hide the agony as much as she could. Judging from his increasing frown, she wasn't succeeding.

"Did you see that dismount?" Amber tugged on Mallory's left arm.

Mallory hissed a breath, closing her eyes and trying to will the misery away. Amber had no idea she'd hurt her, and she didn't want the poor kid feeling guilty.

She never should have come on the trip, not right after another skin stretch.

Amber's eyes went wide. "Are you okay?"

Teeth tugging on her bottom lip, Mallory nodded. Since a tear leaked out of the corner of one eye, there was no way either Ben or Amber would believe her.

"Mal?" Ben put a hand on her back. "What's wrong?"

"I'm just…hurting."

"What did I do?" Amber's voice quavered. "I didn't mean to—"

"It's not you," Mallory insisted, not wanting Amber to blame herself.

"Really? I—I wouldn't hurt you."

"Really, Amber." She would have patted the girl's hand if she hadn't thought it would be condescending. "It's not you at all. I know you wouldn't hurt me." She groped for her purse. "I need to go to the ladies' room."

The pain was incessant. She had no choice but to take the Vicodin. Ibuprofen just couldn't cut it, not for this kind of hurting. At least she'd had enough common sense to bring her meds along.

"Mal? What can I do?" Ben asked, his tone full of concern that touched her deeply.

"Nothing. Really. I'll take something and be right back."

She worked her way across the aisle, grateful several seats were empty. By the time she found a water fountain, the sharp pain had downgraded to an intense throbbing, but she was still going to take the Vicodin. She fished the prescription from her purse, fumbled with the childproof cap, and finally freed the pills. After she spilled two onto her palm, she threw them back into her throat and then drank a fair amount from the fountain.

Since the restroom was close, she made her way inside. At least there wasn't a wait. When the event started, the disparity between the number of men and women attending became evident in the length of the line to get into a ladies' room. Now she could thankfully breeze into one of the open stalls. After locking the door, she gingerly lifted her shirt and camisole, the one she wore since the tightness of a bra would only cause more pain.

The balloon used to stretch her skin gave the left side of her chest a shape for the first time since the mastectomy. It wasn't as large as her breast had been, at least not yet. But there was something satisfying about seeing the bump that would be replaced by a saline implant soon.

If only it didn't hurt so damn bad.

There was no nipple, but she had two choices to correct that—reconstruct it using tissue from her vulva or skin, or she could get a tattoo. She was leaning heavily toward the tattoo.

Had she stayed home, she might have eased some of the horrible ache with cold compresses and a good book. Knowing how important this was to Amber, there'd been no way she'd consider canceling. She'd pamper herself when she got home.

Mallory had almost fished her cell phone out of her pocket to call Jules before she remembered Jules was probably still in a sulk over their lunch squabble. Even though things were better, Mallory needed to clear the air and apologize. Not that she could blame any of her friends for their anger. After having time to think more about things, she knew she'd been taking them for granted.

They'd been there for her through all the bad times, and she'd brushed them aside for a new boyfriend. Had Juliana, Danielle, or Bethany done the same, Mallory would have scolded her and told her just how rude the behavior was. Guys might preach about "bros before hos," but the Ladies Who Lunch were more than mere friends. They were sisters of the heart, and she'd ignored them as though they had no feelings or no stake in all she was facing—both with Ben and with her reconstructive surgery.

She grabbed her phone and sent Juliana a text.

I'm sorry, Jules.

The return message wasn't long in coming.

Sure you are. That's why you're in Chicago with Mr. Rebound.

Juliana could hold a grudge for a century, probably her Irish heritage. Mallory wasn't deterred. With the Vicodin slowly kicking in, she relaxed a little and tried again.

I really AM sorry. Lost myself for a while.

Just about ready to head back to her seat so Ben and Amber would stop worrying about her, she was slipping her phone back into her purse when Jules's ringtone sounded—"Holding Out for a Hero." Something they'd both promised to do in those days after her mastectomy. They'd used the endless time to talk about everything from ex-husbands to hunky movie stars to future guys who might enter their lives. Each had sworn she would settle for nothing but the perfect guy.

Had she found that man in Ben Carpenter?

It was too soon to tell, but the seeds had been planted and were already taking root.

Mallory answered her call. "Hey, Jules."

"Did you find yourself again somewhere in Chicago?"

Mallory heaved a sigh. "Yeah. I really didn't mean to push you away. Danielle or Bethany, either."

"Look, we get it. You like the guy. But he's just a boyfriend. Don't change your whole life for him."

"I didn't mean to. It just…happened."

"You're still in pain," Jules pronounced. "I can hear it in your voice."

As if she could hide anything from her best friend. "The stretcher hurts so badly."

"You had it done again?" Juliana asked.

"Yeah. Yesterday afternoon. Makes my whole chest ache."

"I'm sorry, Mal. You should've stayed home."

"I know," Mallory admitted. "But I really wanted to get to know Amber, and Ben said she was dying to see this exhibition."

"And?"

"She's nice. Typical girl her age with good manners. We haven't talked about much except gymnastics, though."

"Just be yourself. Your students love you. She will, too."

"Thanks, Jules. I needed to hear that."

"You're welcome." The silence stretched between them before Juliana said, "Be sure and text Danielle and Beth. They're worried about you, too. Remember... we're just looking out for you."

"You're worried? Thought you were all still peeved at me."

"Always remember how close love and anger are," Juliana replied. "We don't want you to get hurt. Call me when you get home. We can talk about our Black Friday plans."

"Love you, Jules."

"Love you, too, Mal."

* * *

"I don't know what I did," Amber insisted, her eyes filled with panic.

While Ben wasn't sure exactly what was causing Mallory so much pain, he knew it had something to do with getting ready for breast reconstruction soon. He knew next to nothing about medicine, even less about women's bodies. The only thing he was sure of was that Mallory was hurting, and he wanted that to stop. Immediately.

"I don't think you did anything, Amber."

"But I hurt her."

He shook his head as he moved over a seat where Mallory had been, torn on how much he should explain to his daughter. Amber was a sensitive kid, always had been. Just introducing Mallory to her was a leap forward that showed how seriously he was taking this relationship.

He felt something for Mallory, something strong enough to make him bring her into his daughter's life. Amber sure needed a female role model, but he'd never dated a woman he felt comfortable having around her. Most were only one or two dates, then they were history.

Mallory was different, had been from the moment he met her, especially from that first incredible kiss. She was smart. She was strong. She was a good person. He had no doubt she could be a stabilizing force in his daughter's life, maybe even become the type of woman Amber needed to help her become a good person, too.

Even then, he was uncertain of whether to say anything about Mallory's cancer. It was her story to tell, and she might not be ready to share it with people outside her inner circle. Jules had told him how Mallory had kept the diagnosis quiet and how closely she guarded her feelings. Maybe she didn't want her boyfriend's kid to know she'd survived such a harrowing struggle.

Amber would no doubt be affected by the news. Sure, Mallory was healthy now—at least, he thought so. She couldn't go ahead with the breast reconstruction if she wasn't done with her chemotherapy. She'd told him that much.

But only time would tell if she stayed in remission. He couldn't bear the thought of something happening to her, and he sure as hell didn't want to put his daughter through another ordeal. Hurricane Theresa had done enough damage. What if Amber got attached to Mallory and then her cancer returned?

The thought he could lose Mallory now that he'd finally found her felt like a knife to the heart.

She's well now. She is. She's well now.

He kept repeating it like a mantra.

"Should I go check on her or something?" Amber glanced back to the exit Mallory had used.

He gave his head a shake. "If she doesn't get back soon I'll have you go after her."

Although Amber's attention shifted to the floor exercise area, she spoke to him. "You like her."

"Yeah, I do. I already told you that."

She shrugged. "Are you gonna marry her?"

"Whoa there, darlin'. Aren't you getting the cart well ahead of the pony?"

His daughter only shrugged again.

"Look, Amber... I'm not ready to even think about a step like that. It's too soon."

"Then why'd you drag her along with us?"

"I didn't drag her along. She's the one who got the tickets when she found out you wanted to go. She's trying to get off on the right foot with you."

"That was nice. But you know stepmoms are s'posed to be horrible." She plucked her soda from the cup holder and took a long swig, still staring at the girl in blue flip-flopping her way across the mat.

"Says who? Cinderella?"

"My friends all hate their stepmoms. They try to boss them around and always take their dads away all the time. Gets worse if they have kids."

"So the stepsisters are evil too?"

She ignored his sarcasm. "A lot worse if their dads have kids with their stepmoms. The old kids get forgotten."

After Theresa's bullshit, it wasn't any wonder Amber was full of concerns. Her mother had abandoned her. Now she feared her father would as well.

All he could do was give her a stable home and lots of love, and hope she learned that she could always count on him. "I've only been going out with her for two months, ladybug. We're not getting married, and we're sure not having our own kids."

That gave him pause. Could a cancer survivor even have kids? Had she lost her fertility along with her breast? What kind of future was in store for her?

He had a lot to learn about Mallory's condition.

"But you're old. Old people get married quick and have babies before it's too late."

"Who you callin' old, you young whippersnapper?" He used his best gruff elderly man voice. At least he made her smile. "How about I make you a promise?"

Her gaze found his. "What promise?"

"If I decide I want to get married again, I'll talk to you before I propose."

The pledge was easy to make. Ben's life wasn't entirely his own, hadn't been from the moment he cradled his seven-pound, four-ounce daughter in his arms the day she was born. His heart had been hers for thirteen years. There was no way he'd start a new relationship with a woman, even someone as special as Mallory, if it meant Amber would be miserable.

Besides, he was probably worrying for no good reason. Mallory was a wonderful woman. She was a teacher. Handling kids was her specialty. She and Amber would get along just fine once they got to know each other.

"Really?" Amber stared at him, and he saw the concern written plainly on her face.

"Really."

"And if you and Mallory have a baby? You'll tell me?"

"We won't be having a baby."

"But if you do?"

"Then I'll tell you before we even start trying. How's that?"

She found a tentative smile. "That's nice, Dad."

He held up his pinkie. "Pinkie swear?"

With a smile, she hooked his pinkie with his. "Pinkie swear."

"What are you swearing to?" Mallory asked as she took his empty seat.

"Nothing important," Amber replied, directing her attention back to the floor. Her cheeks had tinted a vivid red.

Ben chuckled at his daughter's embarrassment and then gave Mallory a quick appraisal. "Feeling better?"

"Yeah. Took something strong for the pain." A yawn slipped out. "Makes me major sleepy, though. You're gonna have to drive home. Sorry. I should have asked first."

He took her hand in his and rested them in her lap as she settled back to watch the action. "I would have told you to take it if you hadn't." Unsure of how much she wanted to talk about, he asked a tentative question. "Is it the…um…surgery?"

She nodded but didn't elaborate.

While he still wasn't sure exactly why she'd be in pain now when the surgery was weeks away, he let it slide. They'd have time alone to talk soon.

Then he'd find out exactly what was going on.

* * *

Amber popped her seat belt and leaned forward between the seats. Her face glowed in the green lights from the dash. She stared at Mallory, who'd fallen asleep only moments after they started the trip home. "Are you sure she's okay? I mean, she's out. *Really* out."

"She told me she took something stronger than Advil."

"It really wasn't me who hurt her?"

He shook his head.

"Then what's wrong with her?"

"We'll have to talk about it later, Amber. Okay?"

"I guess... But she really takes drugs? That's not good."

His daughter had a bad habit of leaping to the wrong conclusion, always assuming the worst. Of course, after living with her flighty mom, he understood. "She's a teacher, ladybug. She wouldn't take illegal drugs."

"Phew. Had me worried," she said in a teasing tone of voice as she continued to watch Mallory. "She's pretty."

"I think so, too."

"No, I mean *really* pretty. Wears her hair awful short, though."

"Is really your word of the day?" He'd have winked at her if he thought Amber could see it.

"What's making her feel so rotten? She doesn't act like she's got the flu or anything..."

"She was sick. She's better now, but I think she should be the one to tell you about it."

"Did she have cancer or something?"

The moment he'd dreaded had arrived. The concern in Amber's voice said it all. He was going to have to be honest with her whether Mallory wanted him to or not. He owed his daughter that much.

She had as much at stake in this new relationship as he did. If he and Mallory moved forward as he hoped they would, this woman was going to become a part of Amber's life. Amber deserved to know exactly what they were getting into. He just hoped Mallory would understand why he had to share the news.

"She had cancer." Needing to see her reaction, he chanced a look. Her eyes were wide as she stared at Mallory.

"What kind?" Amber asked.

"Of cancer?"

"Yeah. What kind?"

"Breast cancer."

His daughter's gaze fixed on Mallory's chest.

He could only imagine what was flying through her mind. Did all women worry about losing their breasts to cancer? Was that fear even half as terrifying as ball cancer was to guys?

When Ben had heard about Lance Armstrong's battle with testicular cancer, he'd thought that was as bad as it could get for a guy—to lose his nuts. But did women feel that way about their boobs?

Since Amber obviously wanted to know but seemed afraid to ask, he told her what he knew. "She had a mastectomy on her left side."

"That's the side I hurt." Her hand flew to her mouth. "Oh God. Did she just have the surgery?"

"No. Nothing like that," he replied, hoping to allay her worries about causing Mallory's pain. "She's getting ready to have that side reconstructed. The pain has something to do with that."

"When?"

"When what?"

"When's her surgery? I mean...if she's getting things put back together, it'll be soon?"

"Yeah. Over Christmas break. I might have to help her out."

Amber nodded. "I can help, too."

What a wonderful woman she'd be one day. She barely knew

Mallory, yet she was willing to lend a hand to help. "That'd be nice. I'm sure Mallory would like having another girl around."

"She's not sick now, right?" Amber asked. "I mean…she's not gonna die on us or anything is she?"

The fright in her voice cut him to the bone because he shared it. Niggling in the back of his mind was the concern that he could easily learn to love Mallory. And if he handed her his heart, he'd have to live with the fear of her cancer returning, threatening to take her away.

Could he handle that?

God help him, he wasn't sure. He also wasn't sure he wanted to put his daughter through the type of ordeal.

"Dad?"

"No, ladybug. She's not gonna die on us. Sit back and put your seat belt on. Okay?"

With a nod, Amber did as he asked. "I like her, Dad."

"So do I."

"I know."

He tried to see his daughter's face in the review mirror, but it was too dark to make out what emotions were taking hold. "Is that a problem?"

"Nah. I just…Thanks."

"For what?"

"For promising you'll tell me before things get too serious." She shoved her earbuds back into her ears, dismissing him.

Ben picked up Mallory's limp hand and wrapped his fingers around hers. In going to Chicago despite her overwhelming pain, she'd proven something to him.

She cared.

A lot.

A good thing, because so did he.

Chapter 15

Are you sure she won't mind if we stay over at her place?" Amber had asked the same question from the moment he turned left instead of right off the interstate.

Mallory was in no shape to drive. The mere thought of her trying to get home and to bed without him was untenable. "No, Amber. She won't."

"But you could drop me off at home first."

"She wouldn't want you to be home alone. I wouldn't want you to, either." Ben glanced at Mallory. "I can't leave her alone. She needs me."

"I know, but…I could just stay home by myself."

He shook his head.

"I'm thirteen, Dad. I can be home alone. I won't smoke dope or anything…"

"I know that. I just think it's better if you come with us."

"Dad…"

Pulling into her driveway, he dismissed the argument. "Too late. We're here."

Amber let out an exaggerated yawn as she checked her watch. "It's past your bedtime, old man."

"Past yours, too. I'll open the door." He punched the remote opener. "Go on in. Guest bedroom is at the top of the stairs on the left."

"Need any help with Mallory?"

"We're fine. Go to bed. It's late."

After opening the door, she glanced back at him. "Theresa's supposed to pick me up at nine."

As if she'd actually show up for visitation. "I know. I'll have you home in time." *In case she actually appears.* Snatching his cell phone off his belt, he punched in a new alarm time. "I'll get you up by eight."

"Ugh, too early," she said with a frown before her gaze shifted to Mallory. "Just yell if she needs me."

His daughter never ceased to amaze him. "When did you get so grown-up?"

"When you weren't looking."

She disappeared into the house.

The drive to her house was so familiar now he could have made it blindfolded. He pulled her Escape into the empty side of the garage.

Most of his tools were there since the new job with the homebuilder provided tools. He'd even started storing them in the cabinets and on the pegboard that her ex had left behind.

I wish I could work on her house more often.

Mallory was infinitely patient, and she probably knew he needed the money from the new job. But he hated that she might feel he was putting her last on his list of important things. Far from it. As soon as the construction job ended, he'd throw himself wholeheartedly into making this place beautiful.

Mallory didn't even stir when Ben opened her door.

Her face was soft in the dim light of the streetlamp. She looked younger when she was relaxed, although she wore her age well in general. Having cancer probably aged a person rapidly, but her face didn't show the wear.

Amber was right. Mallory was *really* pretty.

Should he carry her inside? Only fear that he'd hurt something if he lifted her kept him from scooping her up into his arms. Hell, he still wasn't sure what exactly was causing her so much pain.

He brushed the back of his knuckles over her cheek. "Mal? Baby?"

She wiggled her nose but slept on.

Since he had no idea what she'd taken, he didn't know how long it would be before the drug wore off. He would have popped her seat belt, but she'd tucked the shoulder strap behind her, probably because it would've pressed on her left side. If he unbuckled it, he'd have to work it over her left side.

As he rubbed her upper thigh, he tried again with a louder voice. "Mallory. We're home."

Thankfully, she stirred, her eyes slowly opening. "Ben," she murmured, laying her right hand against his cheek. Her fingers were cold as ice.

"We need to get you inside." The tone of his voice was the same he'd used with Amber. When Theresa first left, she'd been afraid to fall asleep alone. Most nights she'd dozed off on the couch. As he'd carried her to her room, he always made sure he woke her enough that she wouldn't be afraid later when she realized she was someplace different.

His gut was rapidly tying itself into knots. It was far too easy to picture himself doing this for Mallory if she was sick—if her cancer returned. He hated himself for thinking about something so chilling, but he was a realist. No matter how badly he wanted to, he couldn't pretend she hadn't had cancer inside her. And cancer had a nasty habit of returning.

How many stories had he heard of people who rallied, fighting the disease until it reasserted itself? Was anyone truly cured, or was it only a matter of time before they had a recurrence?

"Can I help you take off the seat belt?" Ben asked.

"Seat belt?" She blinked her eyes and knit her brows.

"You're in the Escape. We just got back from Chicago. Remember?"

"Hmm. Yeah."

"Can I help you get your seat belt off? Then we can get you to bed."

"Bed. With you." She hummed. "I've been looking forward to that." She hummed a little more as a smile lit her face.

Damn if he didn't blush. "To sleep, baby. Just to sleep. You're still groggy from—what did you take?"

"Vicodin. Makes me sleepy."

He found a smile. "I can see that. If I pop the buckle, will it hurt you if I lift it over your left side?"

"No. No, I'll get it." Evidently his question helped her return to the land of the living. She didn't flinch when she took it off, but she kept her left arm clasped close to her. "Where's Amber?"

"In the guest room."

Mallory's gaze searched his. "You told her."

"Yeah, I did. You're not mad?"

"No. No, she should know."

"Are you still hurting?" he asked.

"Not too bad." She tested her words by gingerly touching her chest. "Nope. Not too bad. That Vicodin's good stuff."

"Want me to carry you upstairs?"

"I'm fine." Her gaze fixed on the open garage door. "Where's your truck?"

"At home."

"But…how are you going to go home?" She was thinking hard about that simple dilemma, which meant the drug was still holding tight. "I guess I need to drive you back."

She wasn't going anywhere. He blocked her path when she stepped toward the back of the SUV. "You're not driving."

"But…" The fact she swayed on her feet probably didn't even register with her.

"No way. You're not in any shape to do anything except sleep." He came up on her right side and put his hand on her back. "I'm gonna pick you up."

"Ben, you can't—"

As gently as he could, he lifted her into his arms. She didn't wince or flinch, but she did pull her left arm close, cradling it over her stomach. "This is good? I'm not hurting you?"

Although she didn't answer, she nuzzled her face against his neck. Her warm breath brushed over his skin, sending heat shimmering through him. She smelled sweet; the lingering scent of the perfume she'd worn at the mixer clung to her skin.

Twirl. His little spin at the dance helped him remember.

He made his way to the master bedroom, grateful to see she hadn't bothered to make the bed. After he laid her down, he took off her shoes and set them on the floor. When he looked back at her face, he was surprised to see she was still awake.

"Thank you," she said.

"You're welcome." Her clothes were loose and comfortable, so Ben saw no purpose in trying to help her get into pajamas. He pulled the fuzzy blanket up over her legs and middle. "Do you need any more pills or anything?"

"No. I'm not hurting now. I think the skin finally stretched." She gave him a lopsided smile. "That or the Vicodin's still working well."

"What do you mean about the skin stretching?"

She patted the spot next to her, so he sat down. Then she took his hand in hers. "It's something the surgeon has to do to get me ready for the reconstruction procedure."

"Stretch your skin?"

"Yeah. He put this sort of balloon under the left side of my chest. Every so often, he pumps more air in to help the skin expand enough that it'll cover the implant."

Things finally made sense. No wonder she hurt so much. He hated the idea of her putting herself through that kind of pain for something cosmetic. "You think you have to have the breast done?"

She nodded.

Although she'd told him she wasn't doing this for him, Ben couldn't help but think things weren't that cut-and-dried. "You know it doesn't matter to me. Right?"

She gave him no reply, save the thinning of her lips into a tight line.

"I mean it, Mal. You don't have to put yourself through this if you're doing it for me. I don't give a shit if you've only got one breast."

Her scoff caught him off guard. "You say that now, but…you don't know, Ben. You have no idea."

"No idea about what?"

"How…*ugly* it is."

"The scar?"

This time she let out a haunting laugh. "A couple of stiches leave a scar. I'm a—a *horror movie*."

"What are you talking about?"

"I look like some piece of meat carved up by Freddy Krueger."

He gave her hand a squeeze. "It can't be that bad. Why don't you show me?"

* * *

"No way." Mallory was wide-awake now. Meds or not, she was meeting this confrontation head-on.

And that was exactly what this was: a confrontation.

Ben had no idea what he was getting himself into. She'd been lying to herself when she thought she'd ever have a chance to be anything more than a "date" with him or with any man. No one could find her desirable now. Shit, she couldn't even stand to look at herself in a mirror.

Even when her breast was reconstructed, it would have scars running across the top and the middle. Dr. Dowell had shown her the pictures of other reconstructions. Mallory had stared at each, telling herself the scars would fade over time, lying to herself that the fake nipple wouldn't appear all that different from the real one.

No, he had no idea.

"I wouldn't care, Mal."

"Trust me, you would."

Not only would he run away if he saw her hideous chest, Ben wouldn't want to face the five-year ticking clock. Why would he put himself through that? Why would he want to hang around, waiting to see if the cancer was hiding somewhere in her cells, looking for the right moment to come out and start attacking her body again?

Who would want to put himself through that kind of nightmare?

"I—I think you should go," she insisted.

The frown he threw at her was fierce. "I'm not going anywhere."

"Go home, Ben. I'm tired. I need some rest." Once he was gone, she'd ignore his calls. There were other contractors. Robert would help her find someone else to fix her house.

Fuck the house.

Who would fix her heart?

Ben wouldn't let go of her hand, even when she tried to pull it back.

Mallory bordered on a panic attack. Her heart was pounding a rough rhythm, roaring in her ears. This was exactly what she'd hoped to avoid—some relationship that exposed her emotions, leaving them blistered and raw. "Please. Just…just go away. I want you to go away."

She hadn't realized she'd started crying until Ben wiped a tear from her cheek. "No, you don't."

"Why won't you leave me alone?" The question came out in a nearly breathless sob.

His shrug sure wasn't what she expected.

What exactly did she expect? Did she want Ben to drop to his knees and declare his undying love? Did she want him to swear it didn't matter if she looked like some grotesque Frankenstein project? Did she want him to promise it didn't matter if the cancer returned, that he'd still be at her side?

The tears came in earnest, so she squeezed her eyes tightly shut. Mallory jerked her hand away, rolled to her right side, and pulled her knees up. "Go away, Ben."

The mattress shifted. She prayed he was finally doing as she asked.

God, she hated crying. Not only did the sobs make her chest ache, but she loathed the indulgence of self-pity. But she couldn't seem to stop.

Suddenly, the blanket was pulled away. The mattress dipped behind her before an arm snaked around her hips, pulling her close.

Her eyes flew open and she glanced over her shoulder. "What are you doing?"

"Holding you." He tugged her closer, molding his thighs to the backs of hers. His broad chest pressed against her back.

"Why?"

"You ask some silly questions, Mal." He nuzzled his face against her neck. "I love that perfume."

"I—I want you to leave."

"No, you don't." Ben's hand left her hip to smooth down her cheek. "You need me."

"I don't!"

"Bullshit. Now hush up and get some rest. We'll talk in the morning."

Part of her wanted to shove him away, to demand that he leave right now. She didn't need him. She didn't need anyone.

He rubbed soothing circles down her hip and thigh. Then he dragged the blanket over them, letting his arm rest over her waist.

When she realized he was being careful not to touch the left side of her chest, she almost burst into sobs again. She swallowed hard a couple of times, willing away the threatening tears.

His warmth quickly surrounded her, drugging her almost as effectively as the Vicodin. He was banishing the cold that had been a constant companion since her first chemo treatment.

Needing to borrow more of his wonderful heat, Mallory put the soles of her feet against the tops of his. She wished for a moment he'd taken off their socks, too, so she could feel his skin against hers.

"Your feet are like ice cubes."

She would have jerked away if he hadn't locked his ankles around hers, anchoring her.

Anchoring me.

That was what Ben Carpenter was rapidly becoming: an anchor in the storm.

He brushed his lips against her neck before kissing her earlobe. With no warning, his tongue traced the shell of her ear.

Mallory shivered.

"Get some sleep, baby."

He was breathing deep and even in a matter of moments.

Since she had no strength to fight him, she surrendered, letting sleep scatter her thoughts.

Chapter 16

The incessant sound of an old-fashioned telephone ringing woke Mallory. She was lying on her back, staring at the cathedral ceiling of her bedroom, but she barely remembered getting home. Blinking a few times, she tried to clear away the lingering medicine haze.

The ringing droned on.

An alarm?

Not one of her clocks. They all buzzed. Her cell's alarm was an annoying three-tone chime.

Where was the sound coming from?

Ben's scent and warmth still surrounded her, pushing aside the rest of her confusion. He'd stayed the night, making sure she got home and to bed, which was the only place she belonged when taking painkillers. Her heart warmed to his gentle care and how he'd assumed the role of her protector. With a vicious finality, she drove away the last thought of how she might become a burden to him. She was healthy now. And she'd continue to regain her strength. Soon, she'd be whole—would have restored to her what cancer had snatched away—and be able to share with him the intimacy she needed. They could make love.

Why wait? If Ben was truly the man for her, shouldn't he love her, scars and all? Judging from his passionate kisses, he would be on board for becoming lovers. Heaven knew she was ready. Past ready.

So why not now? Why not find out once and for all if he was telling her the truth, the truth he gave such importance? Why not show him what she looked like before the reconstruction so she'd know if Ben was just another Jay?

Her heart told her he was different, that Ben wouldn't run away when the going got tough. He deserved to know everything about her, and she desperately needed to show him and see his reaction.

Baring her scar to him took on a new importance, and though she hated to admit it, she would be testing him.

Please let him pass that test.

The ringing had to be his cell phone, and it thankfully quieted. If it was a typical alarm, it would sound again soon. If he'd missed a call, he could return it later. What she didn't know was whether it was a call or an alarm. Maybe he needed to get up early.

Mallory was loathe to wake him up. He snored softly, and she loved having him so close. If she tried, she could almost pretend he was hers and that she could wake up exactly like this every day. The security of being in his arms was something she could easily learn to depend upon.

He lay on his stomach, his arm draped over her chest. When it dawned on her there was no pain, she breathed a relieved sigh. Exactly as the first time the surgeon had blown up the stretcher, the agony left as quickly as it had arrived.

Slowly rolling to her side, she eased his arm down to her waist and stared at his face, squelching a sigh of contentment so she wouldn't wake him. Light brown stubble covered his cheek and chin, and her fingers itched to trace the shape of his jaw. His mouth was open ever so slightly. All the worry lines were gone, and he looked at peace. His hair was getting a little too long, and it was mussed in a way that made him appear as though he were resting after a satisfying romp in bed.

She wanted to run her palm over that heavenly butt. Whenever he bent over while working, she had to squeeze her hands into fists to keep from groping those round cheeks. She'd been deeply in lust with him from the moment he took her in his arms to dance. That lust gave her courage, letting her lightly rub his lower lip with her fingertip.

Ben woke up smiling. "Hey, you."

"Hey."

He smoothed his hand over her hip, making her suck in a breath as his touch sent her heart into a faster tempo. "Sleep well?"

"Yeah. You?"

"Yeah." His brows knit. "How you feelin'?"

"Good. Pain's almost gone." The way he scowled made her add, "Really. It's almost gone. The truth, remember?"

Instead of replying, he moved to face her, tugging on her waist until their groins were pressed together.

He had an erection. Mallory would have found it flattering if she didn't know from experience that guys woke up hard most days. But then Ben gently drove his hips forward to rub his cock against her.

"I want you," he murmured a moment before his lips captured hers.

The kiss started out gentle, like a whisper. Her heart smiled when he let out a low growl, put a palm against her ass, and pressed her harder against him at the same moment he thrust his tongue into her mouth.

Kissing him was like taking more Vicodin, making her feel as though she were floating. She grasped his tongue with her teeth, gently tugging. His growl made her whole body flush. The kiss grew, filling her with an urgency she hadn't felt in a long, long time. Her core flooded with heat as her breast tingled. Funny, but she could almost feel a tickle in her left breast, too.

Sexual need guided her actions as Mallory stroked across his hip to slip between their bodies. Then she rubbed her palm against his hard cock.

Ben broke off the kiss, groaned, and rested his forehead against hers. "You're killing me, Mal."

That made no sense. "Why?"

"Because I want you so bad I'm about to jump you right now."

"Who's stopping you?"

"Dad?" Amber's sleepy voice called only a moment before his cell alarm sounded again.

He dropped his head back against the pillow and groaned again.

Mallory rose over him to brush a quick kiss over his lips. "What's the alarm for?"

"Amber's with her mom today. She's supposed to pick her up at nine."

She glanced to the clock. "Then you two better get going. If you want a shower—"

With a shake of his head, he sat up.

She looped her arms around his neck and kissed him again.

When he finally broke away, they were both breathing hard. "I need to go. But how about I bring back breakfast?"

"I'd like that." Mallory flopped back on her pillow and tugged the blanket over her legs. "I'll just lounge around in my nice, warm bed 'til you get back."

"Dad?" Amber's footsteps sounded on the hardwood of the hallway. She knocked on the bedroom door. "Are you up?"

"Yeah," Ben replied. "Go get your shoes on and we'll head back home." He smiled at Mallory. "Anything special? Donuts? Pastries?"

"I'm good with anything." If he was going to the trouble to bring back breakfast, he had to believe they were going to end up in bed again. Just to be sure he understood what she wanted, she decided to be bold. "Do me a favor, Ben?"

He quirked a tawny eyebrow.

"Come back with at least two things?"

"What two things?"

Mallory tossed him what she hoped was an inviting smile. "Coffee with extra cream and a hard-on."

* * *

Ben was speechless the whole drive home. Since Amber was quiet, probably because she hated being with Theresa all day, he didn't have to try to fake a conversation. Whatever he said would probably come out nothing but babble anyway. The only thing on his mind was Mallory.

Had she meant it? Did she really want him to go back to her place and make love to her? Maybe he was reading too much into her words.

Coffee with extra cream and a hard-on.

How could any man possibly misinterpret *that*? It was an invitation, the same welcome he'd seen in her smile.

"She's actually here." Amber's words pulled him from his pleasant reverie.

Theresa was standing by her vintage POS, leaning her ass against it while she took a long drag on the cigarette—a habit she'd dropped while they were married—she cradled between her fingers. She was dressed in a clinging, low-cut shirt and jeans that had rips and tears, as though she were young enough to get away with a teenaged look. A quick glance at the dashboard clock told him she was on time, probably for the first time since he'd met her.

Sweet Lord, had he actually been married to this woman?

She pushed away from the car, dropped the cigarette, and ground it into the concrete with the toe of her shoe. Folding her arms over her breasts, she glared at him as he pulled Mallory's SUV into a parking spot a few spaces away.

Killing the engine, Ben stared at his daughter. "You ready?"

Amber nodded.

"She needs to have you back by eight."

"By seven. I have homework." She glanced to her mother and then frowned. "Maybe six would be better."

"I thought you told me you got your homework done."

"So what? I have other stuff to do, too."

He sighed. "If you tell her you have homework, I won't rat you out." The court order gave Theresa ten hours every other Sunday. Not that she wanted more, and half the time she showed up late if she bothered to show up at all.

Amber crawled out of the Escape, slamming the door behind her.

Ben rolled his eyes. His daughter didn't show her temper

often, but when she did, she was a slammer or a thrower. Since there weren't any glasses handy, she'd inflicted her anger on Mallory's SUV. It was tough enough to take it.

Theresa stepped up to his side of the Escape, her scowl hot enough to melt the window.

Although he had nothing to say to her, he lowered the glass because she clearly had something to say to him.

Might as well get this over with…

"Where the fuck did you get the money for a new car?" she demanded as if she had any right to know anything going on in his life. "Where's the fucking truck?"

"It's sitting right there." He pointed to row of autos parked under the parking canopy, where his ancient Ford waited.

"So you're bitching at me all the time about helping pay for the kid's stuff and you're out buying whatever the fuck you want?"

Refusing to answer would be childish. Tempting though it was to let stew in her curiosity, he said, "It's not mine." Too late, he realized what a big can of worms he'd just opened.

"Who's it belong to, then?"

"Mallory," Amber replied as she went to her mother's side. "Where are we going today?"

Theresa didn't even bother to acknowledge her own child, the one she always called "the kid." She was far too busy shooting daggers at Ben with her angry blue eyes. "Who the fuck is *Mallory*?"

"She's none of your business," he replied.

She shifted her gaze to Amber. "Who's Mallory?"

"She's a friend of Dad's," Amber replied as she gave him a pathetic glance.

"Friend? What kind of *friend*? A fuck buddy?" Theresa's tone dripped with disdain.

Ben bit his tongue hard enough he could've drawn blood. Since Theresa saw nothing wrong with hopping from bed to bed, she was dumb enough to assume everyone else did as well. His life had ceased to be any of her concern the day they'd signed divorce papers, and he wasn't about to let her taint what was growing between him and Mallory with her snide insinuations.

"Shouldn't you two get going?" he asked. "Amber needs to be back early enough to finish her homework. Maybe by suppertime would be good."

"I can keep the kid out as long as I damn well want."

He wasn't about to get into a pissing contest with the queen of the harpies. He'd learned from experience the more he protested, the harder Theresa dug in her heels.

Like a two-year-old.

"Where are we going?" Amber asked again.

"Out" was all Theresa said in reply. Then she popped a pack of cigarettes out of her purse, tapped one out, and held it between her fingers as she pointed it at Ben. "If I find out you've been fucking this Mallory bitch when the kid's around, I'll have you back in court before you can blink. The kid can come live with me."

An empty threat. Theresa didn't want custody of her daughter any more than she wanted a sexually transmitted disease. But where Amber was concerned, Ben wasn't about to take any chances. Hopefully Amber was bright enough not to share anything about what happened last night with her mother.

"I hope you two have a fun day." Ben wished he could spare his daughter the ordeal.

"Let's go." Theresa grabbed Amber's arm and dragged her away.

Ben would have told his daughter to call him if she needed anything, but that would alert Theresa that he'd gotten Amber a new cell, which she'd undoubtedly take. The best he could give Amber was a smile that told her he'd be happy to see her when she got home and that he'd do his best to soothe away any hurt Theresa inflicted.

She hadn't changed. Not much. Her face had aged, probably because she tended to spend a lot of time in tanning beds. Her language had gotten worse. She'd always had a habit of cursing—something he used to do more often before Amber was born. Now it seemed like his ex tossed an f-bomb every other word.

As Theresa drove away, he couldn't help but compare her to Mallory. Dark and light. Mallory's brown hair and brown eyes so in contrast to Theresa's peroxide blonde and ice-blue eyes. Yet his dark lady had the soul of an angel while the fairer woman had a heart as black as night.

Mallory waited for him, and he dismissed his ex from his thoughts. If it weren't for Amber, he'd never think about her again. He had more pleasant things to consider like the invitation, the *challenge*, Mallory had tossed at him before he left.

Should he run inside and take a quick shower? Brush his teeth? Grab some cologne?

No. Mallory wasn't the kind of woman who'd want him to go to so much trouble. He could get one of those one-brush toothbrushes when he stopped by the store for some condoms. Although she'd only specifically asked for coffee, he'd bring along breakfast, too. No healthy food. Donuts with icing and sprinkles. His lady had a sweet tooth she tried to hide. He would indulge her.

Ben fired up the engine and headed toward Dunkin' Donuts. He needed to get some coffee.

The hard-on wouldn't be a problem.

Chapter 17

Mallory stayed in bed for a good, long while, wondering if she could follow through with the sensual promise she'd made Ben.

She'd never been shy where sex was concerned. Being coy or cautious wouldn't bring a woman any satisfaction, so she'd always been vocal about what she wanted. Some guys might find that a bit brazen, but she refused to fake an orgasm just to stroke some guy's ego. Not that she'd had a lot of lovers. Five, to be exact. Yet she'd taught each of them to be conscious of a woman's needs, telling or showing them what they could do to please her.

Would Ben like that? Would he appreciate her open attitude about sex? Would he be the kind of man who felt intimidated by a strong, assertive lover?

Standing right next to that concern was the one about how he'd react when he saw her chest. Mallory had a little more shape now thanks to the stretcher, but the scar remained, appearing an angry red next to the pale white of her skin. And there was no nipple.

Since there was nothing she could do to change it, at least until the reconstruction, she refused to let a stupid scar be an excuse to put Ben off. She'd tossed the challenge at him, and she had every intention of following through.

Condoms.

There wasn't a single one in the house. When Jay had finished fetching his stuff, Jules had helped Mallory purge the house of any reminder of him. He'd left behind everything from condoms to cologne to a ratty pair of boxers. Every bit of it ended up in trash bags to be hauled away with the rest of the garbage, except for the love letter he'd written her and a couple she found to another woman. She and Jules burned them while toasting each other with Diet Cokes.

She'd never expected to need condoms again, especially not after the mastectomy.

Maybe Ben would remember. He seemed rather savvy where romance was concerned, so he had to practice safe sex. Although the thought of him in the arms of another woman turned her stomach, she was honest enough with herself to acknowledge he wasn't the kind of man who had trouble attracting female company. No doubt he'd been… active since his divorce. Surely he'd remember to pick up a pack of Trojans. There wasn't an abundance of places to get good coffee in Cloverleaf, but there were two CVSs and three Walgreens in the small city. Grabbing some rubbers would be simple.

Good heavens, she was going to make love with Ben.

Mallory scrambled from the bed to brush her teeth, slap on some deodorant, and comb her hair. She was just coming out of the bathroom when she heard the garage door rising. Her heart jumped in her chest, pounding hard and fast as excitement raced through her.

This is really happening.

Should she jump back on the bed and try to take a seductive

pose? Should she just strip and let him get a good look so he could call an end to their romp before it truly began? Should she throw herself at him the moment he walked through the bedroom door and not give him a chance to turn her down?

She'd never been so nervous about making love, not even when she'd lost her virginity. That rather awkward affair had taught her that it was better to be honest with a lover about what she liked or didn't like rather than leaving the bed unfulfilled. And she always made sure her partner was every bit as satisfied.

But what about Ben?

What if he wasn't ready to be intimate?

Judging from his wide eyes and open mouth when she'd told him to come back with a hard-on, she'd shocked him. But he hadn't said a single word. He'd simply blinked a few times and then...left.

Don't be an idiot. What kind of man turns down sex?

A good man who might think she'd made her offer out of some sense of gratitude for taking such good care of her. Ben could easily make that kind of assumption. He would never accept her invitation if she couldn't convince him she was sincere in her passion, her desire.

With a shake of her head, she pushed her troubled thoughts aside. What would happen would happen. Overthinking it would only ruin the experience. She focused instead on how wonderful his kisses made her feel and how much she wanted to praise his body with her hands and her lips.

"Mal?" he called.

"Coming!"

Mallory raced down the stairs, trying to figure out what Ben had shouted back because his words had been muffled. She skidded to a stop in the kitchen, chuckling at what was before her.

Ben had two cups of coffee, one in each hand. A donut with chocolate icing and multicolored sprinkles rested on the lid of one cup. His words had been hard to understand because he'd cradled a cruller between his teeth. An open box of more donuts rested on the counter.

When he tried to speak again, she laughed and took the cup and donut from his hand. "I can't understand a word you're saying."

He bit off a good section of the cruller and smiled as he chewed.

"Slow down or you'll choke," she cautioned.

"Wanted to bring you breakfast in bed," he said through his full mouth.

"That's so sweet." The donut smelled wonderful, so she took a bite, letting the chocolate fill her senses.

"Good?"

She nodded with a little hum.

"Wasn't sure if you liked flavored coffee, so I chose something fun for you." A quick sip of his own ended with a stream of "hot, hot, hot" as he fanned his mouth while holding his half-eaten cruller.

Instead of burning her own tongue, Mallory took a bite of her donut. But her curiosity was killing her. What had Ben chosen for her? Hazelnut? Caramel? Chocolate? She sniffed the steam rising through the small opening in the lid.

"French vanilla." He took the cup from her hand and set it next to his, which now rested on the counter. "Far too hot for you to drink right now."

"We should probably let it cool for a little bit." She nibbled on her bottom lip.

Ben took her hand and tugged her closer, wrapping his arms around her. "How's the pain?"

"Gone."

"Will it come back? I mean…I don't want to hurt you or anything."

She shook her head while her pulse did a little giddy-up at the note of concern in his voice.

"I did as you asked," he whispered before pressing a quick kiss to the tip of her nose.

"Oh?"

"Yeah. I got the coffee, so my job's done."

Teasing had always been one of her favorite things, and she loved that he was keeping the moment light. "But you won't even let me drink it."

"I told you. It's too hot."

"I believe I asked for one other thing." Mustering up her courage, Mallory fit her hands between them, smoothing her palm over the front of his pants. His erection strained the front of his jeans, stretching the buttons on his fly. "Oh my. It appears you paid attention and got *exactly* what I wanted."

"I always listen to my clients."

"As much as we pay you? You should."

He snatched up the small CVS sack that sat next to the donut box. Before she knew it, he'd shoved it in her hands and swept her into his arms.

***

While he normally loved trading witty banter with Mallory, Ben wanted nothing more than to get her naked, needing the skin-to-skin connection to prove this was really happening. The way she'd caressed his cock had him wound as tight as a spring, and the time had come to make her completely his.

He hurried up the stairs, heading straight to her room.

She hadn't made the bed, making it easy for him to lay her on the sheets. Then he came down on top of her, stretching out as he pushed her legs apart with his knees to nestle his pelvis against hers. Tangling his fingers through her hair, he smiled down at her. "Do you know how long I've waited for this?"

"Every bit as long as I've waited. So shut up and kiss me."

Brushing his lips over her, Ben took his time, wanting this to last forever even as he wondered how he could possibly take things slow. Everything inside of him was screaming to get her clothes off and bury himself inside her as he'd imagined doing a million times.

No way. Mallory deserved a patient, giving lover. The woman was the kindest, sweetest creature he'd ever known. He'd make love to her. Slowly. Gently. Deliberately.

Even if it killed him.

Holding himself up on his elbows he stared down into her eyes. Such pretty eyes that sparkled with life. And passion. "You're so beautiful."

A blush tinted her cheeks.

"Doesn't this feel great?"

"*More* than great," Mallory replied in a breathless whisper. "*Perfect.*"

He shook his head. "Not yet, it's not. But I'm going to make sure it will be."

Pushing back, he crawled off her to kneel on the mattress. His fingers opened the first button of her shirt, the same one she'd worn to Chicago and slept in all night. A second opened. A third.

Mallory put her hands over Ben's. "Wait."

"Wait? Why?"

"Are you sure you want to see…everything?"

He cupped her cheeks. "You don't need to be afraid."

"But—"

He gave her a kiss full of everything that was in his heart—his passion, his desire, his need.

His *love.*

Ben didn't stop to examine his revelation. Yes, he loved Mallory Hamilton. He loved everything about her, from the top of her head to the soles of her feet. And now he needed to show her.

When he pulled back, her eyes searched his. She gave him an almost imperceptible nod.

Slowly he finished unbuttoning her shirt, then he spread it open, revealing a white camisole. He helped her sit up and shrug out of the shirt before tossing it to the floor.

To level the playing field, he jerked his own shirt over his head. It landed on top of hers. He ran his palms over her shoulders and down her arms, raising gooseflesh in his wake. Her skin was smooth and white as a china doll's. Touching it was sheer joy, the type he'd never known before.

His own fault. Sex for him had always been by-the-numbers. A touch here. A caress there. He knew how to help a woman feel pleasure and bring her to climax. None of his lovers had been unsatisfied.

Yet as he made love to Mallory, he realized *he* hadn't been truly satisfied. The time he'd spent with other lovers was like a fast-food meal. Filling and satisfying, but leaving… something wanting.

Being with Mallory was a feast of prime rib that he intended to savor.

He wanted this to last forever, but he also found himself in uncharted territory. Never before had his feelings been so entangled with his body. That separation was what had made all of his past affairs so cold.

After briefly clasping hands and then pinning her wrists to the sheets, he reached for the hem of her undershirt. As he tugged it up and over her head, she lifted her arms to assist him.

He didn't look, instead doing his best to hold her gaze until the fear in her eyes slowly died. Only then did Ben allow himself to see what cancer had done to his Mallory.

The scar ran from under her armpit almost to her sternum. While the red stood out like a beacon against her pale skin, it wasn't anything extraordinary. Just a scar, no different from any other. The only true difference was the significance of why it was there and what it could mean to her future.

Banishing his worries, he focused on easing her fears. He pulled her up until she knelt in front of him. He put his hands on her hips and nuzzled her neck, pressing kisses to her skin, loving her scent and the way she shivered. He trailed his lips downward, kissing her collarbone and the valley between her breast and the stretcher before touching his lips to the gentle slope of her scar.

Mallory threaded her fingers through his hair and tugged. "You don't have to—"

Ben lifted his head and kissed her once. "Hush." Then he brushed his lips over her scar.

She choked out a sob, so he wrapped his arms around her and held her tight against him. "What's wrong?"

She wouldn't answer him.

"The truth, Mal."

"You aren't repulsed?"

Easing back, he grabbed her hand and flattened her palm against the front of his jeans.

A gasp slipped out before she rubbed his length.

"I want you, Mal. I don't give a shit if you've got a scar. You're the most beautiful woman I've ever known."

"Kiss me. Kiss me and I won't think about it."

"Whatever the lady wants..."

* * *

When he kissed her, Mallory could forget her worries. All she could do was feel, and she wanted to drown in each sensation. His tongue tickled her lips until she opened up to him. The kiss made heat shimmer over her skin, swirling until it settled in her core and created a need she knew had to be fulfilled.

She fumbled with the buttons on his waistband and fly. They each gave up the battle until she was able to shove the jeans over his hips.

He broke away long enough to crawl off the mattress and peel the garment down his legs. He dropped his boxers and kicked off his socks.

He was built like an athlete. All muscle, not an ounce of fat. His pecs were covered with brown hair she was dying to touch. A thick, rather intimidating cock rose from a nest of dark curls.

Ben smiled as he snaked an arm around her waist and lifted her off the bed.

Mallory started to pop the button on the waistband of her khakis, but he pushed her hands away. "Let me."

He quickly had her pants off. After he dragged her pink panties down her body, he bent down to take off her socks. Rising to his full height, he put his hands on her shoulders, held her at arm's length, and stared at her. His eyes raked her from head to toe with a lazy speed that could only be deliberate.

"Damn," he finally said.

She quirked an eyebrow, stopped by something in his tone.

While she didn't want to think poorly of Ben, that one word frightened her. "What's that supposed to mean?"

"That means I'm the luckiest man on the planet."

"Make love to me, Ben Carpenter."

"I love how bossy you are."

"You ain't seen nothin' yet."

He scooped her into his arms and set her in the center of the mattress before coming down on top of her again. "Damn."

His skin was hot against hers, his body so hard—everywhere. "Damn right."

* * *

Ben couldn't stop a smile. He could hear the nervousness in her tone, probably the same anxiety he was experiencing.

How odd. Never once had he ever felt the kind of shaky anticipation that now held him hostage—almost like he was a virgin again, a sixteen-year-old who wasn't quite sure what he'd find the first time he put himself inside a woman.

Slow, Ben. Take it slow.

He kissed her—a long, thorough exploration of her mouth as his hands wandered her body. While he tried to be gentle, he was afraid his weight might bring her pain back. If she put a halt to things now, he'd obey her wishes, but he'd probably be the most frustrated man in the universe.

Just to be sure he protected Mallory, he rolled to her right side. His cock rubbed against her thigh, making him groan against her mouth. Trailing kisses down her neck and chest, he tickled her pink nipple with his tongue. It hardened into a tight nub that he drew between his lips. As he suckled, her hands cradled the back of his head. Her moan made him smile against her skin.

He needed to touch all of her. His hand smoothed over her hip bone, then down her flat belly to rest on her mound. The hair there was soft and fine, and he combed it with his fingers before he slid them between her folds.

He watched her eyes as he teased and stroked, seeking the most sensitive part of her. When he found it, she dug her heels in the mattress and arched her back.

"Easy, baby."

"Ben…"

He rubbed tight circles over the swollen nub. "Do you like that?"

"Yes," she hissed.

"Tell me what you want."

"Faster."

"Yes, ma'am." Ben obliged her, enjoying her uninhibited response as her hips thrust up in a rhythm he longed to match while deep inside her.

A cry spilled from her lips as she strained against his hand. He slid a finger deep inside her before adding another. He captured her mouth, kissing her long and deep as she came. Only when her last spasm ended did he take his hand away.

After a few moments, she eased her mouth back and gave him a wan smile. With no warning, Mallory grabbed his cock.

"Damn." Seemed like that was the only word he could use, but the feel of her warm fingers exploring his body rendered him nearly dumb.

Her thumb rubbed over the crown before she wrapped her fingers around him and stroked. "Damn," she said in a breathless echo.

Ben fumbled for the bag she'd dropped on the mattress. The box was obviously sealed with industrial-strength glue, because it took forever to open. A string of condoms fell out.

"Let me," she whispered, releasing him.

He groaned, wanting her hand right back where it had been.

Mallory grabbed a condom, tore the packet open with her teeth, and awkwardly unrolled the sheath over his erection. Each touch of her hands as she tried to figure the way to make it work was near to torture. A growl of need slipped out as she finally covered him completely.

Instead of lying back against the pillows, she forced his shoulders against the mattress. "I'm on top."

Not caring if he made love to her on top, on bottom, or upside down, he did as she asked. Having her take charge made heat surge to his groin until his cock swelled unbearably.

She grabbed his erection, straddled his hips, and gently led him to her entrance. Slowly, deliberately, she eased down until she was impaled on him and he was buried to the hilt.

Ben dug his fingers into her hips, rocking up as he relished the tight heat of her body. After a few gentle thrusts, he set a hard, fast rhythm, hoping to hell he could hold back long enough to make her come again. As wonderful as her body felt—squeezing his cock as though she'd been made just for him—he was going to lose his normally steely control.

Mallory put her hands on his shoulders, leaning down to kiss him, her tongue wild as it sought his. Her fingernails raked his skin. The stinging sensation coupled with the softness of her body nearly sent him over the edge.

Thrusting faster and harder, he urged her to join him in the release that was building inside him. Just when he feared he would lose his battle, she threw her head back, closed her eyes tightly, and then cried out as her body clenched around him.

Ben buried himself deep inside her, letting the heat of his orgasm wash over him in waves that seemed never-ending. The thrill was even better because of the bright flush on her face and the way she hummed and rubbed her fingers against his chest.

Everything inside him thrummed, matching the pounding of his heart. "Damn."

"Oh, Ben." Mallory collapsed, resting her cheek against his chest. "You're so eloquent."

He grunted, wrapped his arms around her and decided if he died now, he'd die happier than he'd ever been.

Chapter 18

Someone was banging on her front door, loud enough she could hear it the moment she turned off the shower.

Mallory grabbed the towel she'd draped over the shower curtain rod and wrapped it around her. "Ben?"

He'd been asleep when she woke up from their nap. After spending quite a while propped up on her elbow, staring down at him and remembering the wonderful way he'd made her body sing, she'd finally decided to take a shower and face the rest of the day. Tempting though it was to linger in bed, she had—as she always did—papers to grade.

She'd made a fresh pot of coffee and eaten a couple of donuts. Maybe Ben would get up soon and they could go out for brunch. She would've woken him up and asked if he wanted to shower with her if he hadn't looked so comfortable.

The banging stopped then started again, louder. Someone was intruding on their peaceful Sunday.

"Ben?" She stepped into the bedroom to find him sitting up, running his hand over his sleepy face. "Did you hear the knocking?"

He nodded. "Who's here?"

"I don't know. But I'm not dressed for guests," she quipped, tucking the towel closed and fluffing her hands through her wet hair.

He tossed aside the sheet, baring every inch of his muscular physique. "Neither am I."

Mallory couldn't help but stare. The man was a work of art. When her gaze fixed on his groin, his cock started to harden. She stretched an arm up to lean seductively against the door frame. "Is that an invitation?"

This time, the doorbell rang incessantly. Whoever was there wasn't going away.

"Not now, but later? Most definitely." He threw his legs over the side of the bed and grabbed his jeans.

She picked up his shirt and handed it to him as he pulled on and buttoned his pants. "Probably a delivery. Although I doubt they'd be that insistent. Most leave the package on the porch."

"If it's a salesman, I'll send him packing. I can growl very effectively when I put my mind to it." He gave her a no-nonsense kiss and headed down the stairs.

Mallory was just opening the closet door to choose some clothes when she heard raised voices. Having no idea what was going on, she snatched a long terry-cloth robe from a hook. After she dropped the towel, she shoved her arms in the sleeves and tied it closed as she hurried to the stairs.

Ben was standing with the front door open, hands on his hips as he glared at a big-breasted blonde who was gesturing so much with her hands, she could easily hit him. With bloodred nails that long, she'd do some damage if she got any closer. Was that a cigarette between her fingers?

Since their voices had dropped from a shout, Mallory couldn't hear what they were saying, but their body language was easy to interpret. The blonde was pissed but good, and Ben wasn't liking what he was hearing.

Taking it slowly, Mallory crept down the staircase. Fourth step from the top, the board squeaked loud enough to wake the dead.

The blonde stopped midsentence, shifting her gaze to Mallory. The hatred in those blue eyes took her breath away.

"So that's her?" The blonde pointed the two fingers holding an unlit cigarette at Mallory. "That's the whore you spent the night with?"

With a gasp, Mallory pulled the tie tighter and went to confront the enemy head-on. *Theresa, no doubt.* While Ben hadn't told her much about his ex, Mallory was quickly forming her own conclusions. Years of dealing with parents from all walks of life made her a great judge of character. Although she hated to assume anything, she simply couldn't see anything redeemable about the woman. For Ben's sake, and Amber's, she'd keep her opinions to herself and give Theresa a chance. That, however, didn't mean she would allow the woman to call her a whore and think there'd be no response.

When she stood next to Ben, Mallory threaded her arm through his. "We have company. Did you tell her we were busy?" Leveling a hard stare at the blonde, Mallory shot her a cool smile. "And you are?"

"His *wife*," she replied, jerking her thumb at Ben.

"Silly me. I thought he was divorced. That would make you his *ex*-wife."

"C'mon, Mom. We should go." It wasn't until she heard the pleading words that Mallory realized Amber stood on the edge of the porch, one foot already on the steps leading to the driveway. "We were gonna go get lunch. Leave Dad and Mallory alone. *Please.*"

While she wanted to rub Theresa's nose in the cozy little situation she'd intruded upon, Mallory's heart went out to Amber. It was clear her mother didn't give a shit whether she hurt her child, something else Mallory had seen far too often in her career.

How many times had divorced parents come to parent-teacher conferences for no reason other than to pick a fight with their exes? She wasn't about to let Amber get treated like a prize in some tug-of-war.

Mallory pulled her arm back. "Look, Theresa…"

"I'm not talking to you." She poked Mallory's sternum with her index finger. Hard.

Had she still been hurting from the stretcher, Mallory would have been in agony. At least now it only felt like a sharp stab rather than a return of the torture she'd suffered the day before. She winced and quickly pulled her left arm protectively over her chest.

Ben's roar was deafening. He grabbed Theresa's wrist. "Keep your hands off her, Theresa. Or so help me—"

"What?" Theresa challenged. "What exactly will you do, Ben?"

His jaw clenched tight as he narrowed his eyes.

"Nothin'. Just like always. You'll do nothin'." She snatched her wrist away and rubbed it as though he'd hurt her.

It was a wonder she didn't take a few pictures to show how she'd been abused. No doubt Theresa would be repeating her version of this story to her friends and probably the lawyer she kept on a string to harass Ben when the mood struck.

So much for being nonjudgmental…

Mallory focused on helping the only true innocent in the whole scenario. "Amber, why don't you come inside? We'll let your parents have a minute of privacy. There are fresh donuts if you want a snack." She smiled at the girl, hoping she saw the sincerity in wanting to protect her.

When Amber nodded and tried to skirt around Theresa, her mother's arm shot out to block her path. She leveled a hard stare at Mallory. "You're not going anywhere near the kid. Shit, you and lover boy here were fucking around last night right in front of her."

The teacher in her bristled. "I would truly appreciate it if you'd watch your language, especially around Amber."

"Fuck you." Theresa flicked her unlit cigarette at Mallory. It bounced off her chest and landed at her feet.

Mallory kicked it aside like a dead mouse. "Sets a bad example to smoke in front of your daughter."

Theresa's whole face mottled red. "The kid is none of your business. Sure didn't care about her when you and Ben were screwing each other last night, did ya?"

While she was more than ready to blister the woman's ears over why it would be best to shelter Amber from this scene, Mallory held her tongue. She didn't know a whole lot about Theresa, but everything she'd seen so far had been bad. Really bad. If she persisted in her profanity and name-calling, Mallory was going to lose her temper. God help them all then.

Ben put a hand on Mallory's shoulder. "Amber, why don't you go inside with Mallory and let me talk to your mom?"

Amber came up the last step to the porch, but she kept a wary eye on her mother.

"Fine," Theresa snapped. "Go on inside with Daddy's new *toy*."

Once Amber was in the house, Ben stepped out to the porch.

Mallory quietly closed the door, hoping to spare Amber any more embarrassment. Then she headed to the kitchen. She picked up the coffees, dumped the ancient brew down the sink, and tossed the cups away. After she grabbed a couple of plates, she set them next to the box of donuts.

"Help yourself," she said. "I'm gonna make a fresh pot of coffee."

While she worked on getting things brewing, she glanced over her shoulder, wishing she could take away the hurt on the girl's face. Amber was a such sweet kid. She deserved better than a foul-mouthed mother on a histrionic bender.

"Do you like hot chocolate?" Mallory asked. "I could make you some."

Amber just shrugged.

"Maybe a glass of milk instead? Juice?"

"Nah."

"Why don't you take your jacket off and make yourself at home?"

"Theresa'll want to go soon."

Theresa?

Interesting... But not at all surprising.

After pressing the button to get things going, Mallory took two cups off the mug tree and set them next to the pot. Ben would surely want some after his little powwow with his ex. "You sure I can't get you something to drink?"

"Maybe some... Oh, never mind. I won't be here long."

The pain in Amber's voice told her more than enough about the girl's relationship with Theresa. While she tried to help as many students as she could, at least Mallory could leave their problems at school.

Amber needed her.

After what she and Ben had shared, there was a possibility Mallory would be spending a lot of time with Amber, which meant dealing with Theresa. So she'd face it like she did everything—head-on. She'd handled parents a lot worse before. Theresa would never know what hit her.

What had possessed Ben to marry a woman like that?

Mallory didn't bother comparing herself to Theresa. They were nothing alike, from their looks to their personalities. Nor did she bother with worrying that Ben would prefer a brash woman like his ex over someone more mild-mannered. Had Theresa's in-your-face approach to life appealed to him, he'd still be married to her.

What Mallory focused on was Amber. Perhaps it was the teacher in her, but her heart went out to the girl. If there was anything she could do to make this whole awkward situation easier, she'd be glad to give it a whirl.

Opening the box of donuts, she smiled at the empty spots, remembering the goofy way Ben looked when he stood there with a donut between his lips. The only thing that might have improved the view was if he'd been naked at the time. The half-eaten cruller was sitting on the kitchen table, along with the chocolate-frosted donut with one big bite gone.

Mallory tossed those in the trash before picking up one with maple frosting. "I love icing." She smiled at Amber, hoping to relieve the tension. "I'm a bit of an icing junkie. I'll admit to eating cake icing right out of the container sometimes."

"I'm sorry about Theresa."

Evidently the daughter was as blunt as the father. So much for ignoring this elephant.

"You're not her keeper, Amber."

"Yeah, but..." She heaved a sigh. "I shouldn't have told her Dad was with you."

At least that explained how Theresa found out not only that she was dating Ben but where she lived. The only question remaining was why the woman was looking for him to begin with. Since Amber appeared near tears, she let that question go. "I'm sure you didn't expect her to do something like this."

Amber's dark eyes—so much like her father's—found Mallory's. "I should've. Theresa does stuff like this all the time." Her lower lip quivered. "I'm really sorry."

"I don't blame you, honey. Look, why don't you take off your jacket? Grab a donut and have a seat. Let your dad take care of this." She pulled a chair out and sat down. "I'd guess he's pretty good at handling your mom."

The girl snorted, but she picked up a blueberry donut, dropped it on the plate, and brought it over to the table. She peeled off her jacket, sat down, and munched on the donut. Her mouth was still partly full when she said, "Dad does his best, but..." She finished the thought with a frown.

There were so many things Mallory wanted to say to Amber to try to ease her mind, but she wasn't sure it was her place. Sure, things between her and Ben had taken a leap into "serious," but that didn't give her permission to interfere with his child. Her experience told her Amber needed reassurance because she was worried that Mallory was judging her based on her mother's actions. Far from it. If anything, she was impressed at how well Amber and Ben kept cool in the face of Theresa's anger.

She finally decided to speak her mind. "You're handling this situation well."

"You mean Theresa making an ass of herself and calling you dirty names?"

Yep. Amber was truly Ben's daughter.

Mallory nodded.

"I guess I'm just… used to her. If I hadn't told her the car was yours, she wouldn't know about you and Dad." The floodgates seemed to open. "She's jealous. Dad's had dates before, but nothing like… like… you." A smile curved her lips. "Theresa can't stand it."

"Amber, you don't have to talk about—"

She gave her head a shake. "I know, but I want to. I'm not used to having someone to talk to."

Ben had never spoken of Amber's friends, so Mallory bit her tongue instead of asking about her social life. Just because she had the Ladies Who Lunch didn't mean Amber had that kind of support system.

"Once I told Theresa about you taking Dad and me to the gymnastics exhibition, all she wanted to do was ask about you. She hates that Dad likes you so much."

Exactly how much had Amber told the woman? "Did you, um… talk about my… Oh, never mind." *No.* She wasn't going to put the girl in that kind of awkward position.

"I didn't tell her about your cancer."

Some kids grew up awfully fast. "Probably a good thing."

Amber nodded.

The front door opened, and Ben came down the hall into the kitchen. He looked to Mallory first, the apology clear in his eyes. Then he shifted his gaze to Amber. "Hey, ladybug. Your mom wants to take you out for lunch."

"With what? She told me she was broke again." After she blurted out the words, she quickly glanced to Mallory as though mortified she hadn't guarded her response.

"She's not broke now," Ben replied. "Do you want to go? If you don't, I can talk to her and—"

Amber popped to her feet and picked up her jacket. "I'll go."

"She said she'd have you back in time to do your homework." He tossed her a conspiratorial wink.

Amber shoved her arms into the jacket sleeves, dragged up the zipper, and left without another word. Ben followed her to the front door.

Mallory scarfed down another donut while waiting for Ben to return. Part of her wanted to let this whole stupid episode go by without any kind of discussion. Part of her wished they could hash it out now so the problem wouldn't fester. Perhaps his approach of acknowledging the elephant really was for the best.

"Sorry," he said again. He sat in the chair Amber had vacated and picked up a donut.

"Not your fault."

"I didn't want you to have to deal with Theresa. Ever."

"After what happened between us, I don't think that was likely." The words were out before she thought. Just because Ben had slept with her, that didn't mean—

Bullshit. It *did* mean. She wasn't the kind of woman to fall into bed with a guy and not expect that to be part of a committed relationship. Ben knew that.

"You're right," he replied. "Doesn't mean I didn't hope to avoid it for a while." He ate the donut, chewing slowly, probably turning things around in his mind.

"Like I told Amber, you're not Theresa's keeper."

A snort slipped out. "That's exactly what she needs: a keeper—a zookeeper. I got tired of the job pretty quick."

"Then why did you marry her?" Mallory almost groaned at her own stupidity. "Wait! Don't answer that."

"No, it's okay."

"No, it's not. It's none of my business."

Ben took her hand in his and tugged at her until she finally understood and got up. Then pulled her onto his lap. "It's very much your business." He kissed her chin. "At least I want it to be. We've got something exclusive going here, right?"

Mallory cupped his cheeks and kissed him. "I sure as heck hope so."

"Good." He gave her a decisive nod. "Good."

"So why did you marry her?"

"Because I knocked her up," he admitted. "I'm not proud of it. We met at a bar. I let her pick me up. Would you believe she can be sweet when she tries? I never saw the side of her you just saw until after the wedding."

"Lots of people are like that," Mallory said. "They wear some kind of mask or something until they've snared you. Then they show their true colors."

"Your ex like that?"

She shook her head. "But Juliana's sure was. Like Dr. Jekyll and Mr. Hyde."

"Theresa can be a real bitch, but I wouldn't change a single minute of the aggravation because of Amber. She was worth it."

"She's a great kid, Ben."

"She is, isn't she?" He gave her a quick kiss. "Unfortunately, the baggage that comes with her is her impossible mother."

Since he seemed to be in the mood for sharing, Mallory let her curiosity loose. "Why'd she hunt us down?"

"Honestly?"

"Isn't that the only way we do things?"

"Absolutely," he replied. "She's not happy that I've moved on."

That made no sense. "You're divorced. You already moved on."

"We might be divorced, but she knew there wasn't anyone

else in my life. Now that I have you, she thinks she finally lost me."

Looping her arms around his neck, Mallory smiled. "You do have me, you know."

"Yeah, baby. I know."

Chapter 19

Juliana plopped into the chair and sprawled out as though she were at home sitting on a sofa. "One more final exam to give and I can get the hell outta this place. Not even grading 'em. Leaving that for Teacher Work Day in January."

"No way. I'm getting all my tests graded before I head home." Mallory grabbed her lunch from the refrigerator and set it on the table. Her thoughts were on her upcoming surgery, but she needed to find some focus and do her job for another few hours. She sat down and spread out the containers of food. "I've got enough to deal with over break. I'm not about to come back here in January with final exams to finish."

"I'm staying, too." Bethany started pulling her food from her bag. "I have lots of better things to do the first day of a new semester. Seating charts. Lesson plans. Talking to a few teachers about the problems I'm inheriting from their classes."

Danielle all but slammed the door to the break room. "I think my brain just exploded in an avalanche of words—all badly spelled and poorly used. I need to read some Jane Austen to cleanse my mental palate."

"*Pride and Prejudice*?" Jules asked with a grin.

"What else?"

"That's what you get for giving essay finals, Dani," Beth quipped. "I'll take my bubble sheets any day. Run them through a scanner and…voilà!"

"I used those for the literature questions, but…" Danielle sat down and shrugged. "Sometimes teaching English sucks."

"But think of all the good you're doing," Mallory insisted. "Without English teachers, these kids would write in text-speak all the time."

Juliana settled a concerned gaze on Mallory. "Are you ready for your surgery? Are you sure you don't want any help from us?"

"No, I really don't," Mallory replied. "But thanks. Ben's going to stay for a couple of days. You all go and enjoy your breaks. You've earned them."

"What about Amber?" Beth asked.

"You know, she offered to help," Mallory replied. "I really like her."

"She's staying at your place?" Danielle took a bite of her baby carrot.

"No. Theresa's taking Amber to visit her parents for Christmas. They're flying to Dallas Sunday afternoon. Won't be back until after the new year. Ben's going to take care of me and do some work on the house. His regular job's on hold until after the holidays."

Theresa had mellowed some since the confrontation the day after their Chicago trip. Perhaps the shock of Ben seriously dating another woman finally settled in as the weeks passed. She and Theresa had little contact, and from the time Mallory spent with Amber, she'd learned that Theresa seldom mentioned her or Ben. When she did, her main gripe was that Amber spent more time with Mallory than her. Since that was Amber's choice not to be with Theresa often, as well as what the court ordered, there wasn't much to be done to change things.

"I can't believe how long he's been working on your place," Danielle said. "Shouldn't it be done by now?

"Not so long, really," Mallory insisted. "He can only do projects here and there since he started full-time with the builder. He's at my place today, trying to get the gas logs in so the great room is done before I go to the hospital."

"Key Club's decorating the tree at the Community Center this weekend and singing carols," Danielle said. "Any of you coming?"

"Sorry. I can't," Mallory replied.

Jules snorted. "That's why I don't sponsor clubs anymore. Look at the stuff you get roped into, Danielle."

"I like being with Key Club," Danielle insisted. "They're great kids." She shifted her gaze to Mallory. "Sure you can't come?"

Mallory shook her head. "I'm going to try to get the house straightened up, finish the laundry, and shop for enough groceries to last until I'm up and about again."

Danielle smiled at Beth. "How about you?"

"Sorry, hon. I'm out." Beth fished some change out of her purse. "Heading straight to my parents' place after school." She popped up and bought a can of soda from the machine.

"That's right," Jules said. "I forgot you're all going to Vegas."

"Yep. Mom, Dad, and me in Vegas. What was I thinking?"

"You were thinking they offered to pay for the trip," Jules replied with a smirk.

"That and I saved up a nice little bankroll to blow on slots. Maybe I'll strike it rich."

Mallory held up her Diet Cherry Coke in salute. "Merry Christmas, Bethany. May you win enough to retire!"

* * *

"Ben?" Mallory dropped her purse and her tote—now empty because she'd graded every last stupid test—next to the coat closet.

She was almost afraid to go into the great room. Ben would be upset if he didn't get everything finished. He'd kicked up a fuss about getting several things done before her surgery on Monday.

No sounds of work greeted her. In fact, she heard… *Christmas music?*

After shrugging out of her coat, she tossed it on the coat tree and hurried down the hall. When she saw the great room, she gasped in surprise.

A fire burned in the fireplace. The gas logs looked so real, she had to wonder for a moment if he'd changed his mind about using them and just gone ahead and built a wood fire. He'd finished painting the walls, and all the furniture was back in place. Her flat-screen had been hooked back up to the stereo, and a soft instrumental version of "White Christmas" floated from the speakers.

Ben had put up her Christmas tree in the corner. It was fully decorated with all the ornaments she'd collected from the time she'd been a teenager. The multicolored lights twinkled from the branches of her artificial spruce. Gold tinsel hung from the restored oak mantel.

Tears pooled in her eyes. The amount of work he'd done and the trouble he'd gone to in finding her holiday decorations amazed her.

"Merry Christmas, Mal."

Ben's voice coming from behind her made her smile and sniff back the threatening tears. "It's all so...beautiful."

He put a hand on her shoulder, turning her to face him. "Our first Christmas together. I wanted it to be perfect."

"It's not Christmas yet. We've got a few days before the twenty-fifth."

His lopsided smile was intensely charming. "You'll still be laid up on the twenty-fifth. So I figured we'd celebrate tonight."

Wrapping her arms around his waist, she smiled up at him. "How exactly did you think we'd celebrate?"

"How about I take you to a nice dinner? Then we can come back here and make love by firelight."

"I've got a better idea." She kissed him quickly before taking his hand and tugging him into the great room.

"And what exactly is that?"

She flipped off the lamp. Since dark was rapidly descending, the lights from the Christmas tree and fireplace gave the room a cozy glow. As he waited in the middle of the room, she grabbed the afghan from the back of the couch and spread it in front of the fire.

"Why, Ms. Mallory. What are you up to?"

Instead of answering, she tossed him a saucy grin and reached for the top button of his flannel shirt. After opening each fastener, she helped him shrug out of the shirt. She let out a frustrated growl that a T-shirt blocked her access to his skin. She jerked the garment over his head, glad that he grinned in response.

Would she ever tire of looking at him? Her dark knight. So very handsome.

As she ran her tongue around his flat nipple, she fumbled with his belt buckle until she could whip the belt out of his pants. Then she took a step back, enjoying his confused expression.

"Mal?"

Mallory followed up by folding the belt and snapping it hard enough the sound echoed through the room. "You've been a bad boy, Ben Carpenter."

He quirked an eyebrow.

"You haven't finished my house yet."

"Been a little busy. Work and all..." He popped the button on his waistband and unzipped his fly.

She snapped the belt again. "Excuses, excuses. You've been a bad boy, and bad boys need to be punished." A slap of the belt against her thigh accompanied her authoritarian tone.

Ben let out a ragged groan as he dropped his jeans. They pooled around his ankles.

"Tighty-whities, too, mister."

After peeling them down his body, he kicked both garments aside and yanked off his socks. His erection bobbed, drawing a smile from her.

"That's better. *Much* better."

"So where should I be for you to punish me?" he asked, his voice husky.

Mallory's bravado vanished. While it might have been fun to tease, she wasn't sure she could actually hit him, especially with the belt. She was definitely in over her head—*way* over her head.

Ben bent over the arm of the sofa and wiggled his ass at her. "I'm ready."

This time, she was the one to groan at the tempting picture before her. She'd often taken the lead in sex. Why should this be any different?

How could she ever deny him?

She smacked the belt gently against his tight buns. His responding yelp made her jump. "I'm sorry."

"Don't be. Do it again." His voice held a note of desperation she didn't understand.

She found herself in uncharted territory. Sex with Jay had been nothing but normal. Missionary. Her on top. From behind once or twice.

Vanilla.

Watching Ben's eyes fill with desire just because she'd given his ass a light tap left her feeling heady. Empowered. Each encounter, each time they made love, was still so new, so exciting. He took advantage of her small body to take her up against the wall. In the shower. On the backseat of her car. Now it appeared they'd be on the floor in front of a roaring fire.

"Do it again, baby," he said. "Spank me."

She did, a little harder but with a smile on her face.

Ben surged against the sofa, let out a rumbling growl, and then came to her. Without a word, he stripped her quickly and efficiently until they faced each other.

The air between them fairly cracked with anticipation. Mallory was no longer afraid to show Ben her body. From the first time he'd made love to her, he'd shown nothing but appreciation, so why try to hide?

She'd learned that her missing breast didn't define her. Not personally. Not sexually. He made sure she enjoyed each tryst every bit as much as he did. And he *did* enjoy himself, despite her scar. She had no doubt that if she decided not to have the reconstructive surgery, he'd still desire her, still want her, every bit as much as he did right now.

The love swelled in her heart until tears stung her eyes.

How long had she loved him? Mallory wasn't sure.

Love hadn't snuck up from behind and clubbed her over the head. There had never been a moment of clarity that screamed her love. Nothing so deliberate. Instead, he'd stolen her heart in small pieces, claiming a new bit with each kind gesture and loving word.

He reached for her the same time she took the last step toward him. The feel of his skin as he enfolded her in his embrace sent heat shimmering through her veins. She was hot, wet, ready—had been from the first button opening on his shirt. The smack on his butt, tender though it was, lent an air of naughty that heightened her desire.

Who knew the prim and proper schoolteacher enjoyed giving her man a spanking? The school board would be scandalized should they discover the truth.

His kiss was possessive, downright frantic. She matched his need with her own, thrusting her tongue past his lips to mate with his—wild kisses she used to show him what she couldn't find the courage to confess.

Would Ben welcome her declaration?

Probably. But Mallory was going to take the coward's way out and show rather than tell.

She stroked down his body, over the hard planes of his chest and the defined abs until she could capture his cock. Wrapping her fingers around him, she loved the hot feel of the silky skin over the hardened flesh. "I want you."

"Oh, baby. I'm so past that. You've worked me up so much." He glanced at the couch. "Think you can let me go long enough so I can grab a condom?"

"No." She punctuated her word with a few pumping strokes. Then she rubbed her thumb over the crown, smearing the drop of fluid that had pooled at the tip.

"Don't we need birth control?"

She gave her head a shake, figuring it would be easier to reveal the truth at a time when he was so drugged with desire the weight of the words couldn't quite sink in. "I can't get pregnant."

* * *

Ben hadn't expected her to be so blunt about something that might devastate most thirtysomething women. Not Mallory. The woman's spine was made of the strongest steel.

The way she was touching him made it impossible to think, especially about such an important topic. All he wanted was to toss her on the afghan and bury himself so deep inside her they became one.

She released his erection long enough to crook a finger at him. Then she sat down, dragging him with her until he was sprawled over her.

He would never tire of the feel of her skin against his. She'd gained a little weight, enough that her hips and collarbones were no longer so sharply evident. She was round and soft and so incredibly beautiful.

Even her scar. It was such a part of Mallory, in some ways making her who she really was deep down inside. He was sure he wouldn't give a shit if she didn't have the implant or if she didn't have the new nipple tattooed to give it color. While he'd support her through the recovery, he'd have to make sure before she checked in at the hospital that she knew she was doing this for herself. Not for him, because to Ben, it truly didn't matter.

He spread her thighs with his knee, loving how she pressed her core against his leg. She was so open about her desire, something he'd quickly learned to enjoy. To have a woman who knew her own mind and her own body was exciting.

Holy shit, she'd actually spanked him. Mallory had really

followed through and used his belt on his butt. He'd been teasing, figuring she'd back down if he pushed her. He should have known better. But he'd loved it enough he'd probably ask her to do it again.

Probably?

No.

Definitely.

"Tell me what you want, baby."

"I want you to fuck my brains out."

He smiled down at her. "Such dirty talk."

"Shut up and kiss me."

Obeying her was his pleasure. He let his tongue explore her mouth, rubbing over hers before he nipped at her bottom lip. Ben slipped his hand between her thighs to be sure she was ready for him. The wet welcome took away what remained of his control.

He settled between her slender thighs, rubbing his cock against her until he plunged forward. She fit him perfectly, even better without the condom between them, and the feel of her would never grow old.

Her hands covered his backside, pulling him deeper as she lifted her knees. "Damn, I love it when you fuck me, Ben."

Unable to find a voice to answer, he eased back and then thrust forward. Soon he found a fast, rough rhythm that drew gasps and moans from Mallory. Then she sucked in a breath and held it, a signal that she was close to release.

Ben increased the speed of his movements, and when her eyes widened and her body clenched around him, he gave up his own battle, surrendering to his orgasm.

Chapter 20

Ben paced the length of the surgical waiting room yet again. Twenty-two steps up, twenty-two steps back, then a glance to the hallway to see the closed doors to the surgical area.

It was maddening. Waiting had always been difficult for him at best, but this was nothing short of torture. He wished their roles were reversed, that he was facing the surgery rather than Mallory.

She's fine.

He kept reminding himself this was a routine kind of surgery, nothing nearly as bad as what she'd already faced with the mastectomy.

Even thinking about what that had been like made him squirm. The poor woman must have lived through hell. All the Internet sites he pulled up doing research on breast cancer and mastectomies made a point of discussing the pain that the patient went through. And that wasn't the worst of it. The waiting, the days, months, and years of worrying—those could be unbearable.

At least this surgery would only keep Mallory in the hospital one night, and as soon as she was back in her room, he'd stick close to her side. He'd sleep in the chair if he had to, like he'd done when Amber was born.

The delivery had been easy on Theresa, so much so even the nurses commented on how different the experience was when compared to other first babies. How funny was it that a woman who was such a bad mother could so easily squeeze out a baby? She'd delivered around noon and hadn't even wanted to spend the night, but the doctor and nurses convinced her it was better for Amber to be watched for the first twenty-four hours. Theresa suggested she go and Amber and Ben stay. The nurses thought she was joking. Ben knew better.

After checking the clock—*three more minutes gone*—he started counting the tiles on the floor. Anything to keep his mind calm.

Who was he trying to kid? He was a fucking mess. A million horrible things were flying through his thoughts.

Mallory going into cardiac arrest.

Mallory stroking out on the table.

And the one that refused to abate and turned his blood to ice water—the surgeon finding more cancer when he opened her up again.

How did she live with the fear?

Duh. The same way she handled everything else. With grace, elegance, and the strongest love of life he'd ever known. Mallory embraced each day with open arms.

Perhaps her unflinching approach to the world was because she'd looked Death in the eye and that bastard had blinked first. Since Ben didn't know her before the cancer, he could only imagine whether she'd changed with the diagnosis. But he loved her the way she was now, so it really didn't matter what she'd been before the day they'd met.

Now, she was his.

Four more minutes gone.

Ben plucked his cell phone from his belt and almost called Amber. The only thing stopping him was that she'd still be on the flight to Dallas. Probably for the best. He had no business foisting his anxiety off on his daughter. She was anxious enough having to spend the holidays with her mother and grandparents. He'd considered telling Theresa that Amber couldn't go, but a call from his ex-mother-in-law changed his mind. Begging that she get to see her only grandchild, Doris had promised to make things great for Amber and to be sure that Theresa behaved while under their roof. So for the first time since her birth, Ben was missing Christmas with his daughter.

That turned his mood sour, which wasn't a good thing because only another two minutes had clicked by. The tumultuous emotions were almost more than he could take.

A nurse in pink scrubs marched into the waiting room. Ben hurried over. She had to be there for him because no one else was there.

"Ben Carpenter?"

"Yes. Yes." Fighting the urge to grab her hands, he shoved his own in his front pockets. "How's Mallory?"

The woman smiled, her blue eyes full of sympathy. "She's in recovery. She did great. We should be taking her up to her room in about an hour."

He could have kissed her purple Crocs.

She glanced at the collection of empty cups of coffee he'd bought from the vending machine. "Why don't you go grab a bite to eat?"

"I don't know... Shouldn't I stay close?"

"She's fine. Go eat. We've got a great cafeteria."

Since his hands were shaking, Ben figured he should probably have a decent meal to offset all the caffeine. Unless his hands trembled because he worried about Mallory.

The nurse put her hand on his arm. "Go on. Get a bite to eat. Then you can see your girl."

* * *

Although her eyes were open, Mallory didn't seem to understand too much of what was happening.

The orderlies had wheeled her into her room—thankfully a private one—and two nurses had taken over, pushing Ben to the background as they got her settled. She had tubes popping out of her everywhere.

By the time the fuss was over, only one nurse remained—a thin, ponytailed blonde wearing a scrub shirt decorated with penguins wearing Santa hats. She finished taking Mallory's vitals and then clipped a call button on the blanket next to Mallory's hand. "Push that if you need us for anything, hon."

Ben moved closer to the bed, worrying that Mallory looked so fragile in her green hospital gown. The left shoulder of the garment was held together with only one snap, probably to give the nurses quick access to the bandages. Her arms appeared so slender, and the gown seemed to swallow her whole. Her hair was a riot of waves and curls that she'd probably be trying to tame if she could see herself. She wore no makeup, but her face had so much natural beauty, she didn't need any—although a touch of color might have been nice on her pale skin.

"Hey, baby. How you feelin'?" he asked, his voice throaty with emotion. Seeing her so helpless tore at his heart.

"Fine," she murmured. "Sleepy. *Really* sleepy."

"That's the anesthesia." The nurse fiddled with Mallory's IV. "It'll keep wearing off tonight, but you'll have times you still get a little groggy."

"Anything I can do to help her?" Ben asked.

"She's doing great."

Mallory tried to push herself higher up on the bed before hissing out a long breath as her brow gathered and a frown formed on her lips.

"Easy, honey," the nurse said. "I know they explained the PCA in recovery, but…" She grabbed a line from the IV, stretched it out, and put a controller with a red button in Mallory's hand. "When you need something for the pain, push this. You'll get morphine released right into the IV."

"Seriously?" Ben asked. "But what if she pushes it too many times? Won't she overdose?"

The smile the nurse gave him appeared genuine rather than patronizing. "The machine will lock her out until it's time for another dose. She can push all she wants, but it won't release the meds until the right time."

Such an odd concept—the patient controlling her own painkillers. Both he and Amber were seldom sick, so he knew little about medicine let alone surgery.

Mallory pushed the button, and a few seconds later, her whole body relaxed. She even had a lopsided smile on her face.

Ben let loose a laugh. "Good stuff, there, Mal?"

She hummed her answer before closing her eyes.

"She'll be sleeping a lot," the nurse said as she finished adjusting a few more things. "I'll be back soon to check on her. If you want to watch TV, the controls are"—she picked up what he'd assumed was the controller for raising and lowering the bed—"on this."

"Thanks. I'll turn it on if I get too bored."

With a nod, the nurse left, pulling the door closed behind her.

Ben grabbed a chair and scooted it closer to the bed, choosing her right side in case the nurses needed access to her incision. He picked up her hand and cradled it in his. Her skin was soft and warm as he stroked the back of her hand with his thumb. That hand was so tiny, all but lost in his enormous mitt.

With a murmur of something he couldn't understand, she wiggled her nose and then sighed. After her zap of morphine, she'd be out for a good, long while.

The woman sure couldn't hold her painkillers.

He lifted her hand and pressed his lips to her knuckles. "Sleep, baby. Best thing for you. I'll take you home as soon as they let me, but just sleep for now."

No surprise that she didn't reply.

Since she clearly couldn't hear him, he smiled and said the words he'd been holding in his heart. "I love you, Mallory."

Once he got her home, he'd find the courage to tell her when she could actually hear him.

***

Something was squeezing her right upper arm so tight she grumbled.

"Taking your blood pressure," a far too chipper feminine voice said. "Be done in a sec."

Mallory hated the foggy feeling that still enveloped her. Seemed that as soon as the anesthesia wore off, the morphine had taken charge. Hardly remembering anything except the button her nurse had handed her, she took a few deep breaths and tried to orient herself and banish the last of the drug's effects.

No more pushing the morphine button for her.

A quick glance at the clock. 2:10 a.m. No wonder it was still dark.

The nurse who'd come in to check her had dragged Mallory back to the land of the living. Amazing how much the petite blonde could do with such a low level of light. Probably a night-shift nurse accustomed to moving around like a nocturnal creature. In short order, she'd checked all of Mallory's vitals, taken a peek at her incision, and gotten her a glass of ice water.

"Buzz if you need me," the nurse whispered. She smiled as she inclined her head at Ben. He lay sprawled in the easy chair as a soft snore slipped from his half-open mouth. "He's been worried about you. Hasn't left for a minute. Such a good husband."

Mallory almost corrected the woman, but she breezed out of the room too quickly.

Such a good husband.

Maybe one day…

Things between them were going well. They were not only compatible, but they complemented each other in so many ways.

She hated cooking. Ben loved it.

He could be a bit of a slob, leaving tools all over the place or doffing a shirt and forgetting to grab it when he left. But Mallory actually enjoyed straightening things up.

And both had hearty sexual appetites. Sometimes it was hard to let him work on the house because she wanted to strip off his clothes and jump him. Once he'd convinced her that the scar didn't matter, she'd released the last of the shackles holding her back. The way he responded every time he saw her naked ended the last of her worries. Ben let her know with his words, his touch, and his body that he liked everything he saw.

Would he love being able to see her body now that it was made whole? Well, at least it would be once the swelling subsided and she got the new nipple's color tattooed.

The pain had eased enough she considered lifting the bandage to see her new boob. What stopped her was fear of moving in a way that tugged at the incision. The implant wasn't going anywhere, and it would probably be best if she waited to look when all the swelling had eased.

That gave her pause. Ben might be accustomed to her scar, but could he handle the drainage tube that the surgeon told her would follow her home? Would the ugly side of what she'd been through turn him off?

Juliana had offered to help, and Mallory had taken her up on that offer. Ben was supposed to call Jules when Mallory got discharged since the doctor had said it could be one day, two, maybe even three depending on how well she handled the procedure. Once called, Jules would be home waiting for them. While Ben might be great at doing all the messy chores to help her recover, she'd be much more comfortable letting Jules deal with drains and bandages.

"Hey, Mal."

Her gaze caught his. "You're awake."

His dark hair was messy in a rugged way. Add his heavily lidded eyelids, and he was far too sexy for his own good. It was the same way he looked after they made love, and she would never grow tired of her handsome boyfriend.

"You need something?"

"No, I'm fine. The nurse was just here."

"She was?" He glanced over his shoulder at the closed door. "Didn't hear her. What time is it?" An exaggerated yawn consumed his face.

"It's only two. Go back to sleep, Ben."

"You sure you don't need anything?"

"Just some rest."

Settling himself back in the chair, he closed his eyes. "Night, baby." He was snoring again in only a few moments. The man could fall asleep faster than anyone she'd ever known.

Mallory closed her eyes, only to have them fly open again when Ben shifted in his chair and said, "Love you."

"What did you say?"

No reply.

Surely she'd misheard. The man was asleep. He hadn't said what she'd thought. No way. It was the morphine. Or the anesthesia. Or the ordeal of surgery.

She was wide awake now. "Ben? What did you say to me?"

Still no reply.

Shit.

There was no way she'd confront him when he finally woke up enough to answer her question. What if he'd only been talking in his sleep? What if he'd been dreaming that he was talking to Amber or some sexy nymph skipping through his mind?

Moving around to try to get a little more comfortable, all Mallory managed to do was send pain searing through her chest and arm. After only a few minutes of trying to cope, she realized she'd abandoned that little red button just a little too soon.

With a resigned sigh, she gave herself a dose of the soothing morphine. Right before sleep claimed her, she whispered, "I love you, too, Ben."

Chapter 21

Almost home." Juliana steered around the last corner and onto Mallory's block.

Mallory watched the houses on her street pass by through the passenger window, wondering again why she was with Jules and not Ben.

"Ben said he'd be waiting at the house." Juliana gave her a sidelong glance. "Hang in there."

"I'm fine." At least physically, that was true. Mallory's pain was bearable. Her anxiety, however, was spiraling.

She kept reminding herself that Ben had spent the night with her at the hospital. When he woke, he went to fetch an enormous coffee and a blueberry muffin. He ate in her room while she choked down the hospital breakfast. Once the doctor came by and pronounced her ready to head home early that evening, Ben started sending out a flurry of text messages.

Mallory had finally worked up the guts to ask what was going on when Juliana arrived. Ben had given Mallory a quick kiss, told her Juliana would get her home, and then promised to be waiting at the house when they got there. He was out the door before she could even catch her breath and ask why in the hell he was leaving her.

Jules eased her Accord into the driveway as Mallory heaved a relieved sigh. Ben's truck was there, so things were fine after all.

"You thought he was lying to you?" Juliana popped off her seat belt as she shook her head.

"Not…lying. Not really. I just…" A shrug would've hurt her side, so she refrained and let the words hang there.

"You just can't seem to stop comparing every guy in the world to that bastard ex of yours."

Because Jules had always seemed rather reticent for Mallory to get too serious with Ben, it came across as rather odd that she was supporting him now. Why had she had such a change of heart?

"I'm not comparing him to Jay," Mallory insisted.

Jules snorted. "You know, one of the reasons I was so pissy about you dating Ben was because I was worried he'd hurt you."

"So you're not now?"

"No," Jules replied. "I'm not. He's shown me he's a good guy." She crawled out of the car. She came around to open Mallory's door. "Let's get you inside and settled."

After Mallory got to her feet, she leaned heavily against the car, fighting back another wave of dizziness. Seemed like the anesthesia was taking forever to wear off. The nurses had warned her she might get drowsy for the next day or so. What she wanted at that moment was to collapse in the easy chair and go back to sleep.

Then the familiar red car over Juliana's shoulder caught her eye. "Danielle's here?"

"Maybe."

She looked around to see if Bethany's blue Beetle was also there. It was parked just behind the neighbor's sedan. "Beth's here too? I told you not to make a fuss. Why'd everyone come?"

After grabbing the plastic bag with the medical supplies, Jules tossed Mallory an incredulous frown. "Why do you think, silly?"

"I didn't want anyone to go to any trouble," Mallory grumbled under her breath. While she loved that everyone cared for her so much, the idea of having so many people waiting for her was daunting. Especially when she'd expected it to only be her and Ben.

Didn't help that the house was upside down. He'd started on the master bedroom and bath, so her clothes and toiletries were strewn around the great room. She'd been sleeping on the fold-out couch. Because of her pain, the recliner would be where she'd rest for the next few days. She didn't mind the mess, but now everyone could see what a wreck the place was.

Jules led her through the front door instead of the garage. It opened before they were all the way up to the porch. Danielle grinned at them through the storm door as Bethany waited right behind her, holding Rascal in her arms as she stroked his furry back.

Where's Ben?

"Welcome home!" Danielle held the door while they came inside.

Juliana hurried ahead and disappeared up the stairs with the bag of supplies.

"Wait!" Mallory called after her. She'd need the stuff Jules was taking upstairs, and if the master suite was half the chaos it was last time she been up there, they'd never find the supplies again. The bag would disappear in the mixture of paint cans, brushes, rollers, and tarps. "Jules, I need—" The rest of her words froze in her throat when Ben stepped out of the bedroom and came down the stairs, smiling so broadly she almost smiled back.

Not until he tells me what he's been up to.

"Welcome home, Mal." He brushed a kiss over her cheek before bending down to help remove her shoes. "You need to get settled and get some rest. How's the pain?"

"Where were you?" Her voice sounded like some pouty kid.

Ben didn't owe her anything, least of all an explanation. He'd already gone above and beyond the call of duty to stick so close to her after the surgery. For God's sake, the man slept in a chair simply to keep an eye on her all night.

She'd tried to come up with a million reasons he hadn't taken her home from the hospital—anything from Amber's gymnastics to some emergency at a worksite. None of them had seemed important enough for him to let Jules come and drag her home.

The dichotomy of her feelings only added to Mallory's light-headedness.

"Busy," he replied with a smirk. He set her shoes in the foyer closet, took the jacket draped over her shoulder, and hung it up. "Need a painkiller yet?"

"I'm fine." Her tone was harsh even to her own ears.

What's wrong with me?

She'd sworn to herself she wasn't going to be dependent on a guy. Jules, Beth, and Danielle had taken great care of her after her mastectomy, and this surgery was a cakewalk compared to that. She had no business being so snotty to Ben after everything he'd done.

"I'm sorry," she whispered. Maybe he'd think she was still too drugged up to be polite.

"For what?"

"For snapping at you."

"You just had surgery. You're allowed to be grouchy."

The dizziness was still plaguing her, and she was ready to get settled, pop a painkiller, and sleep so she didn't keep biting his head off for no good reason. When she tried to head down the hall toward the kitchen, Ben took her hand in his. "Not that way."

"What are you talking about? I was going to sit on my recliner and—"

Ben tugged gently on her hand. "I have a surprise for you."

"A surprise?"

He nodded. "It's upstairs."

The notion of walking up a flight of stairs seemed daunting, especially when doing something as simple as coming in from the car had sapped most of her strength. "I'd rather go to the great room and—"

He cut her off by scooping her into his arms. His tender touch kept her sore side well protected. "I'd rather you go to your bedroom."

With her three friends laughing and following behind, he carried her up the stairs and into the master suite.

She closed her eyes, afraid to see it was still a disaster area. Although he'd said there was a surprise, she couldn't imagine the place was done. No way. The bathroom hadn't even had the new vanity installed.

"Welcome to your new bedroom," Ben said.

Mallory opened her eyes and gasped at the neat and tidy bedroom. "How did you—"

"This is why I wouldn't let you come up and see the progress last week. I wanted it to be ready for you when you got home."

"It's... it's... beautiful." Tears stung her eyes.

Beth let the squirming cat down. Rascal jumped onto the bed, settled on his usual right side, and watched her. Mallory could have sworn he was grinning.

The room had been transformed from beige and boring to a pleasant, soothing seafoam green. Standing in the middle of the room was the enormous four-poster bed she'd bought right after Jay left. She'd tossed their old mattress out in the trash, sold the bedroom set they'd purchased on their honeymoon, and gotten herself the type of furniture she'd always wanted but he'd nixed.

None of it had been set up yet. She'd had the delivery men leave it wrapped in plastic in the empty guest room, figuring she'd move it into the master when the renovation was done. She'd been sleeping on the mattress and box spring and a cheap frame.

Now the gorgeous cherrywood bed rested in the perfect spot in the middle of the room with nightstands flanking both sides. The matching bureau was next to the bay window, and the dresser was near the closet door. Everything was perfectly placed on the new carpet she hadn't known Ben had installed.

"How did you get this all done?" Mallory asked, her voice choked with emotion.

Ben swallowed hard, betraying that his own emotions were running as high as hers. "Most of it was done before your surgery. Just finished a few details this morning. I couldn't let you come home after surgery and not have a bed to sleep in."

"But all this work..."

"You ain't seen nothin' yet." With a wink, he carried her to the en suite bath.

This time, she couldn't stop the tears from spilling over her lashes when she saw all he'd accomplished. A new whirlpool tub. A double vanity with vessel sinks. A shower with a glass door. While she remembered picking out the light fixture, she hadn't expected it to look so ornate. The walls were a deep hunter green, complementing the lighter shade of the bedroom.

"You're crying," Ben said, his voice full of concern. "You don't like it?"

She sniffled and laid her cheek on his shoulder. "I *love* it."

I love you.

When she'd hired Ben it had been to restore her house. Slowly but surely he was turning it into a place that felt like home. *Her* home. Yet there was still so much of him in every room—just enough masculinity to make the house…perfect.

Jules stepped through the door. "Nice. You did good, Ben."

"Thanks."

"Did you see the bed?" she asked Mallory.

"Yeah," she replied, rubbing her cheek against the soft flannel of his shirt. "It's wonderful."

"Good. Now I can turn down the sheets and prop up some pillows for you. Time for you to rest."

Ben took her back to the bed and set her on her feet. The care he took was evident in his gentle touch. "Want to put on a nightgown or something?"

"Yeah, but…" She cast a glance to Jules and Beth as they fussed over the bed. Rascal hopped down and headed to the bay window to curl up on the new cushion. "The girls should help me."

The surgeon had left a drainage tube that would probably gross Ben out. The thought of him seeing her new breast before the incision was healed bothered her. It was one thing to keep her company in the hospital, but it was another altogether to have him actually care for her incision. When he got to see her new breast, she wanted to be wearing a sexy black negligee.

Danielle picked up the bag of medical supplies. "How about we get her settled?"

Giving her friend a grateful smile, she nodded. "Please, Ben?"

* * *

Although he wanted to show her how well he could take of her, Ben acquiesced. Mallory obviously didn't want him to see her right after her surgery. Part of him was offended that she didn't want his help. But then again, had he been in a similar situation, he might not enjoy her being around when he was at his worst.

When she'd first arrived, he thought he'd made a big mistake not driving her home from the hospital. There hadn't been enough time to get everything finished before the surgery. A few of the details had to be handled today including getting the furniture set up. He'd called in Jules to drive Mallory home and then phoned Robert, Danielle, and Bethany to act as renovation reinforcements. It was the first time he'd met Mallory's friends, but they'd been very helpful in getting the finishing touches in place. They'd completed the last of the tasks only moments before Jules drove into the driveway.

Once Mallory saw the bedroom suite, her whole body had relaxed and a few tears had fallen. Only then did he stop worrying that she'd hate him for not bringing her home.

The place looked great. Her taste in decorating had been spot-on, including the gorgeous four-poster bed. As he and Robert set the mattress on the frame, his friend had made a rather risqué suggestion on how great a bed like that was to tie someone up. Ben snorted a laugh at the comment, but it had put visuals of Mallory tying his wrists to the bedposts and then making love to him firmly into his mind. When she was healed, he was going to suggest it if for no other reason than to see her reaction.

While the ladies got her ready to rest, he headed downstairs. Robert was slipping his arms into his jacket.

"You should've come up," Ben said.

"Nah. She's a private kinda person. I didn't want to intrude. What did she think?"

"She *loved* it," Ben replied. "I can't thank you enough."

"You can buy me a beer next time we catch a game at the bar."

"You've got a deal."

They shook hands before Robert headed out through the laundry room, shutting the door behind him.

Ben had been so busy working on the master suite he hadn't been in the kitchen at all. Mallory's friends obviously had, because the place was spotless. The great room was as well. Slowly the house was getting done. Soon, Mallory would have her home the way she'd dreamed, just like he'd promised her.

Then where would they be? He'd have no more excuses for seeing her so often.

Together. They'd still be together. A couple. There was no doubt in his mind.

All he'd wanted was a job to keep food on the table for him and Amber. He hadn't been searching for love. Yet here it was in the form of a woman with courage and beauty and a heart as big as Montana.

The time had come to tell Mallory his feelings. Then perhaps she'd confess hers, too.

"Ben?" Jules's voice broke him from his reverie.

"Yeah?" Mallory's three friends were donning their coats. "You're leaving?"

Jules nodded. "She's sleeping. I honestly think she's doing fantastic. This surgery was a walk in the park compared to the mastectomy."

He hated even thinking about all Mallory had endured in that ordeal. "She doesn't need you now?"

All three women shook their heads.

"She'll be fine," Bethany said. "Just needs rest and healing."

"You're staying, right?" Jules asked.

With a nod, Ben offered her his hand. "Thanks for helping get her home."

Instead of shaking his hand, Jules gathered him into a quick hug. "Thanks for getting this place ready for her. The master suite's great. Wonderful, actually."

In turn, Danielle and Bethany also gave him a hug, murmuring their appreciation for what he'd done to help their friend. He hadn't done it for their praise, but their words were nice to hear.

Standing at the front door, he made sure the ladies made it to their cars and exchanged waves with them as they drove away.

"Ben?" Mallory called, her voice weak.

"Coming, baby." He took the stairs two at a time.

She was propped up on a mound of pillows, her eyes weighted as though she'd drop back to sleep at any moment. "Hey."

"Hey." Heading around to her side of the bed, he saw another pillow shaped like a round tube resting against her side, supporting her left arm. "You've got quite a collection of pillows."

"They help. Danielle's sister is a nurse. Her advice on stuff like that got me through the last surgery." A yawn slipped out.

"You should sleep."

Mallory nodded. "Stay with me?"

"Of course. Where else would I be?"

"With Amber."

"She's in Texas, remember?"

Her brow knit before understanding dawned. "Yeah…I forgot."

Leaning in, he kissed her forehead. "Anesthesia and painkillers will do that." His gaze took in the things the ladies had left on the nightstand. A glass of water. Tissues. Mallory's phone. A prescription bottle. Problem was that they were all on her left.

If Mallory was alone, she wouldn't be able to reach with her left hand—at least not without causing her pain.

Good thing he'd stayed. "Need anything?"

"Nah." With her right hand, she scratched Rascal, who was back at her side, behind the ears. The cat had curled up against her hip. Mallory patted the mattress. "You must be tired, too. Come lay down with me?"

Tired? Not a bit, but if it would help her sleep, he'd lie at her side until she drifted off. After kicking off his shoes, he almost flopped on the bed before realizing it might hurt her by upsetting her cocoon of pillows. Instead, he stretched out next to her, trying not to squish her cat by moving too close. Ben took her hand and cradled it against his stomach before closing his eyes.

"Thank you, Ben."

"Stop thanking me."

"Why?"

He shrugged. "Makes it sound like you think I did something special."

"You did. I mean…look at this room and my bathroom. They're wonderful."

"You're paying me for that, remember?" He allowed himself a smile. "I'm glad you like it, though."

"That's why I'm thanking you." Her fingers squeezed his.

While he wanted to tell her he'd have done all of it for nothing, he bit his tongue. Mallory was doped up and in pain. Despite his earlier decision, this wasn't the time to confess that he'd fallen in love with her. She'd forgotten Amber was with Theresa. She'd probably forget his declaration as well.

They'd be able to talk about something that serious when she was better.

On the other hand, the time he'd spent worrying about her in that waiting room had taken a toll. If there'd been any question at all that he loved her, that question would have been decidedly answered by the anxiety he experienced over her well-being and the relief that washed over him when the nurse told him she'd come through the surgery with flying colors.

Ben rolled to his side, wanting to see again that she was doing well. He was surprised to find her staring intently at him. Her chocolate eyes no longer looked sleepy. "Did you need something, Mal?"

"I do."

He pushed up on his elbow. "What? A drink? Some ice chips? What do you need?"

"To tell you something." She swallowed hard before a smile bloomed. "I love you."

His heart slammed in his chest. She took the lead again the same way she did when they made love. Her courage was absolute, clearly much stronger than his own. The only thing spoiling her bold declaration was that her teeth now tugged on her bottom lip, betraying her worry.

He wasn't about to leave her dangling in the breeze. Since she'd boldly declared her heart, he followed suit. "I love you, too."

Her eyes searched his, and her hand trembled. "Really?"

Ben nodded.

"When did you decide you loved me?" she asked. "I—I mean, if you remember..."

"I don't know. No special time. I guess I just...knew." Although he sounded stupid, he couldn't think of any better way to explain it. If he tried too hard to describe things—to tell her he'd known with perfect clarity the first time he'd made love to her—she might think his revelation was based on nothing but sex. Far from it.

He simply wasn't good enough with words to say it so she'd "get it." So he tried a diversion. "What about you? When did you know?"

Her laughter was a surprise. Not a big guffaw, but a sly giggle that made him believe she'd have understood if he'd taken the time to explain. Her words affirmed that notion. "I knew when you let me spank you."

He had to laugh along with her. "Never thought I'd have a woman tell me she fell in love with me because I let her hit my ass with a belt."

"I never thought some guy would let me hit his ass with a belt." Her giggles were interrupted with a wince.

"Okay. Enough for you, little lady. You're getting over surgery. You need your rest."

Settling back against her pillows, Mallory smiled. "Tell me again. Then I'll sleep."

Ben carefully rose over her and pressed a kiss to her lips. "I love you, Mallory."

She wore no makeup. Her hair was mussed. And her eyes were clouded with fatigue and medicines. Yet her smile was breathtaking. "Love you, too, Ben."

Chapter 22

Mallory felt far too exposed sitting there with her new boob hanging out. It had been eight weeks since her surgery. She'd experienced no problems—no infections or trouble with the implant—and had been able to go right back to work in January.

The biggest problem was that since the surgery, she and Ben had only made love in the dark. She wanted him to wait and see her new breast when all the swelling had subsided and it looked much closer to the finished product. Once her nipple finally had some tint, she'd let him see her in the light and hope he liked the outcome.

His patience through everything had been extraordinary. The fact he was a fantastic lover didn't hurt, either. He made her feel normal again, like an ordinary woman instead of like a woman who'd lost an important part of herself. And he loved her, a miracle which she returned with her whole *heart*.

Now she wanted to make love to him with her whole *body*.

At least the only people in the tattoo parlor were the Ladies and the two artists. She still kept a furtive eye on the door, worried about someone strolling in to choose some body art.

"We're appointment only." Her artist glanced up at her and smiled. "Relax. I locked the front door, and no one can see through the window tint."

"Thanks." She gave him a wan smile.

The buzz of the tool he held like a pen started again, drawing her attention back to her chest. The feeling against her skin was more of a tickle than a prick, which wasn't surprising. While she could feel the needle forcing the ink into her skin, the sensitivity level had dropped markedly.

Her real breast had quickly responded to any touch or a change in temperature. The new nipple was constructed of skin, and because the surgery severed some nerves, it wasn't nearly as sensitive. Nor would it contract with cold like a real one. Still… it looked better than if she'd opted for nothing but ink as some reconstruction patients did.

"Not hurtin' you?" The artist glanced up again. This time he locked eyes with Mallory.

Her face had been hot with a blush from the moment she entered the parlor, but every time he made eye contact, her cheeks flushed warmer. "No. It's fine."

He gave her a lopsided smile and got right back to work. She much preferred seeing the top of his navy-blue bandanna than trying to make conversation. Her nudity made her uncomfortable. How could people get tattoos in other, much more private places? Did they really sit on the tables with their asses and genitals hanging out?

On the other hand, the new breast looked great. While it wasn't quite a duplicate of the one she'd lost to cancer, it would do nicely. Mallory was anxious to show it off to Ben.

The tattoo parlor had been recommended by a couple of breast cancer survivors she'd met in the course of her treatment. Both had praised the professionalism and how the owner treated them with respect and patience when he'd restored color to their replacement nipples. Even then, she wished the owner or another artist had been female. No such luck. When she, Juliana, Bethany, and Danielle strolled through the door, they were greeted by two men who had ink from necks to wrists. But once she sat down with the owner, his kindness was evident, and she hadn't even minded showing him her right breast so they could decide on the best color combinations to get a close match.

"You hanging in there, Mal?" Danielle asked.

Mallory didn't even try to turn her head to reply. The Ladies were all behind her, working on some conspiracy. When they'd arrived, Jules announced that Mallory wasn't the only one with an appointment. The owner introduced himself, led Mallory to one of the three workstations, and had her poring through color charts before she could find out what her friends were up to. Her back was to the other stations, so whatever the Ladies were doing would remain a mystery until they were ready to show her or her nipple's tint was complete and she could get up and go to them.

"Mal?" This time the inquiry came from Bethany. "You okay?"

"I'm fine. Just ready to be done."

"Almost there, sweetheart," the owner said, not even glancing up this time.

"No rush. Jules? What are you doing?"

"I told you," she called back, "it's a—Ow!"

"You need to sit still, ma'am," a deep masculine voice scolded.

Mallory stopped thinking about her nipple and let her curiosity take charge. "What are you all doing over there?"

Danielle stepped up to her side. "You can't stand being out of the loop, can you?"

"Why is your chest so red?"

"What?"

"The left side of your chest is bright red."

Her cheeks quickly matched her chest.

"Be patient!" Jules yelled before she let loose a moan like she was in pain.

"Are you getting something pierced?" Mallory asked. Then she remembered something Jules had mentioned, something Mallory had assumed was a joke. "Oh my God. Jules, you're not getting your nipple pierced, are you?"

Judging from the chorus of laughter, everyone in the tattoo parlor enjoyed the question.

"Done." Blue-bandanna man sat back, set down the tattoo gun, and smiled. "I think I nailed the color."

Mallory dropped her chin, trying to get a good look at his work.

"Here." He grabbed a hand mirror and gave it to her.

Taking a breath to brace herself, she positioned the mirror in front of the breast she'd thought was gone forever. But there it was. Right back where it belonged. Same size. Same shape. Same raspberry nipple.

Jerking the other side of her shirt open, she couldn't stop staring at her breasts. With the exception of the thin red line of a scar, a person would have to stare closely to know that the left boob wasn't real. The two of them made a nearly perfect pair of knockers.

Tears pooled in her eyes, and although she tried to blink them away, a few spilled over her lashes.

The battle had finally ended, and she'd emerged scarred but victorious.

She'd really won.

"Oh, Mallory." Danielle leaned down to wrap an arm around her shoulder. "I know it's not perfect, but—"

"It *is* perfect. It's absolutely *perfect*."

The artist grinned, took the hand mirror, and set it aside. "Now, here's what you need to do..."

Mallory tried to listen to his instructions on caring for the new tattoo, but she was too wrapped up in figuring out what her friends were up to. Thankfully, he bandaged the left nipple and then gave her a sheet with instructions before she buttoned up her shirt. On suggestions from the other cancer survivors, she'd left the bra at home.

The artist held out his hand and bowed at the waist. "Let me help you down, m'lady." He even affected a good British accent.

She had to smile at his teasing. "How kind, good sir." She placed her hand in his and let him help her down from the table.

"It's great to know I made you so happy."

"You did," she assured him. "Thank you so much. You did a really great job."

"Sure I can't talk you into a nice butterfly or a pink ribbon, too?" he asked with a wink. "Either would look mighty pretty on your pale skin."

"No, I think I'll skip another one. But thanks."

"You come on back if you change your mind." He busied himself with straightening up his supplies.

Mallory stared at Bethany openmouthed when she came over and hopped up on the empty station. "What are you doing?"

"It's my turn." Beth flashed a smile at the artist when he nodded at her. Then she unbuttoned her shirt. After a timid glance to the artist, she pulled her shirt open to bare her left breast.

"What on earth are you doing?" Mallory shifted her gaze to Danielle. "All of you...what are you doing?"

"C'mere," Jules called over her shoulder.

Coming around the side of the second station, Mallory saw that Jules had her left boob bared as well. The artist was working on some art, but he was bent so close, she couldn't see what he was drawing.

Danielle went to the opposite side of the table. Then she opened the first few buttons on her shirt. Funny, but Mallory hadn't noticed they'd all worn button-front shirts as well.

"We did these for you," Dani said as she flipped open her shirt. "All of us."

Halfway down her breast was a small pink ribbon with "Mallory" written in beautiful scroll right below it. A quick look to Jules revealed the same tattoo almost completed. The buzz coming from the station Mallory had sat at was no doubt Beth getting her pink ribbon.

There were no words to express the love in her heart for these women. They were so much more than friends. They were sisters as close as if they'd all shared the same womb.

"Thank you." Mallory's words were more mouthed than whispered.

"Don't you dare cry," Juliana scolded. "As soon as Beth and I are done, we're all going out for margaritas. Ben's the designated driver. We're supposed to text him when we're good and drunk."

***

"Good night," Ben said as Juliana let herself into her condo.

"Thanks for drivin'." She tossed her purse on the table and shut the door in his face.

Forgiving her was easy since she was too drunk to know she'd been rude. The other women were all home, probably already safe in their beds. The last one, his own Lady, waited in the Escape.

Mallory hadn't acted too awfully drunk, especially compared to her friends. Her speech wasn't slurred, and she hadn't experienced any trouble getting into the car. Bethany and Danielle were probably too wasted to drive, but they negotiated the walk to Bethany's apartment with minimal difficulty. They also swore they'd stay put and not try to go out again. Juliana, on the other hand, was good and soused.

"She's pretty drunk. Should we stay and help her?" Ben asked as he slid behind the steering wheel.

"Nah. She's fine. Did she lock the front door?"

"Yeah. I heard the dead bolt go into place."

"Then she'll go right to bed. Probably in her clothes. She'll probably sleep 'til noon at least."

He pulled into traffic. "How did the tattoo go?"

It wasn't like he expected her to pop open her shirt and show him, but he was curious as to how the finished product turned out. Since Mallory was in such a good mood when he'd walked into the bar, he couldn't help but think she was pleased. Maybe she'd get up enough nerve to let him see when they got home.

Her hand moved to his thigh, and she rubbed closer and closer to his groin. "Thought I'd show you and let you decide."

His body responded so quickly, it was a wonder he wasn't dizzy from the blood leaving his brain. "You've been drinking, Mal. I don't want to take advantage."

"I had three margaritas and more than enough chips and pretzels to make up for the alcohol. Besides, maybe *I'll* be taking advantage of *you*."

The husky sound of her voice sent more heat rushing to his cock. "I'd like to see you try."

Her palm pressed against his erection. "Oh, you will, Ben. You *will*."

Breaking most of the speed limits, Ben headed back to her house. He'd be spending the night, something he didn't get to do often—not nearly as often as he would've liked. He wasn't about to leave Amber alone all night, and Mallory always claimed she understood. She never tried to make him feel guilty when he had to head home. Instead, she always kissed him good-bye and told him what a great father he was.

Her praise meant the world to him, but he ached to be able to spend every night with her. Problem was the house belonged to her. There was plenty of room for both him and Amber, but no way in hell he'd be the one to make the suggestion that the Carpenters move right in. Not only was it tacky, it was downright ridiculous. Mallory was an independent woman who clearly enjoyed her life. He was a big part of it now, but she'd never even hinted that she would welcome such a drastic change in living arrangements.

The idea of popping the question had flitted through his mind on too many occasions to count, but he was still too scarred from his first marriage to want to set out into those choppy waters again. Mallory was nothing like Theresa. Yet the fear of making that kind of permanent commitment remained.

"What're you thinking?" Mallory asked. The way she rubbed had him plenty worked up.

"Nothing much. Just curious." Ben tugged her hand away from his lap and held it in his to try to maintain some self-control. "I've waited a long time to see the results of the surgery."

"I'm sorry, honey. You told me you didn't mind making love in the dark."

He squeezed her hand. "Stop apologizing. I told you it was

fine. Shit, like I said before, it really fired up the psychological part of sex for me. Besides, I see pretty well in the dark." Tossing her a crooked smile, he eased onto her driveway.

"We're home." Mallory tugged her hand away and picked up her purse. She was out of the SUV before he'd even killed the engine. "Give me a couple of minutes, then come up to our room."

Our room.

Wouldn't that be great?

Ben followed her inside. She shed her coat, thrust it at him, and hurried away.

"I'll be up in three minutes," he called after her.

"Funny. I thought you were already *up*," she shot back. A few moments later, the master bedroom door closed.

After kicking off his shoes, he hung their coats on the brass coat tree. Then he took a long look around, pleased at what he saw. The place really was coming together nicely.

The great room and kitchen were done. Mallory had picked beautiful dark granite for the kitchen countertops, and the walnut floor she'd chosen for the foyer extended into the rest of the downstairs. She added several rugs, some new lamps, and once the mantel had been stained and the cabinets painted, the downstairs was complete. Rascal curled up and sleeping on the sofa was the perfect finishing touch.

In fact... the whole house was nearly done. All that remained inside was the spare bathroom upstairs and a good coat of paint on the exterior come spring.

Ben no longer worried about what would happen when her house was done. He loved Mallory. She loved him. They worked well as a couple, and they would be together for a good, long while.

The financial arrangements were also done. He'd tried to lowball the bills along the way. She'd retaliated by adding more without asking him then refusing to write replacement checks. In typical Mallory style, she'd told him he needed to deposit those checks or he'd get nothing at all. The first time he'd waited two weeks before he'd caved, needing money for the last payment on Amber's braces. After that, he stopped fighting Mallory, putting anything extra into a savings account for his daughter's eventual college tuition.

Having given Mallory a solid three minutes of waiting, he headed up the stairs. He rapped on the bedroom door with the back of his knuckles. "Can I come in now?"

"Yes."

The bedroom was empty, the bathroom door closed. But she'd clearly been busy. Several fat candles rested around the room on the dresser, the nightstands, the bureau. The bed had been turned down, so Ben rapidly shed his clothes, dropping them haphazardly on the floor. He slid between the flannel sheets, shivering at the feel of the cold material against his heated skin. As soon as she joined him, they'd generate more than enough heat to ban the early March chill.

"Mal, baby? I'm ready."

The bathroom door opened slowly, and she stepped out, silhouetted in the light. Then she flipped the switch, ending the perfect view of her profile through her nightgown.

It took a moment for his eyes to adjust, but when they did, they widened. She wasn't wearing her typical flannel nightgown. "Oh...my...God."

"You like?"

She was dressed in a pink negligee so sheer he could see her through the iridescent material. Only strategically placed bits of lace kept him from seeing all of her, the tease almost more enticing than if she'd been standing before him naked.

"Yeah, baby," he drawled. "I like. I like a lot." He bounded out of the bed, unable to wait a moment longer to touch her.

She held out her palm. "Wait."

"Wait?" He'd wanted to sweep her into his arms and carry her straight to the bed.

Amazing how much he still wanted her with a passion that sometimes made their lovemaking frantic and hurried. Since she always responded with as much desire and desperation, he didn't worry that she'd think he was only seeking his own pleasure. There were times they could linger and play, provoking and teasing until he often wondered at how perfectly their libidos matched.

"Yeah, wait." Crossing her arms over her chest, she dragged the spaghetti straps down her upper arms. The negligee slipped low, but she caught it just before she bared her breasts. "You ready to see?"

"I'm ready if you're ready for me to see." He put his hands over hers. "You know I love you. You're more than a breast to me."

"I know...I just..." She released a sigh. Then she dropped the negligee and grabbed his hands so tightly her knuckles blanched. The garment slid down her body, not even stopping at the gentle flare of her hips before resting on the floor.

Pulling her hands away, Ben slowly spread her arms. Keeping his eyes locked on hers, he waited until she gave him a quick nod before letting himself glance at her new breast.

Had he not known she'd lost the left breast to cancer, he might have had a hard time noticing that the left was too terribly different than the right. The nipple had a slightly dissimilar shape, probably because her right nipple had pulled into a tight pebble while the left hadn't.

The candlelight dappled her skin, making it glow. Without a word, he dropped her hands, cupped her face, and kissed her. Not a demanding kiss, but one full of all the love her had for her as well as the admiration for the kind of woman she was—strong, courageous. And beautiful.

There would never be another woman who could equal Mallory Hamilton in his eyes.

She pulled back, her gaze searching his. "So?"

"So… what?"

Mallory gave his chest a playful swat.

"I think it's great, Mal."

"Really?"

Ben nodded.

"I like it, too." When she ran her fingers around her new nipple, he groaned. Her smile was brighter than any of the candle flames. "You like that, huh? Me touching myself?"

Like it? It was one of the sexiest things he'd ever seen. He croaked out a "Yeah."

This time, she licked her finger and swirled it around the right nipple then pinched it.

He'd had enough taunting. Between the way she looked in that sexy negligee to how boldly she stood before him in nothing but her skin, he was sure he was going to explode. With a rumbling growl, he scooped her into his arms and took her to the bed.

Laying her down across the mattress so her legs dangled over the side, he let his gaze rake her body. "God, you're beautiful."

When she tried to sit up, he held her shoulders to the mattress. Then without an ounce of warning, he dropped to his knees, spread her thighs, and buried his face against her hot, wet core.

* * *

Mallory gasped, squeezing her thighs together, capturing his head. Ben simply eased them apart again and continued his erotic torture. His tongue stroked between her folds until he found the sensitive bud that made her moan in pleasure. As he slipped a finger deep inside her, she closed her eyes and let the riot of emotions run roughshod over her body.

She'd planned to take charge, to run the show. He'd changed the rules. Sometimes they both loved a lot of foreplay. Not tonight. Tonight, she was so anxious, so tense at hearing his reaction to the results of her surgery she hadn't even realized just how wound up she'd gotten. He obviously had, and with nothing but the repeated flick of his tongue and the way he touched her, he had her on the verge of climax.

"C'mere," she said, tugging on his hair. "I want you inside me."

He ignored her, increasing his attentions until her body was so knotted with need, she thought she'd scream. Drawing up her knees, she braced her heels against the mattress.

"Ben, please."

One hand on her hip, he stabbed his tongue into her sheath as he swirled his thumb around and around the tight nub of flesh.

She surrendered, letting the bliss fan from her core through her body, washing over her as her body spasmed. Ben refused to let up, wringing every last sensation from her.

Panting for breath, she scooted up on the mattress until she could lie back against the pillows. Ben flopped down at her side, rolling to face her with an arrogant and very masculine smile on his face. "Like that?"

She scoffed at the ridiculous question before figuring he might need to hear some praise. "*Loved* that."

He tickled his fingers up her ribs until he traced the shape of her new nipple. "Does it hurt?"

"The new boob?" She gave her head a shake.

"I meant the tattoo. Figured it might still be tender."

"Nah." When he suddenly jerked his hand away, she frowned. "What's wrong? Does it feel funny or something?"

"No, but…should I avoid touching it? I mean…what about infections? Never knew someone who had a tattoo before."

Gently picking up his hand, she settled his palm over her new breast. "You're fine." She let a giggle slip out as he squeezed. "How's it feel?"

"Like a boob."

"A real one?"

"Yeah, baby. Like a real one."

Ben rose over her, laying his body against hers as he supported his weight with his elbows. His erection pressed against her center, sending a thrill tripping through her.

"Seems as though you react like it's a real boob."

His frown was quizzical. "Huh?"

Raising her hips, she put her palms against his tight buns and pressed against him.

"Oh…you mean *that*." He kissed once, hard and fast yet full of meaning. "Like I've been telling you, Mal, you don't need two breasts to make me want you. Just looking at you, just thinking about you, makes me hard as a rock."

Mallory slipped her hand between their bodies and guided his erection to her entrance. "Then show me."

One thrust had him buried inside her, and she kissed him, encouraging him without words to move, to take her body to that place where she forgot everything. Except him.

The rhythm he set was fast, as though he were starved for the feel of her. His lips settled on hers, his tongue passing her lips to stroke and probe as his cock did the same. Too soon, her body tightened in need. She looped her arms around his neck, kissing him ferociously as she tried to drag him along with her in their race for fulfillment. A growl rumbled in his chest as he sped his thrusts.

Mallory wrapped her legs around his hips as she tangled her fingers through his hair. When her orgasm hit, she tore her mouth away to moan his name. Her release shimmered through her, making her feel more alive than any other experience of her life.

She was a survivor.

Chapter 23

Mallory stopped painting and held her breath, although she had no idea why she was so nervous. Everything Ben had fixed worked perfectly. Her house was almost done. This bathroom, the guest bath, was the last item to complete. Surely this toilet wouldn't be the first fixture to have problems.

No, there was something else that raised her anxiety, something that had been on her mind for weeks. The time had come to gather her courage.

Ben turned the knob, letting water fill the toilet's tank. "Voilà!"

"Awesome."

"Want to take the first pee in the new toilet?" he asked with a wink.

"I think I'm past the fun of that. Two times was my limit for excitement at christening a commode." She set her paintbrush down in the tray and went over to close the lid and sit down, putting her closer to Ben, who knelt on the floor, putting away his tools. "You know, if you move in here, I'd be really pissed if you aren't considerate about putting the lid down." She pointed to the toilet paper holder he'd installed on the side of the vanity.

"Oh, and the toilet paper rolls over the top, not under. I'm fussy about that, too."

Ben snorted. "Most women would be grateful if their men remembered to put a new roll on at all."

Not a word about her offer. Perhaps she needed to make things a little more plain. He was, after all, just a man. Most weren't very perceptive.

"Not *this* woman." She tried to convey her sincerity in her expression and decided to be blunt. "Especially when you and Amber move in. I'll expect you both to pull your weight. Keep the place clean. Do your own laundry. Help unload the dishwasher. Stuff like that."

He eyed her skeptically. Since she'd never once mentioned the possibility of them sharing her house, his look wasn't unexpected. She'd hoped he'd pick up sooner on the vibes she'd been tossing him since her breast reconstruction.

"Who says we're moving in?" he asked.

"Me. At least I hope you will."

"Mal..." He gave his head a shake. "I couldn't ask that of you. It would be imposing and—"

She held up her hand. "Wait. Please. Just hear me out. Your lease is up at the end of the month, right?"

"Yeah, but—"

"They're closing the complex for a massive remodel, right?"

He nodded.

"You want Amber to stay at her school, don't you?"

He ran his hand over his face, a gesture she'd seen every time he was frustrated. "I can look for a new place."

She rose, putting her hand on his arm and stroking, hoping to soothe whatever wound she'd inflicted on his masculine ego. "I'm sorry, honey. I just—"

"I'm not a stray dog, Mallory." His voice held a hard edge. "You don't have to take me and my pup in off the streets and toss us some scraps."

"I never said—" She took a deep breath. "You're right. I'm sorry. You want the truth?"

"That's our rule."

"I was using that as an excuse, hoping it would convince you to move in with me."

"Why? Why do you all of a sudden want Amber and me in your house? Especially now that it's almost done?"

"Because," she replied, "I want to share my days with you. All my days. With you and Amber. And my nights. Because I want to spend more time with both of you. Because when you're not around, this place feels so damned lonely." She shrugged, fighting the choking feeling of strong emotion. "Right now it's just a *house*. It's only a *home* when you're here."

Ben gathered her into his arms, holding her close and kissing the top of her head. "I love you, Mal."

Wrapping her arms around his waist, she squeezed. "I love you, too."

"You really want us here? You really want me and Amber and all our baggage?"

"You've carried mine around; why wouldn't I want to help with yours?"

"Theresa might show up from time to time."

"I expected that."

His sigh made her smile against his chest.

She'd won.

"I need to talk it over with Amber."

"I wouldn't have it any other way."

* * *

"So…what do you think?" Ben watched his daughter, searching for some hint of what she was thinking. As usual, her poker face was firmly in place. "It could work for us, don't you think?"

"It could." Amber kept her gaze fixed on what was left of her hamburger and fries.

When the waitress had put the plate in front of her, Amber had eaten as though she'd gone days without food. The moment he'd dropped the bomb about Mallory's invitation, she'd put down what was left of the sandwich and left it untouched. At least she'd nibbled on her fries, so she wouldn't go hungry.

"You could stay at Armstrong Middle."

She shrugged. "Would only be for the rest of the semester. I'll be heading to high school next year."

"Wouldn't you like to go to Mallory's school next year?"

"I suppose…" Amber snatched up another fry, dipped it in ketchup, and then chewed on it for longer than necessary.

"Look, Amber…I know this is a big change, but it could work for us. Don't you like Mallory?"

Although she held her mouth in a tight-lipped frown, she nodded.

"Don't you like her house?" Bribery was a powerful weapon. "You know that blue bedroom? She said you could have it."

"The one with the skylight and the walk-in closet?"

Now they were getting somewhere. "Yeah. And I can finally afford to buy you a new bedroom set. No more mismatched furniture."

"A canopy bed?"

The hope in her voice meant the world to him. "Yeah. A canopy."

"What happens when you two break up?"

Amber was truly his kid. Blunt and grounded deeply in reality.

Having given that question a lot of thought, he gave her the only answer he'd come up with. "What can I say, ladybug? Then I suppose we move."

A tear leaked from the corner of her eye.

"Oh, Amber…stop. We're not going to break up. We won't have to move. Mallory and I love each other."

"I know that," she snapped, rubbing her eyes with the heels of her hands.

"I don't think we'll *ever* leave each other. In fact, if things work out well, I was thinking about asking her to marry me."

"Then do that now!" Her vehement response made several people at other tables turn to stare.

"I don't get it," Ben said. "You're worried about what'll happen if we move in with her, but you want us to just go ahead and get married? Doesn't make any sense."

The look she tossed at him was a typical my-parent-is-stupid frown. "People who live together before they get married are more likely to split."

"And you know that because…?"

"I just do."

The kid was far too smart for her own good. "What are you so worried about?"

"I don't wanna go through what happened with Theresa again."

He snorted.

She narrowed her eyes.

"Mallory is nothing like your mom. Even if we split—"

"But you said you wouldn't!"

Ben put his hand over hers where it now rested on the table.

"You're worrying too much. Mallory and I are fine. We're solid. I wouldn't even consider moving in with her if I didn't believe that with all my heart. I'd never put you through what happened between your mom and me again. I know how awful it was for you, how awful she was to you. You're the first thing I think of when I make any choice, especially one like this."

Amber's gaze caught his, and her fear was crystal clear. "What if her cancer comes back?"

Another thing he'd spent a lot of time thinking about that he had no good answer for. "I don't know. I guess we help her through it. What else could we do? She'd need us."

Even talking about Mallory getting sick again made the meal he'd eaten sit like a lump in his stomach. Could he handle an ordeal like that? Could Amber?

Nursing Mallory through a recurrence of her disease, watching her waste away from chemotherapy or even die, would destroy Amber.

It would destroy him, too.

"She's fine." Ben kept repeating those two words in his mind, hoping they'd calm his nerves.

"But what if—"

"She's *fine*, Amber." Now he was the one snapping.

His daughter stared at him a long time before she picked up her hamburger and started eating again.

He had his answer, and he couldn't have been more pleased.

Chapter 24

"Want to lick the batter, Dad?" Amber called from the kitchen.

"Not with raw eggs in it, I don't." Since the women were busy baking, Ben popped the footrest up on the recliner, stretched out, and changed the TV channel to a football game. "I'll have some brownies when they're done, though."

Instead of watching the Bears, he found himself watching his girls. They moved around the kitchen together as though their dance had been choreographed. They talked and acted so naturally, they could easily have been mother and daughter.

Speaking to each other in light and friendly tones, they fussed over a pan of brownies, playfully arguing over whether "real" brownies had walnuts and frosting. After Amber put the pan in the oven, she smiled at Mallory, who returned the smile as she tucked a strand of Amber's long hair behind her ear.

That simple display of affection choked him up.

Here was what Amber wanted, what she deserved. Instead, the woman who'd given the DNA to create that life had all but abandoned her child.

Ben shoved his anger at Theresa aside, focusing instead on all the good Mallory was doing for his daughter. This move to share her house would bring them even closer together, and if things continued down the path they were all walking, Mallory might one day be Amber's stepmother.

What a shame that Mallory wasn't Amber's biological mother. After all the nonsense Theresa had put the girl through, it was a wonder Amber had ended up being so caring and kind. Not that he could take credit for Amber being such a neat kid. As a father, he simply rolled with the punches and did the best he could.

Children should come with instruction books.

Amber came into the great room and put her hand on his shoulder. "We're still going shopping, right?"

"I thought you and Mal were making brownies."

"We are, but they're almost done. I thought we were going to find me a canopy bed."

Mallory wiped her hands on a dish towel and tossed it on the countertop. Then she drew closer. "Figured we'd grab a bite to eat for supper, do some furniture shopping, and come back here for brownie sundaes for dessert."

"Brownie sundaes?"

"Yeah, Dad," Amber replied in a *duh* tone. "Brownies with ice cream on top."

"Don't forget the chocolate syrup," Mallory added, touching her fingertip to Amber's nose.

"How could I ever forget chocolate syrup?" The smile Amber gave Mallory felt like a punch to Ben's gut.

The bond was already there, stronger than he'd imagined. Convincing Amber to move in had been easier than he'd expected, and now he knew why.

Perhaps when he got around to proposing to Mallory, she'd give in just as easily.

* * *

"I really wanted a canopy," Amber said, leaning her shoulder against one of the furniture showroom's dressers.

Ben was rapidly losing patience. They'd been to three different furniture stores. This was the last store in Cloverleaf that sold decent furniture. Amber was going to have to settle. "It's just a bed."

"It's *my* bed," she insisted.

"There's one more store we might hit," Mallory offered. "And, hey…if the right bed isn't in Cloverleaf, we'll take a road trip, maybe even go to Chicago again."

Ben frowned at his daughter. She clearly had no idea how much Mallory was enduring to help her. The woman hated shopping with a passion, yet she'd good-naturedly gone with them and had even run interference by keeping the much-too-pushy salespeople at bay.

It was one thing to help his kid get the things she needed, but he drew the line with spoiling her rotten. "C'mon, ladybug. A bed's a bed. Besides, your eyes will be closed. What's it matter what the bed looks like? Pick one already."

"I guess…Let me think about it."

Mallory wrapped an arm around Amber's shoulder. "Just because the other stores didn't have canopy beds doesn't mean the next one won't. Right, Ben?" When he rolled his eyes, she jabbed his ribs with an elbow. "Right?"

He let his heavy sigh express his frustration. "Right. I guess."

The saleslady Mallory had dismissed when they'd arrived—

Nita, according to her name tag—hovered a few bedroom displays away. Mallory waved her over. The woman hurried toward them, high heels clicking against the tile floor.

"What can I do for you?" she asked.

"I don't see any canopy beds," Mallory replied. "We had our hopes set on a canopy bed." She inclined her head toward Amber. "She really wants one of those beautiful old-fashioned canopies."

Nita pursed her lips. "Hmm...I can check with my suppliers, but I haven't seen one in quite a few years."

"Probably because most people have ceiling fans in their rooms," Ben added.

Since the only thing Amber had asked for in return for moving was a canopy, he'd hoped to find her one. His daughter seldom asked for things for herself. But, God, the prices of furniture were ridiculous. If he could barely afford any of what they'd seen, how much would a canopy be?

He glanced at his daughter and her forlorn frown. "We'll keep our eyes open, but at least give these a chance."

"I'd be glad to make some inquiries." Nita pointed down the aisle from where she'd come. "If you're looking for something different that still has a bit of show to it, why don't you let me show you the sleigh beds we've got?"

"Sleigh beds?" Amber pushed away from the dresser, her eyes wide. "What's a sleigh bed?"

"Come with me, and I'll show you." Nita waited until Amber was by her side to start walking. "I had a canopy when I was a kid. The fun of it died pretty quick. They're dust traps."

"Oh...hadn't thought of that."

"I think you'll love the sleighs. I'll show you my favorite first. Bought one for myself last month."

As they walked farther down the aisle, Ben reached for Mallory's hand. "Sorry, Mal."

"About what?"

"I know you hate this shit."

She tossed him a concerned frown. "Hate helping Amber?"

"No. I meant shopping."

"I don't mind in this case. Honestly."

Before they reached Amber and Nita, he brushed a quick kiss over Mallory's lips. "Liar."

"Not lying," she insisted. "This is important to Amber, so it's important to me."

"Hey, Mallory," Amber called, gesturing to Mallory to hurry. "You need to see this!" Then she disappeared behind the screen separating that faux bedroom from the others.

A bit flummoxed that his daughter had called his girlfriend instead of him, he turned Mallory's hand loose. "Go on. Amber wants you."

Amber needs *you.*

"You should say that like it's a good thing. She's not calling me to my execution or anything." She softened her words with a wink. "She's not choosing me over you, Ben. That's what you're worried about, isn't it? You think she wants my opinion instead of yours."

Sometimes he hated how well she understood his thoughts. He shrugged, realizing exactly where his daughter had learned that nonchalant response.

"You wanted us to get close. Right?"

He nodded.

"Then celebrate that. Be happy she cares about my opinion and stop chewing over everything like it's a cheap cut of meat." On that advice, she headed toward Amber and the saleslady.

According to the counselor he and Theresa had seen when

they made a last-ditch attempt to patch together their marriage, children living with parents in a troubled relationship often learned how to play one parent against the other to get what they wanted. As a result, one of those parents would try to buy affection by giving a kid anything and everything.

Was Amber playing Mallory, hoping to be spoiled? Ever since they'd made the decision to move in at the end of the month, Amber had been spending more and more time with Mallory. Each time they returned, Amber had something to show for it. A new winter coat. Her first pair of high heels. And with Ben's permission, Mallory had taken Amber to get her ears pierced.

At least Mallory knew when to put her foot down. Amber wanted three earrings in each ear. Mallory made her settle for one piercing on each earlobe.

Amber might claim that she didn't need anyone but her father in her life, but her actions and the rapidity of her attachment to Mallory declared otherwise. He chuckled as he watched the two of them crawl on the mattress, flop on their backs, and giggle.

"Not a canopy," Mallory said. "But it's cool to be encased by wood, isn't it?"

"Yeah. And I love the step to get up onto it. Wonder if your cat could jump up this high?" Amber asked.

"He's got springs on his feet," Mallory replied. "He'll make it. Unless you don't want him in your room."

Amber sat up and stared at Mallory. "You'd let me decide?"

"Why not? It's your room."

"But it's your house."

"Your room is your own, Amber. If you don't want Rascal in there, that's your choice."

* * *

Mallory glanced over at Ben and wondered why he had such an enormous smile on his face. He'd been even more hesitant to shop than she'd been, yet once they got started, the trip had been fun.

Amber was finicky, but that was easy to understand. Mallory had been a picky teenager as well, and when it came to bedroom sets, she still was. She'd handled everything at the furniture stores because she'd learned the tricks while on the search for her four-poster bed. Just like Amber, she'd checked every single store in Cloverleaf.

To see Amber excited about the move warmed Mallory's heart. Ben was important to her. She loved him with all her heart. But now she realized she had another role in his life and Amber's—to be the kind of mother Amber needed. Not that she would replace Theresa in the girl's life. It was clear, however, Amber deserved so much better than what Theresa had ever given her. Mallory would try to heal those wounds.

It helped that Amber didn't saddle her with the evil-stepmother baggage. Some of the students she had from broken families tended to resent their "steps." Not that Ben was ready to marry her, although the topic had come up for discussion. Things were great the way they were. It was better to keep taking baby steps.

Once burned, twice shy.

How unfair to lump Ben into the same category of male as Jay. Yet she had to protect herself. Maybe she'd remarry one day, maybe even marry Ben, but she couldn't help but hold a part of her heart sheltered. She seldom repeated mistakes, especially costly ones.

Men had always let her down. She prayed Ben was an exception to that rule.

"I like this one," Amber announced, jumping off the sleigh bed.

The saleslady's face lit up like a Christmas light display. "Fantastic." She turned to Ben. "We have several types of financing and—"

"I'm buying it," Mallory said, not even giving Ben a chance to protest.

He wiggled one in anyway. "No way. This is for Amber."

"Yes, but... it's for my house. I think it's only fair for me to buy it."

God, she hoped he wouldn't go all macho on her. The set was expensive, something Ben might struggle to afford. Sure, the furniture was picked by Amber, but it would be in Mallory's guest room. She'd have to convince him it would remain there even if things didn't work out with the three of them living together. She didn't want to jinx them by blurting that out and would press her point only if he objected. In the end, she'd ultimately send it with Amber no matter what happened.

Nita kept switching her gaze between Mallory and Ben, probably unsure of where to hitch her wagon. "Would you like a few minutes to talk?"

"Amber, honey?" Mallory smiled. "Maybe Nita here can go get you a drink and let your dad and I figure this out. Okay?"

Amber looked at her father. He replied to her unasked question with a curt nod. Nita led Amber toward the back of the showroom.

"Mal, what you're trying to do is nice, but... I can handle this."

"I never said you couldn't. I'm just trying to be practical."

"Practical? How is your paying for an expensive bedroom set practical?"

"The room's empty now, right?"

Ben nodded.

"If I pay for the furniture, the room's no longer empty."

He rolled his eyes. "That makes no sense at all."

"Well, you always tell me women lack logic."

A stab at humor didn't change his stern expression.

"Look, let's be honest, okay? If you and Amber end up moving out someday—"

"Are you saying we're going to break up?" Ben asked.

Mallory shrugged.

His hand encased hers. "We're going to be together forever, Mal."

"Maybe I'm thinking about when Amber goes off to college." An innocent fib meant to protect his masculine ego. "Either way, the furniture stays with me."

"Either way? So you *are* talking about breaking up!"

After pressing a quick kiss to his lips, Mallory squeezed his hand. "We're both realists, Ben. I love that you think we'll always be together, but—"

"We will."

"It's important to Amber, which makes it important to me. I really want to please her. Besides, I like it a lot. I'd be buying it for the guest room."

"Liar." The amusement in his eyes took the sting from the insult.

"If you were buying her something, it wouldn't cost this much. Right?"

He answered with a brusque nod.

"Then stop fighting me over this. Let's get delivery arranged, check this off our list, and look for a nice mattress."

Chapter 25

Mallory dropped her robe on the bathroom floor before remembering the new hook Ben had installed for just that purpose. As she hung the terry-cloth garment on the silver hook, she smiled both at his consideration and at the fact her house was finally done.

Once Ben and Amber moved in this weekend, it would be perfect.

Trying to get ready to face another school day, she ran her hand through the water pouring down from the new showerhead. She'd never seen one quite as large before, but she loved the steady stream of water and how standing under it she could imagine being in the middle of a waterfall.

The water had warmed quickly thanks to Ben and the installation of a new water heater, which now filled the bathroom with steam. He'd taken one look at her antique water heater and insisted she update. She stepped into the glass shower enclosure, shutting the door and letting the heat of the water wash over her, bracing herself for a long day full of kids who needed her. It wasn't until she was in the middle of shampooing her hair that she realized what she'd forgotten.

Mallory hadn't looked at her reflection. The implant was such a part of her now that she'd grown accustomed to being "normal" again and not having to check her body all the time.

At long last, the nightmare had ended.

She had big plans for Saturday. While Ben and Robert loaded the rental truck with stuff from the town house and then took a good deal of it to the storage unit Ben had rented, she and Amber were going to wait for the furniture company to deliver Amber's new bedroom set and mattress. The new furniture was oak, the stain light enough to be feminine without being prissy. The set would look fantastic in the guest bedroom, Amber's room now.

The walk-in closet stood empty, ready for Amber's clothes. Mallory had purged as much junk as she could from all the closets as each bedroom received a fresh coat of paint and new carpet. Because she'd always held out the hope Ben might want to share her house, she'd made a point of keeping the guest closet empty and had limited her stuff to one side of the master closet.

A bit odd that she was so excited about a guy moving in rather than marrying her. Then again after Jay, she wasn't sure she'd ever find the courage to take that plunge again. Better to keep it simple. Besides, she was confident in Ben returning her affection. Hadn't he proven he was stalwart in the way he'd cared for her through the skin stretching and the reconstruction?

Love didn't need a license and a ring.

Rinsing her hair, she enjoyed the feel of the water beating against her skin. She squirted her scented liquid soap onto her hand and washed her body. It was still a habit to check her right breast, a good habit according to her oncologist. No lumps. No bumps. She ran her soapy fingers over the left breast, loving how her chest once again felt symmetrical. With a contented smile, Mallory smoothed her hands over her tummy.

The lump was on the left side, right below her navel.

It wasn't until she got light-headed that she realized she'd been holding her breath. Then she started panting, unable to draw enough air into her lungs. Her heart beat hard enough she could hear the echo whooshing in her ears.

A mistake. It's just a mistake.

The truth was there beneath her fingertips.

She quickly rinsed the soap from her body, stepped out of the shower, and dried herself. Then she faced the foggy mirror. She swiped it with the towel to give herself a better look. Heart pounding, she ran her trembling hand over her lower abdomen. First right. Next left.

Not only could she feel the large lump, she could see the imperfection in her mirrored reflection.

The anger hit her square in the chest with the force of a shotgun blast. Mallory shouted a guttural noise, a mixture of pain and rage, and picked up the glass resting by the sink. With a scream full of agony, she hurled it at the mirror, making it shatter and rain shards of silver on the countertop and into the sinks.

* * *

The hospital. The last place in the world Mallory wanted to be. The series of buildings was far too familiar, and she took a few moments to summon up her courage before she could even consider going inside.

Where was Ben? She needed him with her, helping her through this, whispering words of comfort and lying to her that everything was going to be all right. She checked her cell phone yet again.

No calls. No texts.

Maybe he was someplace with no cell phone reception.

Maybe his battery had run out.

Maybe he'd accidentally turned off his ringer.

I should've waited. Telling him face-to-face would have been kinder, but she'd been drowning in panic. All she could do was reach out to the man she loved—her life preserver in the storm. So she'd sent him a blunt text.

Found a new lump. Need you.

After phoning her oncologist's service, she'd waited. The doctor had called back almost immediately, sounding sleepy. She'd apologized for waking him so early, but he'd patiently listened to her near-hysterical words and ordered her to drive straight to St. Ignatius Hospital. He was going to make sure she got right in for a CAT scan even if he had to call in every favor owed him.

Mallory called the substitute teacher service, slipped on some clothes, texted Ben to tell him where to meet her, and then drove like a maniac across town. Now that she was in the parking area, she waited, hoping he'd respond to her pleas to meet her in the outpatient lot and go with her to radiology.

She wanted him to kiss her. To stroke her hair. To hold her hand.

To tell her the cancer hadn't returned to ravage her body and maybe claim her life this time.

I won't cry. I won't cry.

Damn it, I won't cry.

There was nothing to cry about. Not yet. Not until the results of the CAT scan were in. Then she could weep enough to fill a river with her tears.

There were millions of explanations for lumps and bumps on the body. Well, maybe not *millions.* Thousands. Or at least hundreds. Anything *except*…

She almost called Juliana to ask her to list a few simply to ease her mind. But she wouldn't call any of the Ladies. Mallory had always leaned on them. Not this time.

This time she needed Ben. She needed his strength, his support, and his warmth to help her through.

Maybe he was lost in another of the hospital's parking lots.

Maybe he was tied up in traffic.

Maybe Amber woke up sick and he was too busy helping her to check his phone.

The sickening knot in the pit of her stomach grew with each excuse she imagined for why Ben ignored her repeated pleas. Didn't he know how much she needed him? Casting aside her pride, she abandoned texting and called him.

"Please, God. *Please.*"

Although she had no idea if she was praying for Ben to answer or for the lump in her lower abdomen to miraculously disappear, she still sent her entreaty to God.

Please.

No answer.

Maybe Ben... was just like Jay.

She took deep breaths, trying to remind herself Ben had been nothing but considerate.

But so had Jay until things turned rough. Ben had yet to be tested. Could he really be like Jay? Would he leave her when the going got tough?

If this was a test, he was failing.

With an angry growl, Mallory powered down her phone and shoved it in her purse. She climbed out of the SUV and marched into St. Ignatius Hospital.

Alone.

***

Ben saw Mallory's empty SUV and pulled his truck up only a couple parking spots away. He jammed the gearshift into park but didn't turn off the engine. Instead, he gripped the steering wheel until his knuckles turned white and his hands ached.

Time had little meaning, its passage marked only by the pain flowing through his heart and his mind. His phone rested next to him on the bench seat. When Mallory's ringtone played, he'd stared at her smiling face on the screen, unable to answer after the blood-chilling texts she'd sent. Al Green had warbled "Let's Stay Together"—the first song they'd danced to—and the irony of the words filled Ben's mind.

Lovin' you whether times are good or bad, happy or sad.

He should've taken the call. He just couldn't, not until he could wrap his mind around what was happening. Once he'd realized this wasn't some horrifying dream, he'd raced to St. Ignatius, hoping he'd get there before Mallory went inside. But he was too late, had wasted too much time, and he couldn't seem to force himself to get out of his truck.

She'd become more to him than he'd ever imagined. She'd banished the bad memories of his past. She'd filled the hole in his heart he hadn't even known was there. She'd become a beacon of light in a dark world.

Now cancer would extinguish that light.

A tear hit his lap, soaking into the denim. Afraid to give in to his desire to weep—to scream at the unfairness of someone like Mallory being sick when there were so many horrible people in the world who deserved to suffer—Ben banged his head against the steering wheel. Hard.

"It's not fucking fair." First he whispered it. Next he shouted it.

He glanced at the hospital. She was inside, probably dressed in a baby-blue gown, being led to a cold room with a loud, intimidating machine to have her body scanned. He should be sitting next to her, holding her hand before the attendant led her away. Then he should be praying while he waited in an uncomfortable waiting room full of two-year-old magazines.

But he couldn't make himself get out of his truck. As long as he sat by himself, he didn't have to face this disaster. He didn't have to find the right thing to say, as if there even *were* a right thing to say.

How could he ever come up with a way to break the news to his daughter?

Amber. Sweet Jesus, he'd promised her Mallory would be all right. How in the hell could he possibly look his daughter in the eye and tell her Mallory's cancer had most likely returned?

No more drama. He'd promised his daughter that there'd be no more drama.

"Damn it!"

Instead of keeping his word, he'd plunged Amber right into the deep end. Now she might have to face death up close and personal. He'd ruined her life by letting her bond with a woman who might be dying.

After all of Theresa's head games, Amber had recovered. Mallory had helped make that recovery complete.

Mallory's death would destroy Amber as much as it would destroy him. She'd already lost one mother. No way could she stand to lose another.

Ben needed to make this better for both of his girls, but he had no idea how, or even if he could.

One step at a time. Isn't that what people told him when

Hurricane Theresa hit? Take on what he could control and leave the rest to God.

Are you there, God? I sure hope so, 'cause we need you. Bad.

Mallory would be in the CAT scanner by now. Then she'd head home to wait for the results. Since he wouldn't be able to help her now, he decided to go to the person he could help.

Amber.

He tapped out a quick text message that Mallory probably wouldn't receive until she was done, then he backed out of the parking spot.

Can't get to you right now. Will be at your place soon as I can.

Driving away from St. Ignatius, Ben didn't even glance in the rearview mirror. Mallory was going to be okay. The lump was nothing. Absolutely nothing.

There simply was no other way this could end.

* * *

Mallory froze when the double doors swished closed behind her. A smile bloomed as she glanced to the parking lot.

Ben was here. His truck sat close to her SUV. Everything would be all right now.

The CAT scan had been pushed back an hour because of a couple of emergencies. Mallory had been heading out to grab some coffee and a donut since she'd missed breakfast. Experience taught her the hospital cafeteria's coffee was nothing but sludge, so she'd opted for the Dunkin' Donuts just up the street. She'd even planned to check her phone one last time, knowing Ben would've had time to answer her text by now.

She'd been foolish to get so angry at him, and she blamed the panic that had engulfed her when she found the lump. While she was still terrified, she could breathe and think a little clearer now.

Ben wasn't Jay. He wouldn't abandon her when she needed him.

With a smile, she headed toward his truck. If she could catch him, they could go to the coffee shop together. As she walked, she fished around in her purse, searching for her phone. When she glanced up again, she ground to a halt.

Ben had backed out of the parking spot. Maybe he'd seen her and was heading over to pick her up.

She was wrong. So very wrong.

Her phone vibrated in her purse, signaling a text as he sped away.

Chapter 26

Mallory wouldn't answer his texts.

Trying to swallow his panic, Ben tried one more time. All the while he kept coming up with reasons why she wouldn't reply.

Maybe the CAT scan was just getting started because she'd had to wait. Or maybe she was driving and wouldn't read a text. Something was up, but he would figure it all out when he got to her house. He sent a last text while he waited for Amber to come from class and meet him in the main office of her school.

Talking to Amber. Then will come to house.

When he glanced up, Amber was coming through the office door. "Dad? What's wrong?"

He tossed her a fake smile. "Forgot you have to get your braces adjusted today."

"I don't have an appointment."

"Yes," he insisted, inclining his head at the secretary, who gave them the stink eye. "You *do*."

"Um…okay."

"Already signed you out." Ben grabbed her elbow and hurried her out of the office. He was near to desperate to find out for sure if his daughter could handle what they were about to throw at her.

"What's wrong?" She hit him with the question before they got to the truck.

"We need to talk, ladybug." He popped the locks and crawled into the driver's seat while Amber entered from the other side. Since there was no easy way to say it, Ben spilled the news. "Mallory found another lump."

"In her breast?"

"I assume." Pulling his phone from his pocket, he checked her text again. "Doesn't say, but with her history..."

"She's got cancer again." Amber's face blanched and her hands trembled. Her wide eyes filled with tears.

Ben tugged her closer and wrapped an arm around her shoulder. "We don't know that."

"What else could a lump in her breast be?" Although she wasn't crying, her voice choked with emotion.

His own thoughts traveled the same path, but he needed to hold out hope. "A lump could mean lots of things. Might be nothing. We don't know for sure yet. She's getting a CAT scan right now."

Amber pushed away from him. "Then why aren't you with her?"

"Because I needed to talk to you first. I was worried how you'd react."

"Why?"

"I know how close you and Mallory are..." *And I'm afraid this news will destroy you.*

After wiping her sleeve over her eyes, she glared at him. "Can we go to her now?"

"I think it'd be better if we kept things as normal as possible.

At least for now." He looked her over unsure of whether she was hiding her reaction or was simply in shock.

His own shock was wearing off, leaving him with a mound of worries and feeling guilty he hadn't stayed at the hospital. The fact Amber was handling this so well only added fuel to the guilt. He should've stayed with Mallory.

This was tearing him in two. Driving away from the hospital had been a knee-jerk reaction, but one born of years of protecting Amber, of always putting his daughter first. Somewhere he'd missed that she'd developed into a young woman who was handling the news with much more maturity than he was.

You screwed the pooch on this one, Ben, old boy.

"What do you want to do, Amber?"

"Could we go buy Mallory some flowers?"

"How about you go with me to the florist, we pick out some roses, then I bring you back to school? You can see Mallory after."

She considered a moment before answering with a brusque nod. "I'll take the bus home. You can text me to let me know what's happening. Okay, Dad?"

Ben gave her shoulder a squeeze. "Sounds like a good plan."

***

With his heart and flowers in his hand, Ben punched in the code to Mallory's garage door. She had to be home by now, and he desperately needed to hold her.

When the door didn't budge, he tried again. As flustered as he felt and with the river of anxiety racing through him, he'd obviously put in the wrong code. A second attempt was no more successful than the first.

Was the power out?

"Changed the code."

Juliana's voice drew Ben around to the front porch where she stood, arms folded sternly over her chest.

"What did you say?" he asked.

"I changed the code." She rubbed her upper arms against the chill. "You need to go." Her voice bore the same harsh tone as any drill sergeant. "Now."

"What are you talking about?"

"You abandoned her."

His heart plummeted to the ground. "I *what*?"

"Cut the bullshit." Juliana scoffed. Her features were pinched and angry.

He held up the roses, hoping they'd sway her. Sure he'd made a mistake. But he hadn't fucked up so badly that Mallory would lock him out. "I came to be with Mallory."

Juliana's snort came out in white tendrils that curled in the cold air. "You're too late, asshole."

His heart seized in panic. "Did she go back to the hospital?" God, what if she was sicker than she'd let him know? "What do you mean 'too late'?"

Before she could answer a shiver ran the length of Ben's spine as he felt Mallory's eyes on him. He glanced up to the master bedroom's bay window, catching a glimpse of her before the drape fell back into place.

"Mallory!"

"Go away, Ben. She doesn't want to see you," Juliana scolded.

"I'm not going anywhere." He kept his eyes on the window. "Mallory! I'm sorry! Come talk to me!"

Juliana jerked the storm door open. "You're an asshole. You know, I thought you might be different, but you're not. Not one fucking bit."

"Different? What are you talking about?"

"You were supposed to be different from her ex, from my ex, from every other idiot guy. But you're not. You're just like all the others. When Mallory needed you, you bailed."

"I didn't bail! I couldn't get to the hospital in time, so I went to tell Amber what was happening."

"She saw you."

Those three words bore so much weight they hardly registered. *"What?"*

"Don't play dumb with me, shithead. You were there. But you didn't go in. You just drove off."

Trapped in his own lie, he had nowhere to turn. "I fucked up. Is that what you want me to say? Fine. *I. Fucked. Up.*"

Juliana stood like a statue.

"I'm here now!" Ben spread his arms wide, smacking the roses against the railing and sending petals falling on the snow-covered grass. "I want to see Mallory. Look, I know I left. I was scared. I was terrified. I needed to see my daughter. But I'm here now."

"Too little, too late, asshole." Juliana stepped inside, let the storm door close, and then stared at him.

"Please, Juliana…I need to see Mallory. I need to explain."

Mallory would understand. Mallory would forgive his mistake. Mallory loved him.

"Please."

Juliana shut the door, and the dead bolt clicked as loud as a gong's chime.

***

Mallory couldn't have hurt more if someone had beaten her.

She threw herself on the bed and reached for Ben's pillow. The tears wouldn't come. Too many emotions swirled inside her to settle on one. Anger. Hurt. Fear.

Devastation.

Juliana strode into the room. "You okay?"

"Did he leave?"

"Yeah. But he really wants to talk to you."

Since he'd shouted almost everything he'd said, she had a good idea of what had happened. A few important holes remained. "Did he say why he left after coming to the hospital?"

"Something about needing to talk to Amber first." Juliana leaned her shoulder against the tall bedpost. "I think his courage evaporated when he got to the hospital. He just couldn't make himself go in."

Mallory frowned. "Exactly like Jay."

Ben showed a yellow streak in the face of cancer—that in and of itself was a wound to her heart. The lie only made her pain worse.

Why lie about being there? What purpose did that serve?

Other than to shatter her trust into a million tiny pieces.

Love was easy to give, especially to someone as wonderful as Ben and Amber. She loved them both. But trust?

That was another matter entirely. After Jay pulled the rug out from under her, Mallory had learned the lesson well. Men spoke of the truth, demanded the truth. They demanded trust. But they clearly couldn't give what they required.

And she'd let him in anyway, only to be betrayed in the same way.

Never again.

"Did the doctor call yet?" Jules asked.

"Not yet."

Giving her a maternal frown, Jules pushed away from the

bedpost. "Are you sure there's nothing I can do? We could talk if you want. About the CAT scan. Or Ben."

"I...can't. Not...not yet."

There weren't any words anyway. Nothing but pain and worry.

"Okay." Jules stopped at the bedroom door. "Want me to make you some tea? Chamomile, maybe? And a few cookies?"

Although she had zero interest in eating or drinking anything, she nodded.

"I'll bring it up in a little bit." Then Juliana was gone, leaving Mallory alone with her troubled thoughts.

Soon the phone would ring. Not Ben calling, though. Oh, he might try, but she'd already blocked his number. No, this call would come from her oncologist. He would let her know if her life was once again being flung into the world of cancer limbo—where a person couldn't be sure how many more tomorrows would come. For a control freak like her, that world was every bit as punitive as hell.

She'd lived there once before and survived to rejoin the living. Her race was supposed to have been run. Evidently that had only been act one in a play that would go on much longer than she'd anticipated.

Could she do this again? Could she face the weeks of uncertainty? Could she show the world that stiff upper lip others needed to see to maintain her privacy?

Ah, but this time the ordeal wasn't private. Not in the least. This time her health had affected Ben and Amber.

Her heart went out to Amber. That bond was so strong there was no doubt the girl would be hurt to hear the news. Mallory thought for a moment about going to her, soothing her fears away just as she'd hoped Ben would've soothe her own. But as much as she loved Amber, Mallory couldn't face Ben. At least not now. Maybe someday, but not today. Not for the foreseeable future.

How unfair! Mallory was the one who'd been wronged, yet she still felt guilty for not being with Amber.

Rolling over, she buried her face in Ben's pillow. His scent filled her nostrils, making tears sting her eyes. He might never understand exactly how much he'd hurt her or even why she saw this as such a betrayal. It all came back to one thing.

Trust.

One of the most convincing things Ben had done to make Mallory accept his attention, and ultimately his love, was to mandate honesty. She valued that trait above all of Ben's other good qualities. It was also the hardest thing for her to give him in return. Yet she had. And he'd shattered her ability to ever trust again. Jay Hamilton might have been a coward, but he'd never lied to her.

She'd trusted Ben with her heart, and he'd thrown it right back in her face by lying the very first time she put him to the test. When she needed him the most, he'd sat there in the hospital parking lot and typed out a text about not being able to get to her.

Her cell rang. She snatched it up, checked who was calling, and let out a heavy breath.

The oncologist was going to give her the CAT scan results.

Chapter 27

Ben dragged his fingers through his hair. The frustration was becoming unbearable—a whole week of silence from the woman he loved. Save one text that came the night of her CAT scan.

Good-bye. Tell Amber I'll miss her.

The message had frozen his blood. There was no clear way to interpret Mallory's words. Was she saying farewell because she was breaking up with him? Or could the word "good-bye" hold more insidious meaning—could she be telling him her cancer had returned and was going to take her away?

Whenever he thought about her dying, he had to fight to stop himself from throwing up. Picturing his beautiful Mallory lying in a casket made tears blur his vision. All he wanted was to wrap his arms around her and protect her from anything that could harm her.

The week had been lonely and terrifying. Since he and Mallory moved in different circles, he couldn't even send out feelers to find out if anyone knew the results of her CAT scan. Ben wasn't living.

He was barely surviving.

After her text, he'd driven like a maniac over to Mallory's house and pounded on the front door. The house had been dark, and no one answered. For all he knew, she was in the hospital. He'd called St. Ignatius, but stupid privacy laws wouldn't even let them tell him if she was a patient. He knew nothing about what doctor she'd be seeing or whether she'd need more surgery or more chemotherapy.

Stone wall after stone wall left him feeling impotent and angry. Sure, he'd made a mistake. He should've gone to her. He shouldn't have lied. But this punishment didn't even come close to fitting the crime. Until Mallory could let him explain, apologize, and try to mend this fracture, there would be no end to his frustration.

Ben slammed his truck door. Since Mallory wouldn't talk to him, he'd come to find someone close to her who would.

Striding to Bayside Church's social hall, he jerked the doors open and stepped inside. His gaze scanned the people gathered for the mixer, searching for the familiar red hair. Juliana looked up the moment he spotted her.

At least she didn't run away as he hurried across the floor, dodging the dancing couples. She scowled at him, but she stood her ground. Robert was with her, his frown no less fierce than Juliana's.

Ben stopped directly in front of Juliana. "I need to know about Mallory. Where the hell is she?"

"Haven't you caused enough trouble? You have no business coming here," Juliana barked.

"I need to see Mallory."

"Yeah, well... too bad. She sure doesn't want to see you."

He tried Robert. "C'mon, buddy. Help me out here. I'm worried sick about her."

When Robert opened his mouth, Juliana shot him a glare that could've ignited a fire. "Don't you dare!"

"I just want to talk to her," Ben insisted. "I need to know what the CAT scan showed and—"

Juliana narrowed her eyes as she interrupted. "If you would've found the balls to haul your ass outta your truck and go in the hospital, you'd know what the CAT scan showed."

"I need to find her," Ben insisted. "Is she in the hospital? I don't even know where she's staying or whether her cancer is back."

Robert kept shifting his gaze between them, clearly torn over what to do.

"Can you at least tell me that?" Ben pleaded. "Is the cancer back? Is she going to lose the other breast?" *Is she going to lose her life?*

"That's none of your business," Juliana said. "You need to leave. Now."

As if he'd even consider walking out of that place without at least a few answers. "Why isn't she home?"

Robert elbowed Juliana, jostling her drink. "You can answer that one at least."

Her eye roll was a drawn out affair. "Fine. She's staying with me."

At least someone was taking care of her. "Thank you," Ben said.

"I don't need thanks for being there for someone I love." Her expression held nothing but disdain. "When you love someone, you do what's right for them. You're there when they need you. Shit, you're no better than her ex, running away at the first sign of trouble."

Ben struggled to hold his temper. "Could you at least hear

my side of all this before you pass judgment and brand me the world's biggest asshole?"

Juliana gave her head a shake. "What could your side even be? She asked for you to be there for her, and you drove away." She snapped her fingers. "Wait! You lied to her and *then* you drove away."

"There's a lot more to it than that!"

"I don't give a shit." On that pronouncement, Juliana sipped her drink and destroyed Ben with her eyes. If looks could kill, he'd be nothing but a rotting corpse.

"*I'd* like to hear your side," Robert said.

Juliana gaped at him. "Robert—"

He held up a hand. "Just stop."

A rumbling growl rose from her. "Robert..."

"I mean it, Jules. I wanna hear what Ben has to say." He nodded at Ben. "What happened?"

Unsure of where to begin, Ben realized that each way he planned to explain came back to one revelation—he'd made the biggest mistake of his life. So why whitewash it? "I had every intention of going into the hospital until I got there. But...I couldn't open the door."

"Why not?" Robert asked.

"Because he's a pussy," Juliana replied.

"Because I was so worried about Mallory, I started thinking about Amber," Ben said, as if that made any sense to anyone but a parent.

"Gee, Robert," Juliana said with a sneer. "Didn't that clear up things nicely?"

Ben needed to ignore Juliana's taunts or he'd never be able to explain. Besides, he deserved some of them, so he'd take his medicine. "When Mallory told me she'd found a lump, all I could think of was Amber. She went through hell with my ex."

"What's that got to do with you sitting in your truck?" Juliana asked.

Robert smacked Juliana on the ass, drawing a yelp from her. "For shit's sake, Jules. Will you let the man tell his story?"

She shrugged. "Whatever."

Ben pressed on. "Amber and Mallory have gotten really close. Part of me wanted to run inside and hold Mallory's hand, but the dad in me made me think of what would happen when Amber found out. I mean, if Mallory's cancer was back, she might... might... die." Just saying it aloud was like a knife to the heart. He swallowed hard to hold back his raging emotions. "Amber thinks of Mallory like a mom now. She'd be devastated. I don't know how to explain it, but I had to get to my kid. I just had to."

"What about Mallory?" Juliana asked. "She needed you more than Amber."

At least she was listening. "I was torn in two. I couldn't be with both, so I went after Amber because Mallory had been there long enough I figured she'd already be in the CAT scan. I wasn't leaving her alone. I was just going to talk to my daughter first."

"Then why lie about it?" she asked.

"I didn't want her to think I'd abandoned her," he replied. "I didn't know she could see me. I honestly didn't mean to hurt her." A rueful chuckle escaped. "Two minutes with Amber and I realized I'd really fucked up."

"Why?" This time Robert asked the question.

"Because I realized my daughter was okay. She wasn't the one who needed me. She wasn't half as freaked out as I was, and she told me to get my ass back to the hospital."

Robert nudged Juliana. "What do you think?"

"I think Mallory was devastated and never wants to see him again."

"Please let me talk to her. I want to help," Ben insisted. "I want to fix this. I love her, damn it! Can you get her to just talk to me?"

The only hope he had was that Mallory would listen and forgive. The woman had a heart bigger than the ocean, but if he couldn't talk to her, he could never get her to understand. If after he told her what happened she wanted to end it, fine. It would kill him to let her go, but he would.

But not now. Not like this.

From the pained expression on Robert's face, he was close to caving in. His furtive glances at Juliana proclaimed why he wouldn't say anything. The woman had intimidation down to an art form.

When she turned to talk to some blond guy who'd just tapped her on the shoulder, Robert inclined his head toward the doors and quickly held up three fingers. That added up to meeting him in the parking lot in three minutes.

As the man who'd talked to Juliana walked away, she turned back to scowl at Ben. "You're still here?"

"Look, just do me one favor. Okay?"

"Why should I?"

"Because you know deep down that I love Mallory and you know we're good together."

When she took a few moments to think that over, he feared he'd misjudged her. Juliana had always seemed smart, maybe too smart. Despite her earlier reticence, she had to know he and Mallory belonged together.

Had his story softened her heart at all?

She heaved a resigned sigh. "What do you want me to do?"

"Tell Mallory I'm not giving up on her. Ever."

* * *

It took a hell of a lot longer than three minutes for Robert to join Ben in the parking lot. Ben leaned against the tailgate until Robert came through the double doors. He pushed away and waved so Robert could find him.

Robert returned the wave and made his way to the truck.

"You gonna help me out here?" Ben asked.

"Depends."

"On what?"

"On you convincing me that I'm doing the right thing in helping you."

"I love her, Robert."

Robert snorted. "I knew that."

"Then why do I have to convince you of anything? I told you what happened and—"

"You hurt her, Ben."

Ben swiped his hand over his face, near to shouting in frustration. It hurt to have everyone think he was nothing but an asshat like her ex. He'd made a mistake. One mistake. And it was costing him everything.

Swallowing his pride, he nodded. "I know. Now I want to fix it."

"You hurt her again, and so help me God, I'll blacken both your eyes."

"Fair enough. Can you tell me if you know what her CAT scan said? Is her cancer back?"

"Would it matter?"

Ben didn't even hesitate. "No. Not one damn bit. I love her. I want to be with her for whatever time she has left. If that's sixty years, fan-fucking-tastic. If it's six months, then I want to make them the best six months of her life."

"I don't know what she found out," Robert said. "She's back

at work, but she looks kinda…wounded. Reminds me of a bird with an injured wing."

"No…" Ben's stomach churned. The news had been bad. No doubt in his mind.

Mallory would have celebrated had it been nothing. As she'd conquered each step of the breast reconstruction, she'd celebrated each baby step toward being done. If she was withdrawn and quiet, that meant her mind and her spirit were carrying a heavy burden.

"Don't go jumping to conclusions," Robert scolded. "She might just be puny because she misses you."

Ben hung his head. "I fucked up, Robert."

"Yep."

"I love her so much. Thinking she might have cancer again, that I might lose her…" Voice choked with emotion, Ben couldn't say any more.

A hand settled on his shoulder. "I have an idea."

"And?"

"She's coming to the game tomorrow."

"Game?"

"Tomorrow is senior night for the girls' basketball team. The seniors invite a teacher they want to honor. Mallory will be there."

Ben found his first smile. The situation was ripe with possibilities. "Any chance I could get your help on something?"

"I suppose." Robert stroked his chin with his thumb and index finger. "You know…I've got an idea. Goes with something Bethany's been working on."

"What are you thinking?"

"Oh…I'm not sure yet. But I can be a clever bastard when I want to be." He leveled a hard stare at Ben. "You willing to let Mallory's friends help with this?"

Ben snorted. “As if. Juliana acts like she’d like to see me castrated—would probably lop them off with her own hand and a rusty knife.”

“You need to learn to look past the Juliana she wants everyone to see and look at the real Juliana.”

“Meaning?”

“Meaning she’s hard on the outside, but the inside is nothing but soft,” Robert said. “And yes, I think they’d help. How about I give Bethany a call and get her to meet us at Frankie’s? We can have a beer and talk about how she can play Cupid. She loves shit like that.”

“Are you sure, Robert? I mean…I might only get one shot at this.”

“Well then, if you’ve only got one shot, we’re gonna make it a bull’s-eye.”

Chapter 28

Relax, Mallory," Juliana said. "You promised Taylor you'd stay for the game."

"I know. I just..." Mallory sighed.

Sitting in the middle of a crowd full of happy people was almost more than she could bear. She couldn't put into words the sadness that blanketed her heart. Each day was a struggle. To get up. To force some food down her throat. To make herself go to school.

School. Her one reprieve from her worries. When Mallory was at school, she was truly alive. Just being with her students was the best medicine in the world, as though she fed off their enthusiasm and affection.

So she was here in the middle of the gymnasium for senior night, the last home game for the girls' basketball team. After the national anthem, each senior player had been introduced as her parent or parents stood at her side. Then one by one, the girls named the teacher who they believed made them a better person. Taylor Engle had asked Mallory to come to be honored, and there was no way she could decline such a wonderful invitation, no matter how miserable she felt or how much she'd rather be wrapped in an afghan and pretending that her life hadn't gone straight to hell again.

Ben was gone. She'd pushed him away, shoved him out of her life with both hands. Yet she still needed him, still thought about him every time she considered what the future held. How could she face all the days that lay ahead without him?

Why did he have to be like Jay? Why couldn't he have held on to that knight-in-shiny-tool-belt personality she'd fallen in love with? Why did he have to be a lying coward?

Lying coward. That seemed too harsh to describe a loving man like Ben. In a moment of utter honesty, she'd realized she'd made up her mind to lock him out without ever listening to his side of the story. Not that his reason for running away from the hospital and lying about it would be sufficient. A lie was a lie, and he'd told a whopper of one at a time she'd needed him.

When the pregame festivities were over, the basketball court was cleared for the game. Before Mallory could get back to the stands, retrieve her coat, and make a hasty exit, Taylor had grabbed her hand. With a sweet smile, she'd asked Mallory to stay for the game. While she wanted nothing more than to go home, she'd sighed in resignation and nodded. She'd never been able to deny any of her students.

Now she sat with Juliana and Danielle in the stands. They both cheered with the crowd, but Mallory paid very little attention to the game. For once in her life, she was letting sadness rule her every moment. Not that she'd slipped into a full-blown depression. Yet the grief was always there, just below the surface, as though no pleasure or promise remained in her world.

"You okay?" Danielle asked.

She was sick and tired of hearing that question. She always

wanted to shout that she wasn't okay—that she'd never be okay because she'd never be with Ben again. "Fine." Since the game held no interest for her, Mallory let her gaze scan the crowd. "I thought you said Bethany would be here."

"I did," Danielle replied. "But I also said her kids had something planned for halftime."

"You mean her Service Learning class? What are they up to now?"

Service Learning, Bethany's "baby." The students who enrolled in her class pledged themselves to participate in projects to help their school, their community, even the world. Beth kept them hopping, always having a variety of things for them to do, from helping homeless families to visiting senior citizen centers to decorating the school hallways with information about the dangers of texting while driving.

Danielle frowned at Mallory. "I already told you all about it." Dani held up her wrist to show her pink silicone bracelet. "It's something to do with breast cancer."

"Good for her." At that moment, Mallory would've been glad to march down the stairs, take the microphone from Beth, and tell everyone about her battle with the disease. Keeping things private had robbed her of something she'd needed…support. The Ladies had always been there for her, but in many ways Mallory had cheated her friends, colleagues, and students.

People knew she'd been struggling. She could see it in every worried glance, hear it in every unasked question. Why hide it? Why not let people help her carry the load?

Why did she suddenly need so much support?

Because Ben had taught her just how important support truly was.

She should go to Ben and talk to him. If nothing else, she

owed Amber that much. The only thing keeping Mallory from jumping in her SUV and driving right to Ben's place was her fear of handing him her heart again. The poor thing was still battered and bruised enough to keep her from risking that kind of hurt again.

Maybe in time...Maybe someday...

Maybe not.

"I told you all about it," Dani insisted again. Her frown went from annoyed to concerned. "I'm worried about you, Mal."

"I'm fine."

What was she supposed to say to her friend? That the world resting on her shoulders weighed more than she could bear? That each hour was agony to survive, especially knowing that there would be no relief from the pain that ate away at her?

Ben's face was fixed in her thoughts. She missed him so much she ached. Despite what had happened, she still loved him—probably as much as she ever had. They'd been apart two weeks, and she'd felt his absence every single minute.

The furniture she'd bought for Amber had been delivered. Right after the delivery men left, she'd made the bed with the fresh, feminine sheets she'd found as a surprise for Amber. Then she'd stared at the beautiful furniture until she'd burst into tears.

Amber would never sleep in the big sleigh bed, the one she'd loved so much. She and Ben would never move into the house and share Mallory's life. Unable to bear the loneliness of the house, Mallory had packed a bag and hightailed it to Juliana's place. She'd been bunking in the guest room ever since.

She was done hiding. The time had come to go home and face life again, difficult though it was.

The halftime buzzer broke into her thoughts. "I'm really tired,

Jules. I'm gonna slip out and head back to your place to get my stuff."

"Your stuff?"

"Yeah. I think I should head home tonight. Okay?"

Both Juliana and Danielle stared at her, their concern clear.

"At least stay through halftime for Beth," Jules said. "She said the stuff the kids were planning would be a lot of fun."

Mallory groaned.

"C'mon, Mal," Danielle said with a smile. "After halftime we'll grab Beth and go out for nachos and margaritas."

Although it was the last thing she wanted to do, Mallory nodded. If she could pretend to have a life after Ben, maybe that miracle might someday happen.

The announcer's voice boomed over the speakers. "We've got something special for the halftime show tonight. Let's welcome the Stephen Douglas High School Service Learning class! Take it away, Ms. Rogers!"

Bethany ran onto the center court, holding one end of a large tarp. Three of her students held the other corners. They spread the cover out over the middle of the floor, covering the enormous SD logo as another kid carried out a stool.

Bethany strode to the announcer's table and grabbed the microphone as the rest of her students, twenty-some juniors and seniors, spilled onto the court. They all wore pink T-shirts and each held two large plastic jars with no lids, one jar labeled YES, the other NO.

With an enormous smile, Bethany walked back to center court, dragging the long microphone cord behind her. "How is everyone tonight? Ready to see our Lady Warriors win?"

The crowd cheered and applauded in response as Beth's students fanned out into the crowd, their pink shirts standing out like beacons.

"See the pink shirts?" She tugged on the hem of her own. "We're here tonight to raise money for breast cancer research. To help us encourage all of you to donate some big bucks, we've got something fun planned. Not only are you giving money to a great cause, you're going to be *voting* with your dollars. See my students with their jars?" She pointed to several of the kids in pink shirts who'd worked their way up some of the bleachers, positioning themselves to reach the majority of the crowd. "They're here to help you vote. Now, you might ask what you're voting for? How about you decide whether we shave a handsome man bald right here at center court?"

"Oh, Good Lord." Mallory couldn't help but chuckle as the enthusiasm of Beth, her kids, and the crowd infected her like a virus.

In the time she'd been teaching, she'd been soaked in a dunk tank, hit in the face with a whipped-cream pie, and dressed up in so many ridiculous costumes she couldn't remember them all. Evidently Beth had recruited someone to her cause, and that poor guy was going to leave the gym tonight bald. "Who did she sucker in this time?"

"Don't know. She told me it's a surprise," Danielle replied.

Juliana said nothing despite the betraying color rising on her cheeks.

"Jules? What do you know?" Mallory tapped her on the shoulder when Jules refused to look at her. "Out with it. Who's doing this? Steve Leonard? Blaine Hancock? Oh Lord, she didn't get your ex, did she?"

All Jules did was shrug.

Mallory folded her arms under her breasts. If Jules wanted to play dumb, no worries. The victim would be revealed soon enough. "What idiot would let himself get his head shaved in front of all these people?"

Bethany's voice boomed through the gym again. "We have a victim who's volunteered to let you decide his fate. Someone he loves is a breast cancer survivor, and he told me he'd do anything for her. So you all get to decide if 'anything' means giving up his hair." She beckoned to the sidelines.

Mallory let her gaze follow to the double doors being held open by two students. A man in a pink polo and jeans came through, waving as the crowd roared. One look at his face and she froze, her heart leaping to such a fast cadence that she grew dizzy.

Ben. Ben was here, jogging across the gym floor, looking handsome and happy.

Her first instinct was to run. Fast and far.

Then she got good and pissed.

How dare he look so happy! She'd been living in a world of emptiness and he'd clearly moved on as though her being in his life had been of no more consequence than a speed bump.

Mallory grabbed for her coat where it rested on the bleachers. She was getting out of there as quickly as she could. No way in hell she was going to deal to him. Not here. Not now. And definitely not around so many people.

Her whole body trembled, as did her voice when she announced, "Screw this. I'm outta here."

"Wait, Mallory," a familiar voice said as a slender hand gripped her arm. "Please."

Mallory whirled to find Amber at her side. "Oh, Amber… Honey, I—I can't. I have to go." Although she couldn't make herself jerk her arm away, she tried to move down the aisle, hoping Amber would release her.

Amber wouldn't let go. "Wait. Please."

Vision blurred with tears, Mallory shook her head.

"Wait, Mal," Jules said. "You need to see what happens."

Danielle joined in as well. "Just watch for a little bit, okay?"

Bethany swept her arm out at Ben, who was now standing at her side. "This is Ben Carpenter. You get to decide if he gets to keep this gorgeous mop of brown hair!"

Ben shook his head much like a dog shedding water from its coat and then raked his fingers through his hair.

Bethany laughed and fluffed his hair with her free hand. Then one of the Service Learning kids handed her a pair of cordless clippers. She flipped them on and let them buzz close to the microphone. "If you want Ben to keep his hair, put your donation in the jars marked 'no.'" She pointed at Ben with the clippers. "But...if you want to watch me shave his head, and you all know you do, put your money in the 'yes' jars!"

"He's doing this for you," Amber said.

Mallory couldn't take her eyes away from Ben. He'd summoned over one of the kids with the jars and had made a show of pulling out his wallet, plucking out some money, and pushing it into a NO jar.

Then his gaze captured hers, and for a few moments, everything else died away. They were the only two people in the cavernous gym, staring at each other as if some rope tethered them together despite the distance between them. She could read pain in his eyes, and he mouthed *I love you.*

She barely stopped herself from shouting back that she loved him, too. Instead, she shook her head and glanced away, sniffling hard and trying to stop tears from falling.

The crowd was going crazy. The Service Learning kids were having trouble keeping up with all the people waving around money. Bills were slammed into jars and passed down rows, and from the looks of things, Ben was about to get scalped.

She considered grabbing money from her own wallet to try to stop Bethany from shaving his hair. She loved his hair. But she wasn't sure a week's salary would be enough to stem the tide flowing into the YES jars.

Her own odd reaction shook her to the core.

"Why is he doing this?" Mallory hadn't meant to let the question slip, but once it was out, she was dying to hear an answer from the three people who'd obviously been in on this conspiracy.

"He's sorry, Mal." That response was the very last thing she'd expected to hear from Juliana.

"Doesn't change anything," Mallory insisted.

But she was wrong. The man was making a sacrifice simply to get close to her again.

"Dad loves you," Amber insisted. "He fucked up."

"Amber!" Mallory scolded.

"Well, he did! Doesn't mean he doesn't love you." Then Amber hit her with the big guns. "You told me that when Theresa messes up I should try to forgive her. You told me people make mistakes all the time, but that doesn't mean they stop loving you."

Having her own words turned on her was unsettling. "That's different."

"No, it's not. Dad made a mistake. One mistake." Amber frowned. "You didn't stop loving him, did you?"

"No." The vehemence of her response came as a shock.

She should still be mad at him. Hell, she should hate him. He'd lied to her and left her alone to face one of the scariest events of her life. Yet the anger was dissolving, vanishing like wisps of fog.

"He went to see Amber, you know," Juliana said. "When he left the hospital, he drove right to Amber's school."

"Why are you defending him?" Mallory asked, resisting the

urge to stomp her foot like an angry child. Then she saw another blush rise on Jules's cheeks. "What did you do now?"

"I didn't *do* anything. He came to the mixer last weekend to talk to me about you."

"And?"

"And... Robert and I listened to the whole story."

"I should've known Robert was in on this," Mallory grumbled.

"Stop pouting and just listen, okay?" Jules pointed at Ben. "Look at what this man is willing to do for you. He's doing his penance right here in front of everyone. He's paying a high price for one mistake."

The Service Learning students were heading to Bethany as two more kids brought out a couple of large clear plastic tubs, each marked YES or NO as well. Beth took the jars from each student, emptying them in the correct tub. Judging from the overwhelming difference in the size of the growing piles of money, there would be no reason to count the haul to find out the results.

Ben was going to get his head shaved.

Chapter 29

Mallory's thoughts became a storm, swirling and churning as she struggled to understand.

Ben was here, ready to have that gorgeous mane of hair shaved off.

For me.

Juliana called it "penance." But why now? Why here? What could possibly prompt him to make such a public display of—

Mallory whirled on Juliana. "You told him!"

Everything suddenly made sense. The halftime show. Ben's sacrifice. Amber standing at her side. There was only one reason all of these things were happening, and it only confirmed what she'd feared.

Ben knew the results of the CAT scan.

"Damn it, Jules! You *told* him!"

Jules had the nerve to look surprised. "What are you talking about?"

"You told him the test results! He's here because of the CAT scan. That's the only reason he'd do something like this. He knows the results."

"Not from me, he doesn't," Juliana insisted.

"Don't lie to me. There's no other reason he'd be doing all of this now."

God, she was a fool.

"Do you have cancer again?" Amber's voice was hoarse, as though she could barely force the words out.

"Didn't your father tell you?" Mallory knew her tone was snide, but she couldn't help herself.

"He didn't have to. We guessed you have cancer again." Her teeth tugged on her lower lip as a tear spilled over her lashes. "We don't care. We love you and we'll be there to help you. Dad says he doesn't care and neither do I."

Mallory had a hard time letting Amber's words sink in. "Your dad thinks I have cancer again?"

Amber nodded, wiping the back of her sleeve over her eyes. "Are you gonna have to have surgery again? Dad wants to help. I want to help. We don't want you to be alone. We don't want you to—" With a small cry, she threw herself against Mallory as sobs shook her whole body. "Please don't die, Mallory. I love you."

Mallory wrapped her arms around Amber and held her close. "Shh. It's okay, honey. I love you, too." She stroked the girl's hair as her own eyes burned with unshed tears. "I'm not gonna die. I promise."

Ben thought her cancer was back, yet he was still here, still telling her he loved her in front of a gym full of people. He was willing to be with her even if it meant holding her hand through surgeries. Even if it meant watching her puke her guts out. Even if it meant a whole lot more hard stuff she didn't want to even consider. He was here. And he was here for keeps.

Suddenly, all was right in the world again.

"Looks like the voters have spoken," Bethany said, drawing

Mallory's gaze back to center court. "You all want Ben bald? Then you're gonna get Ben bald!" She held the clippers high.

With an exaggerated shrug and a goofy smile, Ben sat down on the stool while a student draped a towel around his shoulders.

He believed her cancer had returned. That thought kept slamming through Mallory's brain. Even though he thought she was sick again, he was here, ready to make this sacrifice, this penance, as a way to make amends.

"Amber..." Mallory turned the girl so she could see Ben. "You should watch this."

"And away we go!" Bethany handed the microphone to a student and flipped on the clippers.

Standing beside him, she started at his widow's peak and cut a wide swath through his thick, dark hair, leaving behind a reverse Mohawk.

Ben picked up a large lock, held it up, and laughed as though he were having the time of his life.

The crowd went wild as Bethany continued running the clippers over his hair. The swatches perched on Ben's shoulders and chest or cascaded to the floor. Within a matter of minutes, it was done.

Ben stood up, whipped the towel off like a cape, and held his arms up as the applause rose to a deafening level. Then his gaze searched again, finding hers. With an arrogant smile, he crooked his finger at her.

What was he up to now?

Bethany retrieved the microphone and handed it to Ben. Then she signaled the crowd to quiet down as her Service Learning kids did the same.

"One more act in this play, folks, if you wouldn't mind," Ben said. "I need Mallory Hamilton to come out here and join me." He pointed at her and then crooked his finger again.

"He's insane," Mallory muttered, feeling self-conscious as every eye in the gym turned her way.

"He's in love," Danielle said with a laugh. She gave Mallory a gentle push. "Well, what are you waiting for? Go down there!"

"Let's go, Mallory." Amber took her hand and dragged her down the aisle.

While she could've resisted, Mallory realized her embarrassment would triple if she sat down and refused to move. Better to find out what Ben had up his sleeve and then make a hasty exit.

When she reached the tarp, Amber released her hand, which was promptly picked up by Ben.

He led her to the stool before kissing the back of her hand. His smile made her weak in the knees.

"Have a seat, Mal," he said, holding the microphone away so no one else could hear.

She took advantage of the moment of being close enough to talk to him. "Ben…we need to talk. It's about the CAT scan…"

"Sit now. Talk later."

"But…"

"Please?" His dark eyes begged her to cooperate.

"Fine." There would be plenty of time to talk after this circus ended.

Mallory sat on the stool and put her hands on her knees. "Now what?"

"Now, you listen." Ben winked and then spoke into the microphone again. "I love this woman." He pointed at Mallory as hoots and cheers filled the gym. "And now I need to ask her a question."

When Ben went down on one knee as he fumbled for something in his pocket, Mallory's heart beat so roughly, she feared it would explode. Adrenaline rushed through her, making her tremble.

"Mallory Hamilton... will you marry me?" He set the microphone on the floor and put a small black box on his palm. Then he extended his hand toward her.

The crowd had gone berserk, the noise louder than any pep session ever held there.

Fingers pressed against her mouth, Mallory fought back tears. All of this, especially Ben's proposal, was overwhelming.

"Please forgive me, Mal," Ben asked, his voice gruff. "I never meant to hurt you. Marry me. Let me take care of you. Be with me for whatever time we have left. Six days or sixty years, I want to spend them all with you."

She dropped from the stool, landing on her knees to look Ben in the eyes. Words wouldn't come.

"I mean it. I love you, no matter what happens in the future." He opened the box. "This is for you."

The ring was perfect: a gold band with a square diamond.

"Marry me. Please."

All she could do was cup his face in her shaking hands and press a kiss to his lips. She moved her mouth to say yes, but her voice held no volume. Just to be sure he understood, she nodded.

Bethany's voice filled the gym. "She said yes!"

* * *

Ben pulled his truck up behind Mallory's SUV. She gave him a shy smile after she'd crawled out of the driver's side and stood waiting for him by the garage door.

Robert hadn't been lying when he said he was a clever

bastard. When he'd come with Bethany to the town house to explain their plan for a basketball game proposal, Ben had thought they'd both lost their minds. Mallory had kept her illness so private he couldn't help but think he'd only piss her off more by putting on such a public display. Bethany changed his mind, explaining that so much of Mallory's life was vested in the school, a proposal in front of her fellow teachers and students would please her.

He ran his hand over the light stubble that was now his hair, wondering just how bad he looked. There had to be stray tufts Bethany had missed, and no doubt his sideburns and the back of his neck would need a razor to make a clean line. Didn't matter. Losing his hair was a small price to pay to prove to Mallory that he loved her and was truly sorry for what had happened.

Her hair had grown back. So would his.

The only thing dimming his joy was the knowledge that they still had a battle to fight against her cancer. But fight they would with every ounce of their strength, and he hoped that Mallory would be stronger with him and Amber standing by her side.

"Hey," she said when he got to her. "We need to talk."

Talking was the last thing he wanted to do, but he nodded, resisting the urge to kiss her.

"How about we have a glass of wine?" she asked.

"Wine sounds great." Anything to help him relax.

Ben was wound so tight he wasn't sure he could form too many coherent sentences. He wanted to make love to her, to reclaim what he'd lost with his mistake. He wanted inside her incredible heat, to join their bodies. Repeatedly. On the couch. In the bed. In the shower.

It was too soon. Hell, he didn't even know if they *could* make love. Although she was sick, she didn't look as though she was hurting. He had no idea if she was on chemotherapy or radiation or…*what.*

"Are you sure we shouldn't check on Amber?" Mallory asked.

"She's fine. She has a new friend named Kelsie. They've been spending a lot of time together. Kelsie's mom will keep an eye on her tonight, some sleepover for a few girls." He tossed her a lopsided smile. "I think Amber finally has a BFF. Isn't that what you call it? A BFF?"

"Yeah," Mallory said with a chuckle. "That's what they say. It sounds weird coming from you."

He followed her inside, hovering close as she chose a wine and let him open it. Her cat came to rub against his leg, and he gave it an affectionate stroke.

"Rascal missed you," she said, nodding at her cat.

"I missed him, too."

Watching her closely, Ben searched for anything that might help him know how she was feeling. Nothing appeared to be different. She was the same Mallory she'd been two weeks ago when he'd been foolish enough to hurt her.

"I'm sorry." The words would never adequately express how remorseful he was. How could two words convey the depth of sorrow that had gripped him when she'd locked him out or express the weight on his heart at knowing he'd hurt her so much? "I didn't mean to hurt you. I was afraid for Amber."

"I know that now," Mallory said. "I should've given you a chance to explain." She led him to the great room. She took a seat on the sofa, turning to face him as she sipped her wine. "We need to talk about the CAT scan."

"It's okay, baby. I know. The cancer's back. That's why you moved in with Juliana. But I'm here now."

"You're willing to move in with me? I'm gonna need you close."

"I—I hoped you'd want me to. I want to help you through your treatments, and that's hard to do when I'm all the way across town."

"Good. I want you and Amber here like we'd planned."

"So what does your doctor say?" The last thing he wanted to do was ruin their reunion by talking about her disease, but he needed to know everything he'd missed.

A smile lit her face.

How in the hell could she smile in the face of cancer? The woman was the epitome of courage.

"My doctor doesn't say much of anything," she replied. "I haven't talked to him in almost two weeks."

"What?" The word burst from him in a shout, sending the cat running from the room.

She snatched the glass from his hand, probably to stop wine from flying around with his animated gestures.

"You've gotta get on top of this right away, Mal. I figured you might already be getting chemo. When did he biopsy the lump?"

She put both glasses aside, setting them on the coffee table. "No need for a biopsy."

"No need?" His tone bordered on hysterical. "You had a new lump in your breast! How could there be *no need*?" He couldn't lose her, not now that he'd finally won her back.

"The lump wasn't in my breast, Ben. It was in my abdomen… my lower abdomen."

The words took a moment to register, and once he realized what that development meant, he had to hold back the urge to punch a hole in the wall. It was much worse than he thought. "It's metastasized. Oh God…" When he tried to rake his fingers through his hair, all he got was the feel of sandpaper across his palm.

Mallory took his hands in hers. "It's not metastasized."

"How do you know?"

"Because it's not cancer."

His whole body tensed. "It's what?"

"It's not cancer, Ben."

"It's not... Then what is it?"

A slow smile spread over her beautiful face. "A hernia. The lump was nothing but a stupid hernia."

* * *

Mallory watched him closely, trying to capture every nuanced emotion playing on his face. If he hadn't declared his love, she would have seen it as clear as day in his reaction to her news.

Ben popped to his feet and tugged her up as well. Then he embraced her, near to crushing her against his chest. "Thank God. He answered all my prayers."

To be back in his arms was heaven, even if he was squeezing the breath right out of her. She closed her eyes and breathed in his scent. She'd been so afraid back in the gym—afraid he'd only come to her because Jules had told him she was fine.

Instead, Ben had proposed to her even though he believed she might be facing another long trial by fire, even though he thought she might be dying.

And that revelation swept away every last ounce of her anger.

He really would stay with her through sickness and health. He was still the hero of her dreams.

"Ben?"

"Yeah?"

"Take me to bed," she demanded.

Easing back, he lifted her chin with his finger. “Tell me you forgive me first.”

“I forgive you. Now take me—”

“Tell me you love me again.”

“I never stopped loving you. I want you to—”

“Tell me you’re gonna marry me.”

“Absolutely.” To keep Ben from interrupting her again, Mallory slipped her hand between them and pressed her palm against his groin.

He was already hard.

Grabbing his hand, she laughed as she dragged him toward the stairs.

“In a hurry, there, Mal?”

“Absolutely.”

Once upstairs, she tugged him into the master bedroom and shut the door behind them.

“Now what?” The teasing lilt of his voice made her smile.

“Now we get naked.” She jerked her shirt over her head and tossed it to the floor. Then she unzipped her jeans and shoved them down her legs before kicking them aside.

“Keep going.”

“Your turn,” she insisted.

His shirt and pants were gone before she could pull off her socks.

“Get that underwear off, too,” Mallory ordered as she shed her bra and panties. “Now.”

Naked, they stood on opposite sides of the bed. The tension and anticipation added to her nearly overwhelming desire. “Ready?”

Ben didn’t reply. Instead, he crawled onto the mattress and knelt in the middle, holding his arms open.

Mallory joined him, moaning as he wrapped his arms around her and flesh touched flesh. Although they'd been apart a mere two weeks, she was starved for the feel of him. Their lips met in a kiss that began gentle and loving and quickly turned carnal. Her tongue thrust past his lips, stroking his tongue, tracing the line of his teeth, teasing until he grasped it between his teeth and gently tugged.

Arm around her shoulder, he eased her down on the mattress, letting her stretch out so he could blanket her. The crisp hair on his chest tickled her nipples, making the real one harden. She rubbed her toes against the hair on his legs, reacquainting herself with the wonderland of his body. His cock rested against her core, sending heat racing through her, fanning from her center to the rest of her body.

Ben braced himself up on his forearms and stared down at her. "I missed this."

Mallory scraped her fingernails gently over his shoulders. "Me, too."

"I love you, Mal."

"I love you, too, Ben. Make love to me. *Now.*"

He responded to her fierce command by kissing her hard and gyrating his hips to rub his erection against her. Yet he avoided every attempt she made to put her hand between them and guide him to her entrance.

"*Now*, Ben, please."

"Patience is a virtue." He kissed his way down her throat. Nibbling kisses traced a path across her collarbones to her chest and over her breasts. He stopped long enough to draw her right nipple deep into his mouth before moving lower.

Lost in a sensual haze, ready to receive his intimate kiss, Mallory put her hands on his head. Instead of being able to tangle her fingers through his thick hair, she found rough stubble—a reminder of his willingness to love her unconditionally. Her smile changed to a whimper when Ben reached her core. He tortured her with his tongue and lips until he gently took her sensitive nub between his teeth.

She lost herself in the storm he sent through her body. Heat and need and love, none of which could be contained. Too quickly for her to savor his attention as she wanted, her body knotted in tension.

"Ben! Please..."

He ignored her plea and sent her tumbling into an orgasm that made her gasp and buck beneath him. He didn't let up until he'd wrung every last spasm from her body.

As she slowly came back to earth, his face loomed above hers, a cocky smile on his lips. "Liked that, huh?"

How easy it would be to smack his ego and tell him it was merely *okay*. But after the way she'd sung out, he'd have known she was lying if she claimed nonchalance. "*Loved* that. But..."

"But what?"

"Something's...missing."

He quirked an eyebrow.

"You weren't there with me."

She didn't give him time to ponder her statement. She sat up, pushed his back to the mattress, and kissed each of his nipples.

"Mal, you don't have to—"

Mallory gave his stomach a playful bite, soothing it with a lick. One kiss to his navel as she wrapped her fingers around his erection. Ben hissed, fisting his hands in the quilt.

Having power over such a strong, handsome body inflamed her every bit as much as his intimate kiss. With a smile, she took his cock deeply into her mouth, whirling her tongue around the crown while savoring his rumbling growl. Just to add the coup de grâce, she cupped his soft sac in her hand and gave it a gentle squeeze.

Sitting up, he clenched her upper arms and dragged her up his body.

She tried to protest. "I wanted to—"

Ben flipped her to her back and separated her thighs with his knees. "I want *this*." Ben grasped his cock and rubbed it between her feminine folds. "Now, baby?"

"Oh yes..."

When he plunged inside, her body sprang back to life. Mallory wrapped her legs around his hips, letting him sweep her away with every thrust. There was no teasing, no easy pace. This was a rough race to fulfillment.

Gripping his shoulders, she matched him, raising her hips each time he pushed back inside her until her body exploded in another shower of warmth. He was a few heartbeats behind, growling as he buried himself deep inside her.

Chapter 30

You look amazing," Ben murmured as he took Mallory's hand, cradling it in both of his. Although he wasn't nervous, he worried she might be—after all, she was tying herself to him when she deserved a prince.

Too bad, because he was never letting her go.

A blush tinted her cheeks as she gave him a shy smile. "Thanks. You look like a model."

He had to resist the urge to preen like a peacock in his black suit. His hair—and hers—had grown out in the months they'd taken to plan the wedding. The warmth of June hadn't come fast enough to suit him. "Thanks."

The minister began the ceremony. "Dearly beloved…"

And so it went as Ben stood with Mallory in front of their friends and family to tie the knot. He had a hard time concentrating because his gaze kept drifting back to his bride.

Her dress was a pale pink and fit her curves perfectly, the hem ending just below her knees. She'd worn her hair down. In a few more months, it would touch her shoulders. She was crowned with a small wreath of pink and white flowers. She was everything a bride should be. Beautiful. Happy.

His.

When prompted, he recited his vows in a clear, strong voice, stressing the "in sickness and in health" promise, although he doubted it was necessary. She had to know by now that he would never leave her side so long as he could draw air into his lungs. While the future could be a scary thing, Ben refused to wallow in any worry. Today was a day of joy.

Amber winked at him. She stood behind Juliana, Mallory's maid of honor, but they didn't wear matching bridesmaids' dresses. In her typical fashion, Mallory had wanted to keep everything relaxed. She'd helped Amber find a new dress, but it was appropriate for any occasion. The wedding was small, tasteful, and exactly what they both wanted.

Ben and Robert had helped the women decorate the Bayside Church gathering area the day before. Mallory, Amber, and the Ladies had turned the large room into a festive haven since both the wedding and reception would happen there. The church hall that had been the place of their first dance was awash in candlelight, crepe paper streamers, and flowers—the perfect site for a marriage to begin.

"And now, by the powers vested in me by the state of Illinois, I pronounce you husband and wife," the minister said with a nod, closing his little black book. "You may kiss the bride."

Ben didn't give her a chance to react before tugging her into his arms. Then he kissed her, long and lovingly, until the minister loudly cleared his throat.

"Ladies and gentlemen, I present to you Mr. and Mrs. Benjamin Carpenter."

Amber let out a whoop and hurried to them, trying to hug

them both at the same time. Her enthusiasm made his heart sing. He kissed the top of her head, glad life was looking up as much for his daughter as it was for him. Sure, Theresa would always be a raspberry seed in Amber's teeth, but perhaps with Mallory's guidance, mother and daughter might find a way to make a relationship work. Amber also had a good woman in her life now who loved her and would help her through the changes life tossed her way.

Juliana punched Ben in the upper arm, hard enough to make him wince. "You better be good to her."

"I will."

Danielle and Bethany had moved forward to stand at her side, the three of them giving him a hard stare.

Jules refused to drop the subject. "If you aren't good to her—"

He held up a hand to stop her. "I'll treat her like fine crystal. If I fuck up, I give the three of you permission pound me into the mud."

"Me, too," Amber added.

As if he'd ever want to incite that much feminine hostility. "Good thing I love her so much, then, isn't it?"

"Will you all stop?" Mallory groaned. "I'm a big girl. I can handle myself. He treats me bad, I'll make him regret it. Trust me, I have ways of making him pay that you all don't." She rose on tiptoe to brush a kiss over his mouth.

"That's my girl," Ben said. "If you'll excuse us, ladies…" He dragged her away to greet more of their guests.

***

The time passed in a whirlwind, and Mallory wanted things to slow down. The wedding seemed to whiz by in a heartbeat, and the reception was slipping away every bit as quickly. The guests had been fed. The cake had been cut. All that remained was dancing and socializing until it was time to leave.

Ben's wedding gift to her had been to plan the honeymoon. As soon as the reception ended, he'd be taking her to Chicago. They'd spend their wedding night at the Drake, and in the morning, they'd be flying out of O'Hare to head to Aruba—her first trip to the Caribbean.

Thanks to Ben, she wouldn't worry about her appearance anymore. He'd given her the gift of confidence. She could wear a swimsuit, a new yellow bikini, in public. While the idea of sitting on a beach and sipping margaritas with her new husband was appealing, she wasn't in a hurry. This wedding had been everything she'd hoped for, near to perfect in her mind. They'd made their relationship permanent in the same place it had begun and in the same way—she was in Ben's arms, dancing in their rather awkward style.

The DJ's voice boomed through the sound system. "It's time for the bride to throw the bouquet!"

A squeal rose from the ladies as they scrambled, quickly lining up on one side of the parquet dance floor. Several had kicked off their shoes and were staking out territory with not-so-gentle pushes and glares.

Ben led Mallory to the other side of the dance floor. Amber scurried to the bridal table to grab the bouquet and brought it back to Mallory.

"Thanks, honey," Mallory said, taking the flowers from her new stepdaughter.

"You better wait 'til I get over there to throw it," Amber replied, hurrying away.

Ben and the men stood to the side along with the women

who'd eschewed the tradition. When Mallory saw Juliana plant herself in the middle of the men, she shook her head and pointed to the group of females elbowing each other for a great place to snatch the prize.

Juliana shrugged.

"Jules…get over there."

With a dramatic sigh, she dragged herself over to the women waiting on the toss.

Mallory turned her back to the women, gave Ben a wink, and then waited for the DJ to count down from three.

Then she tossed it hard before whirling to watch the results.

Even though Jules had taken a place on the farthest side of the women, the bouquet landed right in her hands. She stared at the flowers, frowned then glanced up at Mallory while the rest of the women dispersed in a chorus of laughter and a few complaints about the toss being rigged.

"It's fate," Mallory insisted when Jules came to her. "You're next to get married."

Danielle joined them. "That's how it works, Jules."

Bethany nodded as she came over to the group.

"It's ridiculous," Jules retorted. "And hell will freeze over before I ever marry again."

When Mallory thought about all her friends—these Ladies Who Lunch—had done for her, fresh tears formed in her eyes. "Thank you all for making this wedding so beautiful."

"Stop," Beth ordered, dabbing the corners of Mallory's eyes with her embroidered handkerchief. "If you start crying, I will, too."

"Me, three," Danielle added, sniffing hard.

"I love you all so much," Mallory said. "I don't know what I would've done without all of you."

The four women gathered together in a group hug that had to look like a football huddle to the other guests. When they broke apart, even Jules had tears in her eyes.

Then her gaze followed a waiter who'd just passed them with a tray of full champagne glasses. "I don't know about you, ladies, but I need a drink." She hurried after him.

"Right behind you, Jules," Danielle said and she and Beth scurried away.

The DJ waved to Mallory and pointed to his watch.

She shot him a curt nod.

"It's that time everyone," he said into the microphone. "The bride and groom will dance the last dance."

Before she could move, Ben came to her and held out his hand. "I don't suppose you'd... you know... want to dance?"

Hearing the same words he'd used when he'd first approached her filled her heart with joy. "You're asking *me*?"

He took her hand and pulled her close, wrapping his arms around her as he backpedaled until they were on the dance floor. "You and no one else, Mallory Carpenter."

She hummed as she wrapped her arms around his waist. "Mallory Carpenter. I like the sound of that."

"I sure as hell hope so because you're stuck with it now. You're stuck with *me*, too."

"Glad to hear it."

As they danced, she laid her cheek against his chest and sighed in happiness. What would her world have been like if Ben Carpenter hadn't come to her rescue?

Sad and lonely—and she'd still be living in a house that was falling down around her while her heart was in just as bad a state of disrepair. She lifted her head to smile at him. "You know something, Ben?"

"No, what?"

"I remember exactly what you promised me the day we met."

"And what was that, baby?" He nuzzled her neck.

"You told me the bottom line was that you'd fix things for me."

Ben eased his head up, letting his gaze capture hers. "What exactly did I fix?"

"Everything."

He arched a dark eyebrow.

"Well, just look at my house—*our* house. It's beautiful now—all because of you."

"You helped a lot, and you know it. Plus you have really good taste. In everything." He gave her an exaggerated growl and wiggled his eyebrows.

She giggled. "You fixed something else, you know."

His dark eyes were so full of love, she found tears forming in her own. "What else did I fix?"

Mallory stopped dancing and cupped his face between her palms. "You fixed *me*, Ben. My heart was just like my house—a broken-down mess. But you worked your magic on it."

"Did you ever think that street runs two ways?" he asked.

"What do you mean?"

"While I was helping you, you worked a little of your own magic on my life...and Amber's."

Her cheeks flushed warm as a tear spilled from the corner of her eye.

Ben kissed it away. "The bottom line is that we're both damn lucky to have found each other."

"And now that we're married, you will be a lot easier to afford."

"Oh, I don't know about that. I'm kinda expensive."

Mallory tossed him a sultry smile. "Trust me. You're worth every penny."

Turn the page for a preview of the next book
in the Ladies Who Lunch series,

Signed, Sealed, Delivered

Chapter 1

One more thing.

I dare you, universe. Just throw one more thing at me and…

Juliana Kelley growled as she paced down the brown terrazzo in the hallway of her school, tossing faux smiles at any students she passed, subtly checking their hands for hall passes. Her destination—the mailroom, situated about as far from her special-education classroom as physically possible. As angry as she was, steam had to be pouring from her ears. The click of her heels echoed like a metronome, marking the time she'd spent marching these stark corridors.

I mean it this time.

One more thing gets fucked up today, and I'm walking out the door.

If only it weren't an idle threat she'd tossed around far too often. She could no sooner leave her teaching job than stroll on the moon. But after thirteen years of teaching, she no longer found joy in spending time with her students.

She was exhausted. Plain and simple. She'd been hired at Stephen Douglas High School right out of college—a wide-eyed twenty-one-year-old with a sparkling new bachelor's degree and ideas of changing the world of special education. She'd been at the school ever since.

Even though she was only thirty-four, she was the most senior teacher in her department. No matter how much she loved teaching, thirteen years of working with special-needs children was a lifetime, and the burnout of her chosen discipline weighed on her more and more each day.

Unfortunately, she had nowhere else to go and no skills beyond her teaching abilities. Who wanted to hire a smart-ass redhead and the volatility she brought in tow? It wasn't as though switching to a new school would help. Besides, with her years of experience, no other school would touch her. Why hire an exhausted teacher when a fresh-faced kid right out of college could be had for half the price?

One idea plagued her thoughts, put there long ago by her uncle Francis. He'd made a nice life for himself selling real estate. Whenever he cornered her at any family function, he tried to persuade her to move to Virginia, join his firm, and peddle houses. She always listened then politely told him, yet again, that she loved teaching.

Today she'd give him an entirely different answer.

From time to time, usually after a particularly rough group of students, she'd looked into real estate sales as a new career. An online class here. A seminar there. Her overwhelming obsession with HGTV. She'd fantasized more times than she could count of seeing her name proudly pronouncing a house for sale—or, better yet, *sold*.

But could she really leave the teaching profession—especially for something as risky as real estate, where the salary was never guaranteed?

"Hey, baby," a familiar masculine voice called. "How you doin'?"

Juliana heaved a sigh, thinking there should be some law about ex-spouses not being allowed to work together. Ever. "I'm fine, Jimmy." She winced the moment the old nickname slipped out, knowing how he'd react.

"Jim!" He fisted his hands at his sides instead of hitting the wall. At least he was finally learning to control his temper. If he wasn't one of the best wrestling coaches in the state, the administrators probably would've fired him years ago. "It's Jim now. Only boys are called Jimmy."

Then grow up and I'll stop calling you that. "Sorry. Old habits. Blah, blah, blah."

She dismissed her slip with a wave of her hand. Plucking the pieces of mail from her tiny box, she tried to get the hell out of there before her ex could start a real conversation. She'd had little enough to say to him when they'd been married—a good ten years ago. Now he grated on her already frayed nerves like a loud dentist's drill.

"Hey, wait." Jim hurried over and grabbed her elbow. "I wanted to ask you somethin'."

She glared down at his restraining hand, refusing to respond until he took the less-than-subtle hint and let go.

As always, he was slow on the uptake and pressed on. "Heard you were going to the mixers at Bayside Church."

"And that's your business because…?"

He ran his hand over his balding head, a trait that had only developed in the last year but was rapidly overtaking him. "I just…you know…figured if you needed some male companionship—"

She snorted a laugh. "Oh, Jim. I'm not even letting you finish that sentence because you know damn well I'll slap your face if you say what I think you're gonna say."

It wasn't the first time he offered to service her like some male escort, but in the mood she was in, he was going to be the lightning rod she unloaded all her anger on. She needed to get away from him before he became her "one more thing."

Robert Ashford stopped at the door, his gaze shifting between the couple.

The cavalry!

"Looks like I'm interrupting something," he said with a note of laughter in his voice.

"Not at all," Juliana replied. She tossed him a grateful glance.

Jim left the workroom, huffing and puffing as he mumbled under his breath.

"Thank God," she muttered, flipping through the mail and tossing almost all of it in the trash. Most were flyers trying to sell teachers overpriced products they didn't need.

A waste of trees.

"He still hovers, doesn't he?" Robert fished his own mail out of his cubby.

"My fault for working where he works. After the divorce, I should have left, but..." She shrugged. "I liked it here."

"Liked?"

Robert was astute. Always had been. He knew people—something that had helped him earn a huge following for the custom homes he built as a second job. Why he still worked as a shop teacher was beyond her. He had to earn a hell of a lot more money moonlighting.

"Yeah, *liked*. Feeling the burnout bad lately," she said.

"Kinda early in the year, isn't it? I mean...we've got a while before summer break."

"I'm not sure I'll survive that long."

He leaned back against the worktable. "I've been meaning to ask you something."

"Um... ask me something?" The day had held nothing good in store for her, and Robert's tone made her wary.

Then his smile helped her quickly relax. "Easy, there, Jules. You're thinking too hard."

"Probably because Jim just tried to proposition me."

Robert chuckled but shook his head. "I'm not thinking of asking for a date or anything. I mean... you're a mighty pretty lady, but... I go for blondes who don't have quite as much fire as you do."

"Well, then. Ask away."

He stepped over to the door and glanced up and down the hall as though he wanted to make sure they had privacy. That action put her right back on edge. What was so shocking he couldn't ask in front of other teachers or any boss who'd actually taken a moment to come out of his office?

"I'm going to a real estate seminar Friday. Thought you might want to come along. You're thinking about getting outta here, right?" Robert asked.

"How'd you know that?"

"C'mon, Jules. You've got 'runaway' written all over you. I've been here every bit as long as you have. I'm sick and tired of it, too."

She leaned back against the table next to him, sagging to the side so her shoulder pressed against his. That comfort she allowed herself. What she really wanted was someone tall, handsome, and warm so she could lay her head against his shoulder and let him take a little of the weight of the world away. Not that she wanted another husband. But she missed masculine attention, hence the singles mixers that had yielded nothing. Not even an interesting date.

Her fault for living in Cloverleaf, Illinois—translated "Nowhere, USA."

"At least you have something to fall back on if you leave," Juliana couldn't help but point out. "What do *I* have?"

"You're selling yourself short. You've got one really big asset—you're a born salesperson."

Exactly what her uncle Francis always said. "Did I hear you right?"

"If you heard me say you're a born salesperson, you did," Robert replied. "I've seen the way you get all those kids and their parents excited about the European trips. They aren't even your students."

"Yeah," she admitted, knowing how difficult it would be to take special-needs kids to Europe. The biennial overseas adventures gave her a chance to get to know more of the school's student body. "Most of the kids on the trips are from the honors department."

"Those tours cost a pretty penny, but you always take at least a dozen kids with you."

"I never thought about it that way."

Sure the trips were expensive, but the benefits to the kids—the historical sites, the visits to museums, the experiencing other cultures—were well worth the cost.

Robert was right. She had to "sell" people on the idea to get them to pony up the dough. "I sold women's clothing in college," she said.

"See?"

"My uncle is a Realtor. He's always trying to recruit me."

"Serendipity?"

"Maybe... So you really think I could sell houses?"

"Absolutely. I'm taking control of my own life. I'm building these great houses—"

"They're gorgeous, Robert. Absolutely *gorgeous*. If I were rich, you'd be building one for me."

"I do believe that's the nicest thing you've ever said to me." His smile made her smile in return. "I've been thinking for a long time, why shouldn't I profit by selling those houses too? As it is, some realtors pocket seven percent of the profit that should be mine."

"Makes sense," she said.

Real estate.

Suddenly it felt as though the universe had sent her a sign. Her restlessness and her feeling that her life at the school was coming to an end. Robert echoing Uncle Francis, both pushing her toward something she thought she might enjoy doing. The timing of the seminar to learn even more about selling homes as a career. All of it had to be more than mere coincidence. "When did you say the class was?"

"Friday. Six o'clock. I could swing by and pick you up."

"Who's teaching this 'class'?"

"Max Schumm."

"Oh... the guy from Schumm Homes. They pretty much sell every house in Cloverleaf."

"Then he should know what he's talking about. And look at it this way—if we sign up for the class online, they're buying dinner for up to fifteen people. Last I checked, only eight slots were filled. The class is at Byran's Steak House."

"Isn't that the restaurant at the Ramada?"

"That's the one. A steak dinner is worth the twenty-buck fee and an hour or so of your time, don't you think?"

Pushing away from the table, Juliana gave Robert a smile. "Pick me up at five forty-five."

* * *

"I'm thinking about trying something new," Juliana announced when she sat down at the lunch table.

Her three friends, the women she'd shared her lunch and life with for so many years, all turned curious eyes her direction.

Mallory Carpenter was the first to speak. "Something new?"

She stirred her microwaved soup as she eyed the sack Juliana had dropped on the table. The same age as Juliana, Mallory was a beautiful woman—brown hair that barely brushed her shoulders and brown eyes that held both intelligence and warmth.

"No more yogurt and salad?" Mallory asked.

Juliana fished out her lunch, setting the mentioned items in front of her. Strawberry cheesecake yogurt and a tossed salad. "Nope. Guess again."

Bethany Rogers took her turn, her big brown eyes bright and her typical smile lighting her round face, a face framed in a mop of short brown curly hair. "Um…not going to the mixer on Saturday this week?"

"Strike two." Juliana glanced to Danielle Bradshaw, arching an eyebrow. "Care to take a turn?"

Danielle blew a raspberry and then grinned. Blonde and blue-eyed, the woman was a no-nonsense realist whose disposition kept her feet firmly on the ground. "I suck at guessing games. Besides, we've only got twenty minutes left to eat. I'd rather you tell us 'cause you seem pretty excited, which means it must be something good."

Now that she'd decided to explore this new path in her life, she was anxious to share it with her friends. Learning to sell real estate might seem like a pipe dream, but the more she thought about it, the more Juliana began to believe she might have found her bolt hole—her escape route from the hell that the school had become.

Yet she suddenly realized what she could lose.

The Ladies Who Lunch.

The four friends had given their ragtag group that name. Even other teachers called them that now, the way they used the name always seeming a bit envious of the closeness the women shared.

It was no wonder they were close. They shared everything from horrible love lives to Mallory's heartrending battle with breast cancer. They were survivors, every single one of them.

And that was what forced Juliana's honesty. If she was thinking of jumping ship, her friends deserved to know. "I'm thinking about getting the hell out of this place."

Mallory stared at her, blinking several times as her gaze searched Juliana's. "This isn't just blowing off steam because of a bad day." A statement, not a question. Mallory knew her far too well.

"No, it's not. I'm just so… *tired.*"

"You're a special-ed teacher," Danielle said. "It's no wonder. I mean, we all deal with kids, which takes a toll. But the kids *you* see? Shit, Jules, I think you're a candidate for sainthood."

"She's right," Bethany insisted. "I might get some bad things tossed my way, but I've never had to change a student's diaper or help them into a padded area while they flipped out."

Juliana shrugged. "It goes with the job. I could have chosen something else, but I wanted to work with special-needs kids. I always figured they needed me."

Mallory was still staring holes through her. "So what's the plan?"

"Robert's taking me to a real estate seminar."

"Real estate? Interesting..." Bethany took a sip of her soda. "You know, that might just work for you. You're a born salesperson."

"That's exactly what Robert said." *And Uncle Francis.*

The universe was definitely sending her a message.

"Well, think about it," Bethany continued. "You're gorgeous. That red hair, those green eyes. When you put on a business suit, you look like you could take on corporate America and win. You show someone a house, you'll have them buying before they see every room."

Bethany's eternal optimism was a blessing. While that trait sometimes bordered on naïveté, this time it helped Juliana feel stronger about risking a change. "Thanks, Beth."

Beth saluted her with a mock toast of her Diet Coke.

"You haven't mentioned this to the principal yet, have you, Jules?" Mallory asked.

"Not that stupid," Juliana replied. "Besides, it's just a seminar. Who knows if I'll even decide I want to give it a whirl?"

"You can use summer break to get a good start," Danielle said.

Juliana nodded. "That's what I thought, too. I'll just head to the seminar with Robert, see what Max Schumm has to say and—"

Mallory choked on her Diet Cherry Coke. "Did you say Max Schumm?" The anger in her voice came as a surprise.

"Yeah...why?"

"Ben hates that guy."

Ben. Mallory's husband of a little longer than a year. The two of them had a bit of whirlwind romance that started when he renovated her house, which turned into true love when they connected at the Bayside mixers.

If only Juliana could be so lucky to land a hunk like Ben Carpenter. "What happened that made Ben hate him?"

"Schumm screwed up the paperwork on the house he sold when he got divorced. Cost Ben a pretty penny to get things straightened out. The lawyer told him Schumm doesn't know his ass from a hole in the ground."

"Then why is he head of the biggest real estate firm in Cloverleaf?" Juliana asked.

"Because there's not much competition," Mallory replied. "The other firms are national chains, and you know how tight-knit this town is."

"Always use a local," Danielle said, stating the town's informal motto.

"Look," Juliana said. "I'll go to the seminar. Find out what I need to do to get licensed, and see if I can stomach Max Schumm. Then I can make some hard choices."

About the Author

Sandy lives in a quiet suburb of Indianapolis with her husband of thirty years and is a high school social studies teacher. She and her husband own a small stable of harness racehorses and enjoy spending time at the two Indiana racetracks. She has been an Amazon Best Seller and has won numerous writing awards, including two HOLT Medallions.

Please visit her website at sandy-james.com for more information or find her on Twitter or Facebook at sandyjamesbooks.